Command Decision: Project Gliese 581g Book 1

By S.E. Smith

Acknowledgments

I would like to thank my husband Steve for believing in me and being proud enough of me to give me the courage to follow my dream. I would also like to give a special thank you to my sister and best friend, Linda, who not only encouraged me to write, but who also read the manuscript. Also to my other friends who believe in me: Julie, Debbie, Sally, Jolanda, and Narelle. The girls that keep me going!

—S.E. Smith

Montana Publishing
Science Fiction
Command Decision: Gliese 581g Book 1

First E-Book Published April 2016
Cover Design by Melody Simmons

Summary: An unlikely Navy commander is given a new mission in space, one that he might not return from.

ISBN: 978-1-942562-71-9 (Paperback)
ISBN: 978-1-942562-72-6 (eBook)

Published in the United States by Montana Publishing.

{1. Science Fiction Romance. – Fiction. 2. Science Fiction – Fiction. 3. Fantasy – Fiction. 4. Romance – Fiction.}

www.montanapublishinghouse.com

Synopsis

In a world gone crazy, it is often the humans who are at fault, seeking answers to questions we are not yet ready to understand...

Lieutenant Commander Joshua Manson's focus was on his career which has taken him to many places; just not the one he has always dreamed of going – into space. His sometimes controversial methods during missions gives him the reputation of being a soldier who doesn't always play by the rules.

A summons to Washington, D.C., after a challenging mission, leaves him questioning if he'll have a career at all; but once there, Josh is surprised when he is offered the chance of a lifetime, to command a mission in space to investigate an unknown object. The more he learns, the more determined he is to lead it, even if it means a one way ticket.

Cassa de Rola's family has lived for centuries in the quiet valley where they farm. Her family has tried to remain untouched by the growing unrest between the intergalactic military forces fighting for control over their planet. All of that changes when an unusual object falls from the sky and Cassa finds a strange male in the container. She knows that taking him in will endanger the lives of everyone close to her, but she can't leave him defenseless. Now, the military forces on both sides want to discover the origins of the container and its missing contents.

When the fight between the Legion and the Gallant Order escalates to all-out war, a new rebel leader emerges from the stars that will change the galaxy, and Cassa's life, forever.

Table of Contents

Prologue

Twenty Years earlier:
Kennedy Space Center: Florida

Joshua Mason stood on the stands across from the launch pad in stunned disbelief. His gaze was frozen on the sky above him. Tears suddenly burned his eyes. They weren't caused by the brilliant sun or the chilled wind trying to cut through his jacket, though. No, the burning in them had to do with the unusual trail that followed the liftoff that was supposed to take his dad into space for the last time.

At almost eighteen, he and his dad might have had the occasional clash of wills; well, maybe more than an occasional one, but the fact remained that he had never missed one of his dad's launches. Even the fight they had last night over whether Josh should finish college before enlisting in the military hadn't prevented him from coming to silently support his father.

His dad wanted him to finish his degree first, and then join the Navy. Josh wanted to enlist in the Army at the same time as his best friend, Ashton Haze, so they could still do things together. It had been a stupid fight.

Josh really didn't know what even started it. It was like a red flag had flashed in front of his face when his dad started talking on the phone last night.

He had argued with his dad about everything. Now, he wished he could take back his angry words; words he hadn't really meant. Pain pierced him at the thought. He stared at the sky with a growing sense that his mind was playing tricks on him.

"I'm so sorry," a voice whispered behind him.

Josh remained stunned, nodding his head in acceptance of the sympathy even though the words couldn't penetrate what his mind was acknowledging. The Space Shuttle was gone, exploding in a fiery ball leaving spiraling ice crystal contrails in its wake as it fell into the ocean below. The sounds of crying echoed around him.

He jerked when he felt a hand on his arm. Blinking in an effort to focus, he saw a staff member of NASA security standing beside him, a grim expression on the man's face. The man said something, but Josh's mind couldn't decipher what he was saying. It wasn't until the man repeated his request that Josh nodded in understanding.

"Follow me."

Josh moved numbly down the narrow steps of the bleachers, his gaze darting to the fading remnants of the shuttle's last path. Other family members of the crew were being guided to a large bus. He waited as several people entered ahead of him before he climbed the steps, almost choking on the heat inside the bus.

Sliding into a vacant seat, he stared out of the tinted windows. His father was gone. The last member of his family. He was alone in the world except for his best friend, Ash. His gaze jerked down when he felt his cell phone buzz. He flipped the top and looked at it, recognizing Ash's phone number. Pressing the connect button, he held it to his ear.

"Is it true, man?" Ash asked in a slightly husky tone.

"Yes," Josh replied in a tight voice.

"I'm sorry," Ash finally replied with a sigh. "I'm here for you."

"I know," Josh muttered, looking down so he didn't see the long line of cars and the people standing around talking about what just happened. "Thanks."

"I mean it," Ash said bluntly.

"I know," Josh replied, closing his eyes. "I'll talk to you later."

"'Kay," Ash said. "Hang in there."

Josh pushed the red button. He could feel the reaction of shock hit him like a rogue wave. Opening his eyes, he stared out at the launch pad's skeletal tower standing in the distance. His dad loved being an astronaut. He had once told Josh that there was nothing like seeing the earth from above to give you an appreciation for just how alone and isolated we were in the vastness of space. Right now, that space felt big, scary, and lonely to Josh.

"Goodbye," Josh murmured when the first wave of real grief hit him. "Aw, shit. I love you, dad. I hope you knew that. I love you," he choked out, closing his eyes when a fierce wave of pain swept through him.

Chapter 1

Ten Years later:
Outside Flagstaff, Arizona:

"Dad, do you need anything else?" Julia Marksdale asked as she stepped into the Observatory.

"No, thank you. I have everything I need at the moment," Harry Marksdale replied in an absent-minded voice.

Julia shook her head and sighed. For the last week, her father had been distracted. She chuckled when she saw that he had placed the remains of his sandwich in his coffee cup by mistake instead of on the plate. He was bent forward over the computer in front of him, studying it with a frown.

"What's wrong?" She asked, walking forward to stand behind him.

Julia watched as her father rubbed a hand down his face and leaned back to gaze up at her through blurry eyes. He shook his head and released a tired sigh. She reached out and touched his shoulder when he closed his eyes for a moment.

"I'm not sure," he admitted in a tired voice, slowly opening his eyes to look up at her. "It could be nothing. I need to take more photographs and check them."

"Are you still studying the Gliese system?" Julia asked, pulling a small, metal, folding chair closer to the table where several different computers were hooked up.

"Yes," Harry replied as he gave Julia a distracted smile before he turned to study her for a moment. "You look so much like your mother when she was your age."

Julia resisted the urge to roll her eyes like she used to do when she was a teenager. He had been saying things like that more frequently. She was beginning to think that the lack of sleep was making him a touch loopy.

At twenty-two, she was used to being the one to take care of him. Her mother left them when she was ten. Living in the desert outside of Flagstaff, Arizona was not the place her mother - Carry Marksdale wanted to spend the rest of her life. The fact that her father spent more time gazing at the stars than he did at his wife didn't help matters. When her mom gave her the choice of going or staying, Julia stayed. She loved the desert and the stars as much as her dad. In the end, she suspected her mother was relieved, because the only time Julia ever heard from her mom was on her birthday.

"So, what are you studying so intently?" Julia asked instead, glancing at the fuzzy images on the screen.

Harry glanced back at the monitor and frowned. "I'm not sure," he admitted. "It may be nothing. I have a new telescope coming, so I hope that it will help."

Julia raised her eyes to the old fourteen inch Cassegrain telescope. It was currently the largest telescope her father owned. The other two were a smaller eight inch and a refractor. They were each housed in separate smaller observatories on the property.

"I'll help you set it up tomorrow night after I finish with the class I'm teaching," Julia said with a smile. "How much more do you have to do tonight? I was going to fix some dinner."

Harry glanced at the computer screen with a sigh before he smiled at Julia. For a moment, she saw his eyes glaze over as he lost himself back in whatever he was thinking before they cleared. The crooked smile told her that she had won the battle with the stars this time.

"I'll be up in a few minutes," he promised with an affectionate grin. "I just need to check the everything one last time before I come in."

Julia rose out of the chair and bent to brush a kiss across her father's forehead. With a sigh, she picked up the remains of his lunch in the stale coffee. A soft chuckle escaped her when she saw a grimace flash across his face.

"If you aren't, I'll be back," she said with a shake of her head. "I love you, dad."

"I love you, too, honey," Harry absently replied, already lost in what he was doing.

Julia glanced at the computer screen once more, a frown creasing her brow. Her dad was an excellent astronomer. He not only taught astronomy and ran the planetarium program with the undergraduates at Northern Arizona University; he had an impressive private set up. She had recently finished her PhD in Astronomy and Physics, taught classes at NAU and volunteered at the Lowell Observatory. Her love of the universe had been nurtured by the fascinating stories her father told her as she was growing up.

"I'll see you in a few minutes, dad," she said again.

..*

Harry stared at the images he had on the screen before his gaze moved to the glossy pictures he had printed out earlier. He had already forgotten his promise to Julia to not be very long. Picking up the eyepiece he used to magnify the objects on the paper in front of him, he leaned forward and looked at the smudge on the photograph. He did the same with the other hundred pictures he had taken over the last several months.

"Tomorrow, I'll have a better chance of seeing what you are," he whispered, sitting back and staring at the computer screen.

Rising stiffly out of the chair when his stomach growled, he turned toward the door. He would come back after dinner for a few hours. The telescope and camera were already set up. All he would need to do tomorrow was process the images.

He paused at the doorway of the observatory, his gaze drifting back one more time to the images. There was something out there, something unnatural that wasn't supposed to be there. He could feel it in his gut. He just needed more proof.

..*

Pentagon, Washington, D.C.
Eight years later:

Lieutenant Commander Joshua Manson tucked his hat under his arm as he entered the Pentagon's main entrance and passed through the rigid security. There would be several more security checkpoints before he reached his destination. Security continued to be tightened as the war against terrorism escalated; a war that he had recently experienced first hand.

He kept his gaze straight as he continued down the corridor, turning right at the main intersection. He walked past the Administrative Assistant Offices of the Army, noting the changes that had been made in the last year. A quick glance at his watch told him he would still make it to his meeting on time. His gaze briefly swept over the different personnel that he passed in the corridors, but he didn't recognize anyone. Turning right, he soon found himself in front of a set of stairs that would take him down several flights.

The constant renovations at the Pentagon made the journey to the Navy's side of the building a challenge. He had given up trying to memorize the interior layout. Every time he thought he had it down, he would discover that the new commander in charge would order changes. It was nothing for a stairwell to abruptly end or a corridor to lead to nowhere.

"Josh," a voice called out behind him.

Josh turned and he saw a familiar face. His eyebrow lifted as he waited. Ashton "Ash" Haze strode down the corridor toward him with a worried expression on his face. The sinking feeling in the pit of Josh's stomach started to grow. If Ash was worried, then that meant everyone should be concerned. Ash was known for his "no worries, be happy" personality.

"What are you doing here?" Josh asked when Ash stopped in front of him. "I thought you were home on leave."

"I was, but I received a call to come here," Ash replied with a shrug. "I thought with the investigation over things would settle down."

Josh's mouth tightened into a straight line. "So had I," he responded lightly, turning back in the direction he was heading. "You never did tell me why you're here."

Ash shrugged. "Admiral Greenburg's Assistant sent a notice. There was no explanation, just that I grace the Admiral with my charming presence. I've done a lot of stupid things in my life, most of them from following you, but disobeying a direct order from an Admiral is not one of them," he retorted with an easy grin. "What about you? I expected you to be doing latrine duty after the way Captain Horne ripped you apart."

"Us… He ripped both of us apart. I wasn't the only one he was threatening, remember?" Josh replied with a grin before it faded. "He understands that we had no choice in the matter. Our mission was to protect the plane that we were escorting and we did."

"That still doesn't mean it didn't cause an international incident," Ash replied dryly as they turned left before making an immediate right into the Administrative Offices for the Navy.

Josh nodded before opening the door. His mind flashed back to the recent investigation that had grounded him and Ash. They had been providing a military escort for a group of dignitaries when two fighters appeared on their radar. Repeated efforts to warn the fighters to turn away had proven fruitless, so he and Ash had engaged. The fighters had been stolen from an undisclosed military base in Saudi Arabia. The issue came up when the news blasted it all over the world that the United States had attacked two allied military fighters.

It would have been nice if the media could have given the whole story instead of one that would create the most controversy so they could sell ad time, Josh thought bitterly.

His and Ash's life had been on hold for the past six months while the investigation was underway. To hide the lapse in security, the true details of the findings were sealed. Unfortunately, until the Senate released the final findings, he and Ash were both grounded.

Stepping up to the front desk, Josh handed the woman behind it his security badge. She swiped it before reaching for the one Ash was holding out. She was silent for several long minutes as she stared at the computer screen in front of her before she gave them a brief, polite smile.

"I will let the Admiral's assistant know that you are here," she said. "Please have a seat."

Josh gave her a curt nod while Ash sent her one of his easy – I'm-pleased-to-meet-you – ones. The woman pointedly ignored Ash's flirtatious grin and returned to whatever she was doing before they came in. Ash's pained expression drew a smirk from Josh. He hadn't missed the faint white line around the third finger of the woman's left hand or the slightly hostile look in her dark brown eyes.

"I must be losing my touch," Ash complained as he walked over to sit down next to Josh.

Josh leaned back and closed his eyes for a moment. The pounding in his head was getting worse. He had caught an early morning flight and was working on a couple of hours of sleep. Cracking an eyelid, he saw the calculating look in Ash's eyes as he stared at the receptionist.

"Forget it," Josh murmured under his breath. "She isn't too happy with men right now."

Ash leaned back and crossed his arms. Josh could feel his friend staring at the woman with a frown now. He shot Josh a glance and scowled.

"Okay, how do you know?" Ash grumbled.

Josh shook his head and opened his eyes to stare at his friend. "You'd think by now you'd learn to look for the clues," he replied dryly. "The third finger of her left hand still has the outline of her wedding ring and the indent from it. She just took it off. I suspect if you looked in her desk drawer, or better yet, the trash can, you'd find it."

"So, maybe she took it off to wash her hands and forgot to put it back on," Ash reasoned.

Josh shook his head. "No, she took it off on purpose. The indent showed it wasn't something she did often. She's also wearing more makeup than she normally wears. The picture on her badge and the one on the wall behind the desk show that she doesn't normally wear very much. Her bottom lip is swollen as well, as if she had repeatedly bitten it and her eyes are slightly bloodshot from crying. Also, the picture on her desk has recently been changed. She used to have a picture of her husband in it. Now, she has a picture of a dog. It is crooked under the glass. If you look closely, you'll see the smudge mark from the ink on it. The dog isn't hers, by the way. There is no dog hair on her uniform," he added.

"Sometimes I really hate your attention to detail. You take all the fun out of the chase," Ash muttered, looking at the woman again. "What other clues did you see, Sherlock?"

A soft chuckle escaped Josh and he shook his head again. "Her lips tightened when you gave her the smile and I swear if she had a gun, you'd be sporting a bullet wound in your ass right now," he said. "No, I suspect her husband finally got caught cheating on her and she kicked him to the curb."

Ash sighed and released his breath. "I hate to admit you are probably right – again," he snorted when the phone rang and the receptionist picked it up. She hissed out a few strong words before hanging it up with a slight bang. "Of course, I'm always open for being the rebound. I'm great at giving comfort."

Josh was about to reply when the door leading into the internal offices suddenly opened. A stiff looking young Yeoman stood in the doorway. Josh rose when the man turned his attention to them.

"Commander Mason, Commander Haze, Admiral Greenburg will see you now," the young man said.

Ash rose behind him. The Yeoman stood stiffly as he and Ash walked through the door. Once they were clear, the man turned on his heel and led the way through a series of inner offices until he stopped outside the rich, dark wooden doors with Admiral Greenburg's name attached to it. The Yeoman opened the door and announced their arrival.

Josh walked in first, followed by Ash. He heard the slight click of the door when the Admiral's personal assistant quietly closed it behind them. Both he and Ash stood at attention until the Admiral finally looked up several minutes later. Josh's mind raced through all the different scenarios as to why he and Ash were there. Each one kept coming back to one conclusion, they were both about to find themselves on a different career path than what they were expecting – probably not a favorable one at that.

At thirty years old, Josh had passed his thirteenth year in the Navy. He planned on staying the full thirty. His hope of joining the astronaut program a few years ago had slowly disappeared after several rejection letters, but his love of flying hadn't. While he had excelled at it, his tendency to do things his own way had gotten him in trouble more than once, even if he had been right more often than not.

"At ease," Admiral Greenburg finally said with a nod of his head. "Sit down."

Josh sat in one of the plush chairs that had been moved in front of the desk while Ash took the other one. He sat stiffly as he waited for the admiral to speak. His gaze flickered to the open folder on his superior's desk. If he had to guess, it was either on him or Ash.

Admiral Greenburg sat back in his seat and studied them carefully for several long seconds before he leaned forward again. The expression on his face clearly said he wasn't pleased with what he saw; another sign that this meeting wasn't going to be a pleasant one.

"You've both applied to the astronaut program multiple times, why?" Greenburg asked in a blunt tone.

Josh frowned. This was not a question he was expecting. It wasn't often that he was taken by surprise, but the start of the conversation had definitely done that.

Josh shrugged. "You are aware that my father was in the program," he said. "He went on three missions into space. It only seemed natural that I would follow in his footsteps."

Greenburg turned his attention to Ash. "What about you?" He asked.

Josh felt his friend give him a quick look before he redirected it back to the admiral. A part of him wanted to grin at Ash. He wondered how his friend was going to answer the question – truthfully or with a politically correct answer. Knowing Ash as well as he did, he doubted his friend would be able to keep his foot out of his mouth.

"Josh bet me that I couldn't get in," Ash admitted.

Yep, truth every time, Josh thought.

It was just as well, Ash wasn't a very good liar. He was a damn good pilot and friend, though. That was what made them excel as a team.

"He lost the bet then. You are both to report to Lyndon B. Johnson Space Center tomorrow morning," Admiral Greenburg stated.

Josh blinked in surprise. Ash drew in a sharp breath. Sitting forward, Josh stared at the admiral in confusion.

"Why?" He asked in a blunt tone.

The admiral studied Josh's hard face for several long seconds again before he responded. His lips were tight. Josh glanced down at the file on the admiral's desk again. At the top was a subheading in large, bold letters that said Family. Neither he nor Ash had any living relatives. That was another common thread that bound them. Ash had been adopted by an older woman, but she had passed away almost five years ago.

"For a top secret mission," the admiral stated. "I was asked to pick two candidates that would be crazy enough to take on a suicide mission. You two came up. You'll find out the details when you arrive tomorrow morning. My assistant has made all the arrangements. You are dismissed."

Josh rose slowly out of the chair when the admiral closed the file in front of him. Almost as if the Yeoman was listening at the door, it opened. Ash stood up beside him and shot him a puzzled look before saluting the admiral and turning sharply on his heel. Josh did the same and followed at a slower pace. He paused at the door when he heard his name being called.

"Commander Mason," Greenburg called out.

Josh turned. "Yes, sir," he responded.

Greenburg rose from his seat and walked around it to stand at the corner of the desk. Josh noticed he was holding the two files. His eyes lifted to the admiral's face.

"I knew your father. He was a good man and a great astronaut. He would have been proud of you. Whatever happens, don't dishonor his memory, or me," Greenburg ordered.

Josh stared back at the admiral for a moment before he replied. "Yes, sir," he said in a quiet voice.

Stepping out of the office, he strode down the hallway where Ash was waiting for him with a puzzled expression on his face. They both waited impatiently as the admiral's assistant handed each of them a packet before explaining that they would be catching a military hop to Houston at 0500 the next morning.

Neither one of them said anything until they had left the office. Ash grabbed his arm once they reached the outer corridor. Josh turned to look into Ash's dark face.

"What the hell is going on?" Ash asked, holding up the envelope. "I thought we were about to get our asses handed to us on a platter and instead we are suddenly being sent to astronaut training. What the hell is up with that?"

"I don't know any more than you do, Ash," Josh replied with a frown, glancing down at the folder before looking up again.

Ash blew out a long breath and scowled at him. "When you are taken by surprise, I know shit is about to hit the fan," he muttered, turning away. "I need a drink."

"You aren't the only one," Josh said. "I'm staying at the Plaza. I'll meet you at the Boundary at nineteen hundred."

"Sounds good," Ash replied as they passed through security. "And, Josh…"

Josh paused and turned back as he was about to go down the steps. "Yeah," he responded.

Ash gave him a slight grin. "I expect you to have it figured out, man. You know I don't like shit taking me by surprise," he replied in a half teasing, half serious tone.

"Neither do I," Josh retorted before turning. "Nineteen hundred. Don't be late!"

Chapter 2

Lyndon B. Johnston Space Center, Houston, Texas: 0800.

Josh held out his hand to retrieve his security badge and picked up the small bag holding his belongings. His gaze flickered around the huge reception area of the compound before narrowing on an older woman that was walking toward him and Ash. She paused to speak with one of the guards, glancing at the two of them several times before she nodded.

"Commander Mason, Commander Haze, welcome to the space program. My name is Lydia Gaines. I'm one of the senior scientists that will be overseeing your training. Please follow me," she said with a warm smile before reaching out to take two badges that the security guard was holding. Turning back to them, she held one out to him before giving the other to Ash. "You'll need to keep that with you at all times. If you don't, you'll find yourself locked out."

"Dr. Gaines, can you tell us what this is all about?" Josh asked with a frown. "The information we were given was little more than an order to report here."

Lydia smiled over her shoulder as she swept her badge across a lighted post and stepped through. Josh did the same, following her. Ash glanced at Josh with a raised eyebrow as he did the same.

"Everything will be explained shortly, Commander. I apologize for the lack of information given to you so far. I've, uh, scheduled a briefing within the hour," Lydia assured him, pausing outside a bank of elevators. "I think it would be best if the entire team is present."

"Team?" Ash asked, watching as the doors parted.

Josh watched as Lydia Gaines nodded her head and stepped into the elevator. He followed and turned. Ash raised an eyebrow at him again. It was Ash's way of asking him if he had figured out anything. Josh gave a barely visible shake to his head.

He stepped to the back so that he was standing behind the woman. She was in her mid-sixties if he had to guess. His gaze swept down over her. She was wearing a pair of tan dress pants and a dark red blouse with a wide, matching red belt around her waist. Her feet were encased in a pair of sensible, tan loafers that matched her pants. Except for her badge, she didn't appear to be carrying anything else. The lack of information was frustrating to Josh.

"How long have you been in Houston, Dr. Gaines?" Josh asked politely.

Lydia glanced over her shoulder with a smile. "Almost, uh, ten years, Commander," she replied. "Why do you ask?"

"Just curious," Josh said with a shrug. "I imagine the weather isn't much different from Louisiana."

Lydia's soft chuckle filled the elevator as it began to slow. "Very good, Commander. Can you tell me which part of Louisiana I came from?" She asked with a curious expression of her own.

"Outside of New Orleans, perhaps the Metairie area," Josh replied. "You have a slight French accent on some of your syllables and often use the term 'uh' which is common in the south Louisiana dialect."

Lydia's eyes widened and she nodded in approval. "Your files indicated that you were a smart man, Commander Mason. You'll need to be for this mission," she added before turning around and stepping out of the elevator.

"I wonder what in the hell that file says about me?" Ash muttered under his breath. "How the hell did you know where she was from?"

Josh's lips curled into a smirk. "The last woman I dated came from New Orleans and said 'uh' in just about every sentence," he admitted with a mischievous grin. "I immediately recognized it. It isn't something you forget, especially when it is inserted repeatedly between exclamations of passion."

Ash chuckled and shook his head. "Only you would pick up on something like that," he muttered.

..*

Josh walked down the long corridor following their escort. Each room they passed was filled with people. What was strange, they all paused when he and Ash passed by to stare at them before bursting out in excited conversation.

"Something is up," Ash whispered, glancing at the rooms as they passed. "I swear I'm getting the feeling that we are about to be fed to the lions or something."

"It's the 'or something' that has me worried," Josh retorted under his breath.

He slowed his stride before coming to a stop when Lydia paused outside of a room. Her hand gripped the door handle and she smiled at the two of them with a hint of pride and anticipation. Josh was pretty sure she could feel their frustration and curiosity.

"Commanders, I'd like to welcome you to Project Gliese 581g," Lydia said, pushing the door open and motioning for them to step through.

Josh glanced at Lydia before he stepped through the door. His eyes widened when he saw instead of a conference area, they were in what looked like a huge training room. Dozens of people paused as he and Ash stepped inside.

In the center of the room was a strange looking spaceship, or at least a section of it. He walked forward, his eyes glued to the futuristic design. His gaze ran over the outer hull. Small windows around the bottom gave a hint as to what might lie inside. This was far different from the space shuttles that he had seen.

"What is this?" He asked with a frown.

"It's a replica of the Gliese 581 Starship," a soft voice replied. "A long range spacecraft made specifically for extended exploration."

Josh turned to watch as a slender woman in her early thirties walked up to him. She was wearing a pair of faded blue jeans and a white cotton top. Her brown hair was piled up on the top of her head in a messy bun with small wisps fanning her face. Her dark brown eyes were piercing and held a look of curiosity and an intense assessment of them – as if she was evaluating whether he and Ash measured up to her expectations. In her left hand, she carried two binders.

"Dr. Julia Marksdale," she said, holding out her right hand.

"Josh Mason," Josh replied, shaking her hand before turning as Ash stepped up.

"Ashton Haze, but everyone calls me…," Ash started to say with the easy grin that melted most women's hearts.

"Ash," Julia Marksdale finished with a smile. "Your reputation is well documented, as is Commander Mason's. We are honored to have you as part of our team. Lydia, I'll introduce them to the Gliese's command center, if you like, while you let everyone know that they have arrived."

"Thank you. Gentlemen, I leave you in very capable hands," Lydia replied with a smile. "We'll meet for the in-depth briefing in an hour."

Julia nodded. She waited until Lydia had walked away before she turned back to look at them. Josh's eyes instinctively moved down to her left hand – it was bare and there was no sign of a ring having been on it. His curiosity grew when she turned and looked up at the replica. She waved her hand toward it and gave them a smile filled with pride.

"It is slightly different from the aircraft you are used to flying. Would you like to see the inside?" She asked with a smile when both men nodded.

"Is this replacing the shuttles? It was my understanding that private companies were taking over the development of reusable spacecrafts to ferry astronauts around," Ash commented, glancing up at the massive circular pod.

"This is slightly different," Julia replied. "While this has several private backers, this spaceship is designed for an interplanetary mission."

Surprise coursed through him at her words. He glanced at Ash. His friend had a what-the-fuck-does-that-mean expression on his face. He felt the same way as he started forward.

"Project Gliese 581g is an international project that was started six years ago. It is projected to launch in eighteen months, if all goes well," Julia said as she stepped around to a steep, portable staircase.

"What has to happen for it to go well?" Ash asked.

Julia stopped on the fourth step and turned to look down at them. A small smile curved her lips. Josh could feel that assessing look as she scanned both of them again.

"Whether or not you both agree to accept this mission," Julia replied, turning to climb the stairs. "The team needs you, but this mission is on a volunteer basis because of its nature."

"It would be nice to understand what in the hell is going on. Usually the briefing comes first," Josh retorted behind her.

"I second that," Ash responded in a frustrated voice, staring back at Julia. "It'd be nice if someone actually told us why we are here."

Julia bit her lip and nodded. "Let me show you the Gliese 581 and I'll explain what I can before the meeting," she replied, turning to finish climbing the steps.

***

Josh swallowed and looked around the futuristic dashboard. It was like something out of a movie set. His hand ran along the back of the seat as he gazed down at the sophisticated control panel. Julia stood to one side in silence.

"Is this for real?" Ash asked in a husky voice filled with awe.

"Yes," Julia replied. "It is an exact replica of the Gliese 581 control center. I apologize that neither of you were briefed before coming here. There are a few things that have to be approved before I can discuss them in depth. Lydia and I will try to correct that error as much as we can for the moment. I hope you understand the sensitive position that I am in at the moment. I promise to be open about everything once I receive final clearance to do so. Lydia suggested that you both might be interested in seeing the Gliese 581 trainer while she pulled the team in. Some of them are at other buildings on the compound. She thought it might help give a clearer picture of what we will be going over, as well."

Josh nodded, not missing strain in Julia's voice or the hint that there was a lot more to tell then just a mission to space. Whatever was going on, it was larger than a top secret spacecraft. This wasn't an orbiter. Just as Julia said, this type of technology was meant for long distance travel through deep space.

He paused in front of the console, staring through what looked like a large window at the technicians moving around outside the trainer. The interior glass pane didn't match with what he saw outside. His gaze ran over the console in front of him and he noticed a small screen that displayed the same image.

"From below it looked like there were just small windows," Josh commented with a frown.

"What you are seeing is an illusion," Julia said, stepping forward and touching several icons on the console screen. "It is a new technology the Chinese have developed. This will give us a greater view of what we see and help eliminate some of the feelings of being in a small space over a long period of time. At least, that is what we hope," she added, turning off the cameras.

Josh blinked when he saw a curved wall appear in front of him. It looked almost like a large IMAX screen without the cameras on. Leaning forward, he repeated the process that Julia had done just seconds before and a visual of the large room reappeared.

"The resolution is the best I've ever seen," Josh murmured in approval. "There is no distortion that could happen with normal windows. Can you record as well?"

"Yes," Julia replied. "It will be necessary for this mission to document as much as possible and send it back to Earth."

"I'm assuming the briefing will cover this mission? In a nutshell, what is it about?" Ash asked, sliding into the seat next to where Josh was standing.

Julia looked down at Ash. "To discover if we are alone in the universe or not," she replied in a quiet voice.

Josh's head jerked up from where he was studying the controls. In his peripheral vision, he saw Ash's head twist around as well. His mouth tightened at her quiet statement.

"Do you think we aren't?" Josh asked.

Julia glanced at him and nodded. "I know we aren't. The question is, what happened to the others and where did they come from?" She responded before glancing at her watch. "It's almost time to meet the rest of the team. I have more information that I would like to go over with you before the briefing."

..*

Twenty minutes later, Josh and Ash sat in a large room that looked more like a mini-theater than a conference room. Every seat was filled. Julia had escorted him and Ash to the front row and indicated for them to sit down before she had stepped up onto the small platform next to Lydia.

Josh's mind buzzed with the information Julia had shared just minutes before. He glanced down at the binder in his hand. Julia had explained that he had been selected as the commander and Ash had been selected as the pilot for a very special mission into space. While she did not go into much detail due to the limited time, he was piecing together what he had seen. This was a top secret, international mission, possibly to Mars, definitely deep space. He half wondered if the scientists had found something on their nearest planet that hadn't been leaked to the news yet.

"Good morning. Thank you for taking time off of your busy schedules. This morning, I'm happy to welcome the last two members to our team," Lydia announced, glancing at Josh and Ash for a moment before scanning the group. "Lt. Commander Joshua Mason will be the commander of the Starship Gliese 581 while Lt. Commander Ashton Haze has been chosen as the pilot. Gentlemen, I'd like to introduce you to the rest of your crew. You've already met Julia. She is a Mission Specialist and will provide navigation and contact support. While both Mei and Sergi are new to the crew, they are not new to Project Gliese 581g. Dr. Mei Li Hú is from the Chinese space agency. She is a Mission Specialist with a background in computer science, biology, and environmental systems. The last member of the team is Sergi Lazaroff. His specialty is in mechanical engineering, payload, and weapons."

"Weapons?" Josh asked with a frown as he glanced at the spec sheet in front of him of the Gliese

581. "Will the Gliese be equipped with a weapons system?"

"Only in Sergi's dreams," Mei interjected, drawing laughter from everyone.

Lydia smiled at their teasing before she answered Josh's question. "At the moment the answer is no, but we have not eliminated the possibility. The biggest drawback is the technology. We've advanced considerably over the last few decades, but a weapons system is still more science fiction than reality," Lydia said. "This is a review for many of you, but the countdown has begun. In eighteen months, Project Gliese 581g will depart for the Earth's first interplanetary mission."

"Interplanetary," Ash replied with a slight shake of his head. "This is huge. It would have been nice to have more than eighteen months to prepare."

Julia turned to stare at Ash with a strained smile. "I understand your reservations, Commander. The tight deadline is unavoidable," she explained. "The original crew for the mission would have received slightly more time to prepare. It is regrettable that the four of you won't have the same opportunity. On a positive note, both Sergi and Mei have been on several missions to the International Space Station and have worked on the Gliese 581's construction. It helps that they are familiar with space travel."

"What happened to the original crew?" Ash asked with a raised eyebrow.

"They and the backup team were killed when the two helicopters they were on crashed while returning to the compound. There is only one original member of the crew left. I had a meeting in Washington that night and was delayed. It is the only thing that saved me, and possibly this mission. We lost some brilliant men and women in the crash, including my father," Julia replied in a quiet tone that resonated throughout the room.

"I remember hearing about it on the news, but didn't realize the magnitude of it. I'm sorry for your loss," Josh replied somberly after a minute of silence.

Josh studied Julia's pale face. There was more to the story, but something told him it was personal. He could see the shadow of grief in her eyes when she explained the tragic accident that took the original crew members.

Josh caught Ash's glance that told him his friend felt it as well. Turning his head, he stared at the others in the room. He listened while different project managers shared reports, progress, and issues they were having. It wasn't until the end of the briefing, after Julia and Lydia quietly congratulated all of them for their selection as members of the crew, that he felt a nagging suspicion there was still more information being withheld.

"I look forward to the mission," Josh responded with a sharp nod.

Ash was silent for a moment before he sat back in his seat. "Eighteen months to departure, huh?" He replied with a grim smile. "We have a lot to learn."

"Yes, you both have a lot to learn in a short amount of time, but I promise you will also have the best team in the world behind you," Julia said with a relieved expression.

"Does anyone have any questions before we begin?" Lydia asked, stepping up to the front again.

"I do," Josh said with a twist of his lips.

"What is it, Commander?" Lydia asked.

Josh studied Julia's face as he asked his question. "Where exactly are we going?" He asked.

Chapter 3

Josh leaned against the outside wall of the training compound two days later. He drew in a deep breath and rolled his head on his shoulders to release the tension. He had just come back from his early morning run along the flightline.

It was still dark out, but the hint of sunrise was beginning to lighten the horizon. His gaze caught on the movements of another runner. It only took a few seconds for him to recognize Julia. He waited as she jogged closer. He knew the moment that she realized that she was no longer alone.

"Good morning," he called out when she slowed to a walk.

Julia glanced at him and placed her hands on her hips as she drew in deep, steady breaths through her nose to calm her respiration. She gave him a curt nod before she glanced at the fitness watch on her wrist.

"Good morning," she finally replied. "How are you settling in?"

"Not bad," Josh replied with a shrug. "I take it the small accommodations here at the compound are to prepare us for our living quarters in space."

Julia gave him a slight smile and walked in a tight circle as she continued to cool down. Josh watched her as she bowed her head. She appeared to be distracted. Whatever was bothering her, he still got the feeling that he and Ash weren't being told everything and she was struggling with that. Julia had left shortly after the meeting that first day, so he had not been able to confront her about his suspicions.

"There will actually be more room on the Gliese 581 than is normally allocated on a spaceship. Privacy was taken into consideration when the design was finalized due to the length of time we will be gone," she finally said, drawing in a deep breath while standing with her back to him and looking out over the horizon. "I love this time of the morning, don't you?"

Josh heard the hint of wistfulness in her voice. "What's really going on? I think Ash and I deserve to know the truth," Josh demanded in a quiet tone. "What aren't you telling us? I know you explained in the briefing that this was an exploratory mission to test intergalactic travel, but I can't help but feel it is more than that. We aren't heading to Mars as I originally expected, but into a section of the solar system that makes no sense to me from the information in the briefing that you gave us before the meeting. Why? I get the dangers, but I would have thought Mars would have been mankind's first attempt at long distance space travel."

Julia slowly turned to study him. He stared back at her, not breaking her intense gaze. He saw the flicker of uncertainty in her eyes before she released her breath and nodded.

"Yes, you do deserve to know the truth. All of the crew does. I couldn't say anything until I received permission. That took more time than I expected," she admitted. "The original crew knew what they were facing. Because of the classification of the mission, Lydia and I could not share it in the briefing the other day which is why Lydia did not answer your question when you wanted to know where we were going. Besides a very select group, only Lydia and myself are aware of the actual destination. It was important to keep it secret to prevent any leakage to the press. Even Sergi and Mei were not privileged to the information I'm about to share due to the complexity of the mission. It was important to prevent the public from discovering what my father had found," she explained, staring intently up at him.

Josh returned her intense look. "Trust is a very important factor on any mission," he said in a blunt tone. "Without trust, it isn't a mission, but certain death to one or all of those on it. If the government expects us to put our lives on the line, the least they can do is tell us what the fuck is going on."

Julia's jaw tightened before she drew in a deep breath and released it. "My father asked me a question six years ago when this project was first conceived that I will now ask you, Commander. Would you still agree to go on this mission if you knew that you would probably never make it back to Earth?"

Josh reflected on the softly asked question. Would he? What did he have to come back to? He wasn't married. Hell, he wasn't even seeing anyone at the moment. He didn't have any kids or family to return to. The only real friend he had was Ash, if he admitted it. His gaze flashed to the horizon and the soft glow. What would it be like to wake up and see the stars instead of the sun for the rest of his life?

"I don't really have much to keep me here," he replied, turning to look at her. "What about you? Surely you have a reason to return."

Julia shook her head. "Not anymore," she responded in a light tone. "Thank you for your answer. It is only fair that I ask the others the same question. Hopefully, they will feel the same way that we do. I'll . I planned on calling a meeting this morning for the team now that I've received permission to proceed. If you'll meet me in the conference room in half an hour, I'll explain everything. I promise, there will be no more deceptions or half-truths."

Josh reached out and touched her arm when she started to turn. "I knew when I applied for the space program that if I was accepted and sent into space that there was always a chance of never returning to Earth. I still wanted to go."

Julia stared back at him in silence for a few potent seconds before she stepped back. "Admiral Greenburg was right when he said you were the right man for this assignment. The President also agrees. I would say that is a significant level of trust, Lieutenant Mason," she responded with a somber smile. "I've been ordered to answer any and all questions that you or the rest of the crew have. I promise to be transparent in my answers."

Josh watched as she turned on her heel and quietly jogged away. He turned his head and he absently watched the horizon as the sun came up. For a moment, he felt a strange sense of surrealism, as if it was just an illusion before it rose above the curve of the tree line in the distance.

Turning, he headed back to the apartments set up for the crew. He would pose the same question to Ash. Deep down, he hoped his friend agreed because something told him he was going to need Ash's expertise on this mission.

* * *

A half hour later, Josh and Ash stepped into the conference room. Mei and Sergi nodded to them in greeting. The other two members looked as puzzled as he felt.

Julia glanced up when they entered and she released the breath that she was holding. Her eyes swept from Ash to Josh.

"Thank you," she said in a quiet voice. "Once again, I apologize for all the secrecy; I was only given final approval late last night to share the information."

"Don't thank us yet," Josh warned in a slightly curt tone. "Since we were given this assignment, I would have expected that all clearances were approved. I don't like walking into a situation blind or with half the Intel."

Julia nodded. “Normally that isn’t the case. With the sudden deaths of the majority of the crew, it has created a vacuum that was unexpected and had some of our supporters questioning the success of the project. As I told you earlier, Commander, the President has order me to answer any and all questions,” she responded in a light tone. “If everyone would please have a seat, I’ll explain everything from the beginning. I hope to answer any questions that still remain afterwards. It is understood that any information shared here is classified and must remain confidential.”

Julia picked up the remote for the project and turned it on. She knew each slide by heart. They were a combination of ten years’ worth of work. Only a very select group of backers, including some of the highest-ranking officials in the world, knew about Project Gliese 581g.

She swallowed as she turned back to look at Ash and Josh. They were staring up at the slide with a frown. She knew what they were staring at. It had been the same one that her father had presented before the Senate subcommittee during a closed session.

“Ten years ago an astronomer was doing deep space astrophotography in the hopes of discovering a star system that had the potential for Earth-like planets. During his search, he thought he might have found several such systems. Gliese is the eighty-ninth closest star to the Sun and is located in the constellation of Libra. It is a spectral type M3V star, which is also known…"

"As a red dwarf," Ash responded, giving Julia a crooked smile. "What can I say? I love watching the Science Channel."

"Ah, another true science fan, Sergi," Mei teased. "You should be happy now."

"You can learn a lot from the Science Channel, eh, Ash," Sergi retorted with a grin.

Julia chuckled and relaxed. "Yes, it is known as a red dwarf," she repeated with a smile. "It is located approximately twenty light years from Earth and is estimated to have a mass that is about one-third of the Sun. Observation shows that the star may have planetary movement around it based on current evidence. There is speculation of some additional stellar activity that could be the result of mimicking from the radical velocity variations of orbital planets. At this time, there are three suspected planets. Gliese 581c is considered to be similar to Venus." Julia turned and clicked to the next slide. "Rampant greenhouse effects make the planet too hot to be habitable. Gliese 581d and g have come under closer scrutiny, though doubt has been raised as to whether either one has the potential for life. Still, they have not been completely ruled out."

"If there is doubt, why call this project 581g? Why send a mission to explore it when the likelihood of finding a habitable planet twenty light years away is virtually impossible? You'd have a better chance of finding a diamond in the middle of the Sahara," Josh observed, folding his arms across his chest and staring at the grainy image with an ironic twist to his lips.

"Because it isn't the planet that we want to explore," Julia replied in a soft voice. She raised the remote and clicked to the next slide. "My father was looking in the direction of Gliese 581 for planets. Instead, he found this."

Julia watched as each member of her audience frowned and sat forward. Their gaze was glued to the image, or rather, the strange, unnatural object in the image. She clicked to the next slide. This picture was taken just six months ago by a new Russian space telescope. It was slightly smaller, but more powerful than the aging Hubble.

"What the…?" Ash exclaimed, rising out of his seat.

"What is it?" Josh demanded, glancing at Julia briefly before turning his gaze back to the slide.

"It looks mechanical," Sergi exclaimed.

"It is too symmetrical to have been made naturally," Mei whispered, sitting forward in excitement.

"We don't know, but we are going to find out," Julia replied. "This is our destination. The Gliese 581 is almost complete. A select group of top scientists from all over the world have been working day and night for years. This project was too big for just one country and if we find what we suspect is out there, it will affect every person on this planet. This could be the answer to where we came from… and whether we are alone or not in the universe."

Mei glanced at Julia. "If word of this spread to the public, there would be world-wide chaos," she stated in concern.

"Yes," Julia agreed. "In addition, the President thought it best that the launch occurred before the new presidential elections to prevent the project from either being canceled or publicized. That is the reason for the short window of time."

"Good ole politics, ruling the roost again," Ash muttered under his breath. "I'd like to send a few politicians on this one way trip."

Julia bit back a chuckle and nodded. She turned and watched as Josh stepped forward toward the screen. His face was chiseled into a hard mask. She turned to stare up at the screen. It didn't matter how many times she gazed at it, she still felt that yearning deep down inside to know if the object in these images her father took were real, and if they were, why were they there?

"How long will it take to reach it?" Josh asked in a quiet tone.

"Approximately thirteen months," Julia replied. "The object is twice the distance from the Earth to Jupiter."

"Thirteen? What type of propulsion system does the spaceship have?" Ash asked in surprise.

Julia smiled when she heard the curiosity mixed with a touch of wonder in Ash's voice. "A new combination ion-solar propulsion system that was a joint effort between China, Russia, and the U.S.," Julia answered, "The scientists in China and Russia are just as curious as we are to see if it works. Of course, due to the nature of this mission, it is for a different reason. They believe we are going to Mars."

"This is why my father is backing this project. He has always believed that it was possible to go to another planet. Does he know about the true nature of this mission?" Mei asked. "Does he know that I have been chosen to be a member of the crew?"

"He does now. That is one reason I was delayed. Your father's company, and his standing with the Chinese government, was imperative to the success of this mission. I met with the President and your father last night. You are one of the most qualified members of this project to slide into the position. I needed the clearance to not only tell all of you, but also meet with your father. He has agreed to continue to offer support and to remain quiet about the true destination," Julia replied. "I admit, there was some hesitation about allowing you to be a part of the crew because you have a family. Your father wanted me to assure you that he is very proud to have you as a member."

Julia drew in a deep breath and braced herself for the question that she knew was bound to be asked. It was a question she and the original crew members had discussed numerous times over the past several years. She briefly closed her eyes when she heard Josh draw in a deep breath and she stiffened her shoulders.

"None of us have a family, that was why we were chosen, isn't it? There is an expectation that we won't make it back. Why?" Josh asked.

Julia opened her eyes and gazed back at the expression of hesitation and suspicion in Josh's eyes. A rueful smile curved her lips at the corner, but didn't quite reach her eyes. Now was the moment of truth, would everyone still agree to the mission or would they decide they didn't want to take the chance.

"Because my father and I suspected that it might be a gateway. New data continues to support that possibility. If it is, there is a chance we might activate it," she whispered.

"Are you saying like a Stargate of some kind?" Ash asked.

Julia looked back up at the blurred circular object. "Yes," she replied.

"Well, shit," Ash muttered, stepping over to stand near Josh. "I always knew following you was going to get me into a world of trouble. I just never expected it to be out of the solar system."

Josh grimaced. "Isn't that the truth," he muttered under his breath, staring at the image again.

Julia turned at the small group. "So, do I tell the President that it is a go?" She asked in a slightly tense tone.

"Go for me," Josh replied, turning to look at her.

"It's a go for me," Ash said with a nod.

Julia turned to look at Sergi. He was frowning up at the screen before he turned and gave her a crooked grin. She returned his smile.

“Someone has to figure out how to make it work,” Sergi replied with a shrug. “I can fix just about anything. I will go.”

“Mei?” Julia asked in a soft tone. “Out of all of us, you have the most to lose. You have your family.”

Mei glanced at the others before rising and taking a step closer to the screen. She was silent for several long seconds before she turned with a serene smile on her face. Her eyes glowed with determination.

“My family will understand,” Mei said. “My father has always been proud of my achievements. He would never have backed this project if he did not believe in it. It is an honor to go.”

“Thank you,” Julia breathed in relief.

Chapter 4

Eighteen months later:
Baikonur Cosmodrome, Kazakhstan

"The first umbilical tower has separated," Launch Control stated.

"Copy thirty-eight," a woman's voice echoed in the background. "Auto-sequence has been initiated."

"Roger, twenty seconds and counting," Launch Control responded. "The final umbilical tower has now separated. Engines have fired with maximum thrust and we have liftoff from the Baikonur Cosmodrome in Kazakhstan at 1:42 a.m. on their way to Gliese 581."

"Good first stage performance," Josh said sixty seconds later into the microphone attached to his helmet.

"Roll pitch is nominal," Ash stated. "All systems normal."

Josh breathed in and out, in calm even breaths, as the Soyuz rocket went through the different stages necessary before breaking through Earth's orbit. He followed Ash's self-assured movements over the controls as he monitored their flight path and the systems.

"Welcome to the twilight zone, boys and girls," Ash said as they exited the outer atmosphere.

Josh kept his eyes focused on the paper in front of him. This was their second trip into space. The first had been a year ago. That was when he caught his initial glance at Gliese 581.

It had been one of the most magnificent pieces of technology that he had ever seen. He remembered Sergi and Mei teasing him and Ash. It was at that moment when he knew he had made the right decision.

"So, you think we were going to travel through space in a tin can?" Sergi had asked him with a grin. "If it helps, my friend, I felt the same way when I first saw the Gliese. She is a magnificent ship, is she not?"

"She had better be! She has some of the most advance technology known to man aboard her," Mei replied.

Sergi rolled his eyes. "Mei's father's company supplied a great deal of the technology being used," he murmured, before wincing. "She didn't want anyone to know that, though."

"There is no keeping it a secret with you telling everyone. My father has always had a fascination with space," Mei growled in exasperation before she grinned. "Besides, every time Sergi tells someone, it gives me a chance to hit him."

Sergi gave him and Ash a pained expression. "I should never have shown her how to fight," he muttered in pretend resignation.

Mei and Julia's laughter filled the cockpit. Sergi and Mei's constant picking on each other had become a source of entertainment among the crew. They were both intelligent and enjoyed the banter, which made it even more fun to watch as they tried to outdo each other.

"Mission Control, turning over control for core rendezvous and docking sequence," Ash said, jerking Josh back to the present.

"Copy," Mission control responded.

"We can see the pictures. Three hundred meters and closing. Begin fly around," Ash responded.

"We see thrusters are working and we are moving to docking assembly. Copy," Mission Control responded.

Josh watched on the screens as the docking mechanism came into view. Mission control continued to give them information as the two docking assemblies lined up. A few minutes later, there was a soft jerk and the sound of the docking assembly locking.

"Locking assembly has engaged, Gliese 581. Welcome aboard your new home," Mission Control stated.

"Copy that, Mission Control," Ash responded with a grin as he finished the final shut down and prepared to open the connecting hatch. "Let's go take a look at our new home."

..*

Five days later, Josh stood in front of the huge virtual window, looking down at the Earth. Two of the crew members from the International Space

Station had departed an hour before with the capsule that had brought them here. The two cosmonauts would dock with the outlying structure that had been used as a base during construction of the Gliese 581. They would release the last of the tethers. The remaining base would be joined to the International Space Station. At the moment they were waiting for final approval from Mission Control to begin a voyage unlike anything man has ever done before.

"It is good to know that the artificial gravity works," Julia commented as she gripped the handhelds near the doorway and lowered her feet to the floor before stepping inside the main control and living area. "Though, I have to admit floating is fun."

"It is more than fun," Mei laughed as she came up behind Julia. "I missed this part of being in space."

"Not as much as I missed watching you bounce off of things," Sergi retorted with a grin.

Mei turned and pushed Sergi backwards when he tried to come into the control room. Grabbing the handheld, she nimbly lowered her feet to the floor and stepped into the area with the artificial gravity. She glanced over her shoulder and grinned when Sergi stumbled.

"It is not as easy as it looks," he grumbled, flashing a quick grin.

Mei tossed her braid over her shoulder and laughed. "You are just clumsy," she retorted, darting out of Sergi's reach when he started to grab for her braid. "And slow."

Josh couldn't keep the amused grin from escaping. He wondered if those two would be like this the entire journey. Turning back, he stared down at the Earth again as the others slowly made their way over one at a time to join him.

"I wonder if we will ever see it again," Mei asked in a soft voice.

"I don't see why not," Josh replied, shooting a glance at Julia's calm face. "We get out there, find out what the object is, and come back."

"Almost three years in space, a trillion million miles from any other living soul, and totally self-reliant on a massive piece of equipment that looks great on paper, but has never been put to the test," Sergi reflected, rubbing his chin before he dropped his hand and shrugged. "It will be a piece of pie. I would say we have a billion to one chance of making it back in one piece."

"It is a piece of cake," Mei growled, turning and punching Sergi in the arm. "I'm going to go check on my plants."

"What?! What did I say this time? Mei!" Sergi groaned. "Chinese women are too difficult to understand."

Josh watched as Ash hastily moved aside as Mei swept past him. Ash's eyebrows rose when Sergi quickly followed. A grin curved Josh's lips when he saw the expression on Ash's face. It wouldn't be long before his friend joined in the fun.

"What'd I miss this time?" Ash asked.

"Mei asked if we would ever see Earth again," Julia replied before Josh could say anything.

"And Sergi's answer was…?" Ash asked, glancing back at the other two members of the crew who had disappeared through the doorway.

"A rundown of how far we are going in a prototype spaceship with no backup if something were to go wrong," Julia answered with a brief glance at Josh. "I have some tests to run before we get too much further away. Please, excuse me."

Ash and Josh watched as Julia disappeared in the opposite direction. Each person had to deal with the reality of their decision. It didn't matter that they had been training non-stop for the past eighteen months for this mission.

In the end, all the talk, all the planning, couldn't quite prepare them mentally for what was ahead. If something happened, there wouldn't be a damn thing anyone on Earth could do to save them. The knowledge that they would have to depend on each other, and a never-before-tested spaceship on a maiden voyage into the unknown, was unsettling and it would take time for each person to come to terms with it.

Josh understood this. It was one of the things his dad had talked to him about before each mission. For the first time in his life, he could finally appreciate what his father had been trying to tell him. His father's quiet voice rang through his memory.

"Every mission could be your last, son," Edward Mason said. "You can't go into it thinking about that.

You focus on what needs to be done. In the back of your mind, there is always the thought of what could go wrong, that is why we train for it, but we don't let it consume us. If you do, if you quit, then you are doomed to failure and failure in space means death."

Josh jerked back to the present when he felt Ash touch his arm. He pressed his lips into a firm line and nodded. He turned when he heard the sound of the communications console chime.

"Call the others," he ordered. "It's time to go."

Chapter 5

Gliese 581 – Eighteen months; twenty-three days; four hours: 928,081,020 km/6.2 Astronomical Units (AU) from Earth.

"I won't even say the words running through my head," Ash murmured, standing next to Josh and looking at the virtual wall. "I know this is what the mission was about, but damn if I really thought we'd find anything."

"We've been observing it for the last two months, why would you think it is not real?" Sergi asked with a raised eyebrow.

"I don't know. It could have something to do with the huge yellow dancing globes that you programmed into the computer last month," Ash retorted, thankful his dark skin prevented the slight flush he still felt at being caught unaware of Sergi's latest prank.

Sergi chuckled. "It was Mei's idea. She saw you playing the game in the recreation room," he replied with a grin that faded as he grew serious. "This will require numerous space walks, you understand that, don't you, Josh? I need to be able to get up close to study it."

"I know," Josh replied. "Not yet, though. I want to evaluate the situation before we do anything that could compromise any member of this ship or the Gliese."

"It does not look like a ship," Mei reflected, her gaze moving over the large circular structure.

"The new photographs indicate there might be more than one," Julia replied, coming up to stand near the others. "I believe they are lined up in a row."

"A row? Can you bring up the photographs for us?" Josh asked with a frown.

Julia nodded her head. "This is the last photograph that was taken an hour ago. I didn't notice there were others at first. They are in perfect alignment," she responded, touching the tablet and bringing up the image to the upper right of the screen.

Josh studied the grainy image. They should reach the object in another few days. He had been in contact with Earth through the communication beacons that they had deployed as they moved away from the earth. The technology for it had been developed by Mei's father's company. The return messages from earth had been clear, do whatever was necessary to document the object, retrieve it if he could, and return to Earth as soon as possible.

"Have you been able to determine if there is any activity?" Josh asked Sergi.

"No," Sergi replied. "Nothing yet. I need to get closer."

Josh nodded. "How soon until we are close enough to do a spacewalk, Ash?" He asked, not taking his gaze off the image in front of him.

"Two days," Ash replied.

Josh turned away from the screen. "I want everything ready for a first contact. Sergi, you and Mei make sure the equipment for a spacewalk is ready. I also want the escape pods checked. Julia, when we are close enough, I want you to send out the ROSV." He waited for Julia to acknowledge his reference to the Remotely Operated Space Vehicles they had on board before he continued. "We will need all the information we can get. I won't jeopardize anyone. Until we have a handle on what we are up against, then I'll make a decision on the next step. Ash, I want you to work with Julia on the ROSV."

"I'll double check all the equipment and tethers to make sure everything is working correctly," Julia replied in a quiet voice, her eyes glimmering with excitement.

"Proceed with caution," Josh said, turning to look at the image again.

"This is a piece of pie," Sergi said with a grin.

"Cake, Sergi! How many times do I have to tell you?" Mei retorted with a shake of her head and a rueful grin. "And you were picked because they said you were smart!"

"It is because I like pie better," Sergi responded, winking at Josh and Ash as he turned to follow Mei.

"I'll go help those two. You never know what they will get into," Ash replied with a grin.

Josh and Julia watched as the other three disappeared through the corridor. He turned and looked down at Julia. Her face was glowing and her eyes reflected her excitement.

"Your father would be very proud of you," Josh commented.

Julia nodded. "This is a spectacular discovery. It's been almost two years since my dad died, but I feel like he is here with me," she said with a self-conscious laugh. "When he first discovered this, I wasn't sure I believed it was real. At first, it was a long battle to get anyone to believe him. Once he had proof and other scientists confirmed that he wasn't a crazy old man, it still took a while to get support for funding the mission. Mei's father was instrumental in achieving that. He knew and respected my dad. Our government didn't want the Chinese or Russian governments to get their hands on any advanced technology if they could help it, but this was too large a mission for just one country to handle."

Josh nodded. "We still don't know what it is," he stated with a serious expression. "We need to make sure it doesn't pose a danger to the Earth."

"There's no telling how long it has been here," Julia said with a shake of her head. "It is hard to wrap my head around the proof that we aren't alone. Who left this? What is it? Why is it here? Where did they go?"

"Are they friendly?" Josh inserted.

Julia laughed. "Oh, ye of doom and gloom. Don't you understand? This could answer so many questions!" She insisted.

"Or create more," he said in a hard voice. "It's my responsibility to keep everyone on this mission alive. We don't do anything until I'm sure it is safe."

Julia bit her lip, but nodded. "You're right," she finally admitted. "That still doesn't make me any less excited."

Josh didn't respond. Instead, he gazed at the image one last time before turning away. They had a lot to do before they reached the object. He also needed to inform his superiors that it was real. While the question as to whether or not humans were alone might have been answered; the question of who or what left this behind and how long ago still remained a mystery.

..*

Josh leaned over Julia and Ash's shoulder, studying the massive structure as the ROSV moved closer. Small discharges from the nitrogen thrusters sent out bursts of ice crystals.

"Maneuvering to the left," Ash murmured, working in sync with Julia. "Three bursts. Sergi, keep the tether loose."

"Roger that," Sergi replied.

"Julia, go down ten degrees," Josh instructed, leaning closer. "Mei, are you getting the recordings?"

"Yes, commander," Mei replied.

Each of them had reverted back to their professional status as the intensity of the situation sank in. They had reached their objective several hours ago and had immediately been energized at their first contact with an alien device. Josh's mind ran through his meeting with a member of the Joint Chiefs of Staff and his Commander in Chief, the President of the United States.

"It's real?" The President had asked in a calm voice.

Josh remembered the intense intelligence glimmering in the man's gaze. Even though there had been a several hour delay in the conversation, the recorded questions and his responses had been enough to let him know that this was having a major international impact. The mission was still classified top secret/sensitive compartmented information in order to limit it to a handful of people who absolutely had to know. Regardless, the findings shared within the group were causing a ripple effect throughout the different levels as information was sent back.

"Yes, sir," Josh had answered in a clipped tone.

He had answered what questions he could, but there hadn't been a lot he could tell them until the crew of the Gliese could begin their analysis. He meant what he told Julia. He would do everything in his power to keep the crew and the Earth safe. The President had instructed him to destroy the object if it looked like it posed a danger to Earth.

"Look at that," Ash replied with excitement.

Josh jerked back to the present with a frown. He blinked when he saw what Ash was talking about. From the angle that the cameras were positioned, they could see the other circular objects that Julia had mentioned.

"I count six," Julia replied with a grin. "They look to be evenly spaced."

"What is holding them together?" Mei asked, glancing over her shoulder from where she was sitting in front of another console, recording the events. "There is no telling how long they have been here, surely they would have separated."

"Not if they are anchored together," Sergi replied.

"I don't see any type of connection between them. I would estimate they are approximately half a kilometer apart," Julia said.

"I want a map of it, front and back," Josh ordered.

"You got it," Ash replied, releasing a long whistle. "This thing is pretty incredible."

"You can say that again," Sergi muttered under his breath.

Josh watched as the ROSVs moved over the black metal surface. It would take them several weeks for the ROSVs to complete the mapping. Each section would be carefully recorded. Folding his hands behind him, he noted the complexity of the piece of machinery. If each one was the same, he wondered what their function was, who had put them there, how long they had been there, and most importantly, where in the hell were the aliens that built them?

..*

Five weeks passed as they continued to take readings and send the information back to Earth. Josh ran his hand tiredly through his hair. It was getting long again. He would have to see if Sergi or Julia would cut it.

Leaning back in the chair, he knew it was time to take the mission to the next step. During the mapping, they discovered that one of the devices was damaged. It looked like it might have been hit by something. Unfortunately, they were still no closer to answering any of the questions they had written down on the large board.

"So, what's the plan?" Ash asked as he stepped into the small galley. "More mapping?"

Josh watched as his friend poured himself a cup of coffee. He stretched and lifted his empty cup when Ash turned to look at him. Smiling his thanks when Ash filled the cup, he sat forward and stared into the steaming brew for several minutes before he answered Ash's question.

"It's time to take a closer look at it," Josh finally admitted. "I'm going to send Sergi out. The damaged part gives us our first chance of looking at the inside of one of these things."

"Do you want me to go with him?" Ash asked with a raised eyebrow.

Josh shook his head. "No, I'll go," he said quietly. "I need you and Julia to man the ROSVs. Mei can make sure everything we do is recorded."

"What time do you want to suit up?" Ash asked, sitting down at the table.

Josh glanced at the time. It was just after eight o'clock. Sergi was already going over the tools he would need. Time didn't really have a meaning out in space. Without the sun to help keep the body and mind regulated, they had all fallen into the habit of sleeping for short periods of time. It seemed longer than the sixteen months since he had last seen the sun, that he almost forgot what it looked like.

"Twelve hundred hours," Josh replied, taking a sip of his coffee and rising. "I want to go back over some of the data before we head out."

"I'll double check the cameras mounted to the helmets," Ash said.

"I'll have everyone meet in an hour to go over the spacewalk," Josh said with a nod.

"Josh," Ash called out as Josh started to step out of the room.

Josh turned and looked at his friend's concerned face. He knew Ash felt his worry. Relaxing his stiff expression, he smiled back at Ash.

"We've been in some tight situations before. We'll kick ass," Ash stated with a crooked grin.

"I hope you're right," Josh replied with a nod. "See you in an hour."

Chapter 6

The sound of their breathing echoed in the headset as they floated along the outer structure of the Gliese 581. Josh raised his hand to Sergi after he checked to make sure the Russian's tether was securely attached. He grinned when he heard Sergi's soft laugh.

"Life is good, my friend. I finally get to do what I came for," Sergi said.

"What's that, besides driving Mei crazy and pulling stupid stunts on everyone?" Ash asked.

"Just wait until you see what I can do with a wrench! You'll be having nightmares all the way back to Earth," Sergi promised.

"Quit bragging, Sergi," Mei interjected. "His wrench isn't all that special."

"How would you know how special it is, Mei?" Julia asked in a teasing tone, surprising Josh as she usually stayed out of the banter. "I didn't know you were checking out his toolbox."

"Great! You have officially corrupted Julia, Sergi," Mei growled in a dramatic voice.

"It was a piece of pie, Mei," Sergi chuckled. "You owe me a kiss."

"Cake," Mei grumbled in discontent.

"A kiss? This is sounding more interesting," Ash broke in. "She lose a bet with you, Sergi?"

"I never kiss and tell," Sergi replied with a cheeky grin.

"Let's cut the chit-chat for now," Josh ordered as they neared the third circular gate. "Mei, are you getting this?"

"Yes, commander," Mei replied in a calm voice.

"It looks like it is about three meters across," Julia said, staring at the image.

Josh didn't reply. Instead, he focused on Sergi. They had jumped the tethers from the Gliese to him, then to Sergi. From there, they had set up a second tether system to the first gate. They had discovered during their research that each gate was connected by a series of cables. They would use those connections to pull them from one gate to the next.

He didn't bother turning to look at the Gliese 581. It was small in comparison to the massive devices and would be shielded from view at the moment. Instead, he gripped the thin tether and pulled himself along. He and Sergi had a propulsion pack on, but they would only use it in case of an emergency. He followed Sergi as he moved slowly up the first gate to the cable connecting it to the others.

An hour later, they were approaching the third gate. There was a large section ripped open at seven o'clock. He and Sergi worked in tandem as they pulled themselves down the side to the section that was torn open.

"This is incredible, commander," Sergi murmured. "The metal looks different from anything I've ever seen. If I can find a fragment small enough to carry, I'd like to bring it back for testing."

"Agreed," Josh responded. "Be careful as you enter. It looks like there are some sharp edges. The last thing you want is to puncture your suit."

Sergi gave a dry laugh. "That would not be good," he agreed, before he grinned. "I'm sure Mei would bring me some duct tape."

"In your dreams," Mei replied. "Chewing gum, maybe."

"She loves me," Sergi teased with a loud sigh. "I'm going in."

Josh watched as Sergi carefully entered the damaged section. He waited a few seconds before he reached out and gripped the thick edge and pulled himself through into the dark interior.

The lights on his helmet cast an eerie glow. He turned in a slow circle, making sure that Mei captured what he was seeing. Glancing up, he saw Sergi pulling himself deeper into the interior.

"This is amazing," Sergi kept muttering under his breath. "The technology is unlike anything I've ever seen before, but in some ways familiar."

"What do you mean familiar?" Josh asked.

Josh watched as Sergi turned partially to look at him. For the first time, Josh saw a completely serious expression on Sergi's face through the visor. He gripped one of the cross bars to keep from floating off.

"In the laws of physics and mechanics, some things can only work in a specific way. While this is all alien, it still has to be put together with nuts and bolts," Sergi replied. "The circuitry has to work the same. Power comes in, power goes out, whether it is wired in either parallel or serial, it still needs a ground and a complete circuit to function. If an open, or short as many people refer to it, occurs, the power is cut and the connection won't work."

Josh looked at the damaged section. Deep down, he suspected he knew what Sergi was telling him. He glanced sharply at the Russian. He could see the silent question.

"You can repair this," Josh murmured.

"Probably," Sergi replied, turning to look around him. "I need to study the images and see if I can re-engineer what was done. If the power used to work these things is still viable, it's possible I could repair the damage to this and complete the circuit."

"Mei, are you getting this?" Josh demanded. He frowned when he didn't receive a response. "Mei, come in. Shit!"

"It is the metal," Sergi said. "It is probably preventing a signal from getting through."

"Record everything that you can," Josh ordered. "We'll review it once we are back on the Gliese and make a decision then."

Sergi nodded and turned back to start a slow, methodical review of the interior. Josh gritted his teeth and started moving downward. There was no way they would ever be able to bring something this size home. The only thing they could do was document as much as they could and send it back to Earth. Even that would have been little to no help if they hadn't discovered the damage to this gate as they had begun referring to the black objects.

Six hours later, they were back on the Gliese. Josh shook his head to push away the fatigue. He sank down in the seat across from where Mei and Julia were retrieving the cameras.

"We were worried when we lost contact with you," Ash muttered, coming to sit next to him. "The only thing that kept me from coming out there and retrieving your ass was the fact that I knew you wouldn't die without saying goodbye."

Josh gave a dry laugh and smiled as he leaned his back against the wall. "You are all heart, Ash," Josh said wearily.

"So, what was it like?" Ash asked.

Josh's eyes slowly opened and he looked into the expectant faces of Ash, Julia, and Mei. A grin curved his lips when he met Sergi's gaze. He had to agree with the Russian, it was both amazing and incredible.

"You aren't going to believe it," he finally replied. "Let's get something to eat and we'll tell you what we found."

..*

"So, you think you can repair it?" Mei asked, staring at Sergi in disbelief.

Sergi waved his hand as he lifted the fork to his lips. "Yes, I think so," he mumbled.

"This is…," Julia's voice faded as she sat back in her seat. "We aren't really sure what it is."

"This is one way of finding out," Josh said.

"Whoa! If you are willing to do it that means we are going to be in deep shit, aren't we?" Ash asked with a raised eyebrow.

Josh's mouth tightened and he looked around the table. He stared at each person sitting around looking back at him. Drawing in a deep breath, he carefully chose his words.

"On the contrary, I've received orders to proceed with caution, but for us to fully explore the gates," Josh stated. "We've been given the go to see if it can be repaired, but not to actually do it unless we feel confident it doesn't pose a danger to Earth."

"And if it can be, what then?" Ash asked with a frown.

"We are to send out one of the ROSV's," Josh said. "We collect as much data as we can before… if anything happens."

"That doesn't sound so bad," Julia replied in a thoughtful tone. "How long do you think it will take to repair it, Sergi?"

"I don't know," Sergi admitted. "It depends on how bad the damage is and if I can replicate the parts with what is on board the Gliese. I will need to study the video we brought back some more. The last thing I want to do is blow us up."

"I will help," Mei said in a quiet voice, staring at Sergi.

"I'll help Mei with the video," Julia added.

Josh looked around the table again. Each person was quieter than they were earlier, but there was a charge in the air. They all wanted answers to the list of questions that were growing daily.

"Let's do this," he said.

Chapter 7

A week later, Josh watched as Sergi disappeared into the damaged gate again. This would hopefully be the final spacewalk. He passed the section of repaired cabling up to Sergi.

"Two minutes," Sergi said into the microphone. "This should complete the final connection. Whether these things have a built in power supply that is still working is another matter. I've gone through this one and it looks like it's linked to the one before it and the next one, but I never found an actual power source."

"We'll deal with that when we get to it," Josh said.

Josh watched as Sergi struggled to get the cable into place. Releasing his hold on the bar, he floated upward to lend the other man a hand. He was almost to him when Sergi snapped the cable into place.

"What the…," Josh muttered when the interior suddenly lit up with a series of red lights. "Sergi, we need to get out of here."

"Just a minute," Sergi responded, reaching for the tools he had strapped to the bars.

A feeling of dread filled Josh and he turned as the walls began to move. A sense of urgency filled him. Something told him that they needed to get out of there – now!

"Leave them," Josh ordered, reaching for Sergi's foot and pulling him down. "We need to get out of here now."

Josh saw Sergi glance at the walls that were beginning to shift. Sergi nodded and motioned for him to go first. They both turned and used the railing to pull themselves down to the opening. Using their feet, they pushed off and exited through the gaping hole.

"Josh, look!" Sergi muttered, grabbing his arm.

Josh turned in time to see each of the sections light up. He glanced up at the thick cables. Each one was lit a bright red. His gaze narrowed on the second gateway. It was moving as well.

"Josh, we need you to get back to the Gliese now," Ash ordered in their helmet.

"What's going on?" Josh demanded, grabbing the tether they had secured when they first began working on the gateway.

"Those things are lit up like a Christmas tree and are beginning to do some weird shit. I'd feel better if you and Sergi were back inside the ship," Ash replied.

"Can you please define weird?" Josh asked in frustration as he and Sergi pulled themselves along the tether.

"Josh, it looks like the gates are opening up," Julia's calm voice came over the headset. "I think the Gliese being so close to the gate has activated it. We can't move as long as you and Sergi are outside."

"I'm going to have to burn fuel to keep it from being pulled in," Ash's muttered voice echoed in the background.

"No!" Josh ordered. "We barely have enough to get back as it is."

"Josh, if we get pulled in, there won't be any going home," Ash stated in a grim voice.

"Try to keep it steady, we are coming in as fast as we can," Josh ordered. "Sergi, use the Jetpack."

"I won't argue with you on that," Sergi said, reaching to unhook the tether attached to him.

"Watch out!" Josh yelled as the rotating gateway ripped the tether out of his hand just as he unhooked it.

Josh felt his body rotating at a crazy angle for a moment before he fired the Jetpack and regained his orientation. He slowly turned to see where Sergi was when he heard a muttered curse in Russian. Horror gripped him when he saw Sergi being reeled toward the massive gateway as it turned. Tilting his body, he focused on using the propulsion system to push him toward the twirling figure.

"I can't get the tether undone," Sergi bit out in frustration.

"Hold on, I'm coming," Josh replied.

Sergi's nervous chuckle echoed in his helmet. "I don't think I'll be going anywhere," he replied. "Though, I would appreciate it if you can hurry."

Josh pushed forward, working each thrust to move him closer. He didn't want to overshoot Sergi. If he did, he wouldn't have time to turn back around for a second try before Sergi was crushed.

He reached out for the other man as he drew closer. His fingers brushed the back of Sergi's Jetpack.

Gripping the controls of his unit, he calculated when Sergi would rotate again. Pressing the button, he sent a long burst of nitrogen into space and shot forward. This time, he was able to grab the back of the pack.

"Josh, you need to put a move on," Ash warned.

"I am," Josh replied through gritted teeth.

"Josh," Sergi muttered. "Commander, leave me."

Josh ignored Sergi, working on the clip that held the tether onto him as they both twirled closer and closer to the second gateway. With a loud curse, he forced the metal back and slipped it off the belt attached to the Russian.

"Brace for impact," Josh ordered as they bounced into the turning gate.

The impact tossed them in separate directions. Josh was thrown outward while Sergi was pushed up into the glowing cables. Josh saw a flash before a loud cry escaped the other man and his body stiffened.

"Sergi! Josh, I received a spike in Sergi's life support. He flat lined for a moment," Mei said in an urgent voice.

"I'm going after him," Josh replied, gripping the controls to the Jetpack. "How long does he have?"

"I'm getting a weak signal, but his respiration is low," Mei replied.

"I've got him," Josh said, reaching for Sergi's foot. "We are coming in. Mei, be ready."

Josh had a brief moment to see the gateway from a different angle as he turned Sergi around. They were above the first one and each was lit up and turning. It was both an incredible sight and one that scared the hell out of him. Julia's words from almost two years ago came back to him as he turned back to the Gliese, Sergi's limp body in his arms.

Would you still go if you knew you might not come back?

..*

Josh tore off his helmet and hooked it to the shelf near the service bay door. He fumbled with the gloves and shoved them into the net next to his helmet. His right hand instinctively shot out to grab the edge of the shelf as the Gliese violently shook and groaned, even though he was floating.

"The force of the pull from the gate is going to rip the ship apart," Julia informed him with a worried glance in his direction. She had braced herself to hold Sergi's unconscious form steady for Mei. "What happened?"

"His lifeline caught and he was pulled into one of the gates," Josh replied, pulling himself around Julia. Mei was placing an oxygen mask over Sergi's nose and mouth. "I need to get to the command center."

Julia nodded, her face pale, but composed. Josh pulled himself along the narrow tunnels that connected the payload section with the main command and living modules. It helped that this section of the Gliese didn't have artificial gravity. It allowed him to float through the narrow area without having to pause to remove the rest of the spacesuit he was wearing.

"Ash, give me a status report," Josh demanded as he floated through the different sections.

"You'd better get up here," Ash's grim voice echoed through the ship.

Josh grabbed another hand grip and pulled himself up to the last section. He rotated in the air and dropped down onto the control deck. He stumbled when the boots of his spacesuit weighted him down. With a curse, he reached down and undid the top portion of his spacesuit and bent forward. The sound of the heavy, upper section echoed loudly through the room as it fell to the floor.

"What's happening?" Josh asked, glancing at the image displayed in front of him.

"That," Ash stated, nodding toward the huge curved screen.

Josh turned to stare at the image in grim silence. His mind swirled at the scene in front of him. The view of the glowing gates was just as magnificent from inside the ship as it was outside. It also showed the danger they were in.

"Get us out of here," he ordered, sliding into the chair next to Ash.

Ash's mouth was pulled into a tight line. "The force of it is pulling us forward. If I try to get us out of here, it is going to rip us apart," he replied.

Josh's mind ran through all the different scenerios they had talked about. They had two choices. He could detach the front of the Gliese and let it go forward in the hope that it would release them from the pull of the gateway. If he did that, they would never make it back to Earth. It would take out half of their supplies, including food and oxygen. The other choice was to go forward and see where it took them and hoped they didn't get ripped apart.

"Go forward," Josh suddenly ordered.

"What?!" Ash asked in disbelief, glancing at Josh as alarms began to sound.

"Go through the gates," Josh said in a grim voice.

"We don't know what will happen," Ash hissed.

Josh leaned forward and silenced the alarm. He glanced over his shoulder when he saw Julia and Mei holding a standing, but weak, Sergi between them. He knew at that moment what he needed to do.

"I'm making a command decision," he said. "All of you get suited up and into an escape pod. I'm taking control of the ship."

"What the hell?! No! I'm not getting into any coffin while you play space cowboy," Ash said stubbornly.

"I'm not asking, Ash, I'm ordering you and the others to get suited up and into an emergency pod," Josh ordered.

"The others can go," Ash replied in a quiet voice. "I'm your wing man. I cover your back. I always have and I always will."

Josh glanced at Ash before he nodded his head. "If I tell you again, no arguments," he snapped. "Julia, you, Mei, and Sergi get suited up and into a pod."

Julia paused before murmuring in a quiet tone to Mei. Together, the two women helped Sergi turn back the way they came. Josh's jaw tightened and he shot a glance at his friend.

"You have two minutes to make sure they are secure and strapped in before I push us through," Josh said.

Ash gave him a stiff nod and turned the cameras to the emergency pods. Julia was closing Sergi's pod while Mei suited up. Julia was already wearing a survival suit. A moment later, Julia and Mei were both stepping into the long, coffin shaped boxes and closing the lids.

"Three green lights," Ash stated in a soft voice.

Josh nodded. "Let's do this," he said.

Ash winced and gave Josh a crooked grin. "You know, every time you say that we end up in a world of trouble," he retorted with a wry grin.

Josh just nodded and pressed the thrusters to full. In the distance, he could see all the gates open now. At the last minute, he remembered to hit send on the recordings that they had completed. The information would upload and relay between the communications beacons they had released. He didn't know if the scientist back on Earth would get them, if they did, then they would know what had happened to the Gliese 581 and its crew.

"Yippee ki yay," Ash muttered as the Gliese moved forward.

Josh could feel the moment they entered the gateway. The pull on the spaceship thrust them back against their seats. This was far worse than lifting off on the Soyuz rocket or hitting Mach speed in a fighter. For a moment, he felt for sure that the Gliese was going to be ripped apart. The ship shuddered before everything lit up around them and they were pushed forward.

"Shit!" Josh hissed out before he felt like he couldn't breathe from the pressure against his chest.

He tried to turn his head to see if Ash was feeling the same thing, but it felt like his whole body was being held suspended. Opening his mouth, he tried to force air into his starving lungs. Dark spots danced before his eyes. He blinked, as if in slow motion, when the world shifted around him. Seconds later, the combination of the pressure and lack of oxygen were too much and he felt his grip on consciousness slipping away.

..*

Josh woke to the sounds of alarms ringing in his ears. A soft groan escaped him as he shook his head to clear the sound. It took a moment to realize that it wasn't just his ears ringing, but the alarms of the ship. Pushing off the console, he blinked to clear his vision.

Pain coursed down his neck and through his shoulders. Lifting a shaking hand, he rubbed at it as he tried to remember what the hell had happened. As his memory of going through the gateway came back to him, he quickly turned his head, wincing again when it protested his sudden movement. Ash lay against the console, unconscious.

"Ash," Josh whispered before clearing his throat. "Ash!"

There was no response from his friend. Glancing at the controls, he grimaced. Multiple system failures were showing. His gaze went to the front screen. The virtual screen was off. Only the smaller portholes were visible.

Undoing the straps holding him into the chair, he pushed himself up, floating upward and tumbling when the world, or was it the ship, tilted and groaned. Whichever it was, he ignored it for a moment as he tried to get a visual of what was happening. He pushed himself away from the console and floated over the debris that covered the floor. Torn metal and shattered glass from the displays was everywhere.

Josh bumped against the wall near one of the small windows and held on to its rim when the ship shuddered again. He twisted and pressed his face against the clear material covering the window and looked out. A soft curse escaped him when he saw the entire front portion of the Gliese was missing. Excess fuel and oxygen were being ejected into space.

He rotated when the ship groaned again. Bracing his feet against the wall, he pushed off so he could float back to the console. He grasped it and quickly scanned the screens.

Outer hull was failing. The ship was breaking apart. Turning, he held onto the chair he had been sitting in and pulled Ash back in his seat. A thin line of blood dripped from Ash's temple, but he was breathing.

Josh glanced at the console again. The interior camera was still pointed on the emergency pods. Three green lights were reflected.

"Warning, outer hull failure is imminent," the computer stated. "Warning, outer hull failure is imminent."

"Tell me something I don't already know," Josh muttered under his breath even as he ripped the straps off of Ash.

He bent and grabbed Ash's arm as his friend floated upward. One good thing about not having gravity was he could maneuver Ash a lot easier and faster. He reached out and gripped the back of the chair when the Gliese rocked and a portion of the ceiling tiles dropped.

"Time to go," Josh grunted as he began picking his way toward the emergency pods, Ash's limp body in tow.

Josh bounced off the walls in his hurry. It took him several precious seconds when he found a section of the corridor blocked. He had been forced to release Ash so he could move it. As soon as it was clear, he pushed Ash through before following. Minutes later, he was in the section designed to keep them alive until help could arrive.

"As long as it was within fourteen days," Josh muttered as he pressed one of the empty pods opened.

The pods were designed to slow the metabolism and respiration of the person inside to prolong life support. There was technically enough oxygen and heat to keep them alive for thirty days in space. In reality, Josh figured fourteen if they were lucky.

They were also designed with an advanced life support detection system built by a group of students from MIT for extra credit. The group of three students had won a contest to design a program so that if the pod detected a suitable habitat for survival, it would guide the pod to it and open the parachute after entry. In theory, it had sounded great. In reality, the likelihood of finding an alien planet with an environment that could support a human was a trillion to one, by the hundredth degree.

Josh finished strapping Ash into the pod and settled the mask over his friend's relaxed face. A gas with a mixture of oxygen and a sedative would keep each of them in an unconscious state until it ran out. Once it did, they would either be dead or hopefully rescued. Personally, he liked the latter option better.

Closing the lid, he pressed the button on the side, waiting for it to turn green before he pushed it into the chute. He did the same with the other three. Through the clear window, he could see Julia, Mei, and Sergi's relaxed features. They had each slipped into a survival suit. He and Ash didn't have time, though he was still wearing a portion of his spacesuit from earlier.

Floating over to the panel, he programmed the emergency sequence into it. If an outer hull breach was detected, it would automatically eject each of them into space and away from the ship. If not, well, in fourteen days, they would all wake up.

Pushing off the wall, Josh quickly slipped into his pod and pulled the straps over his body to hold him down. Adjusting the mask over his nose and mouth, he reached up and pressed the button to close the lid. Once the lid closed and sealed, the gas mixture would start. Holding the controller in his hand, he pressed the button and felt the pod move into the chute. Almost as soon as he heard the pod lock, he felt the Gliese shake, as if in the throes of a death rattle. A moment later, his stomach turned as the pod was ejected out into space. He blinked several times, trying to clear his vision as the gas mixture dulled his senses. He stared up into the blackness of space and swallowed.

No, Julia. I was wrong, he thought as his mind grew hazy. *I think I would mind if I never saw Earth again.*

Chapter 8

Telsa Terra:

Cassa glanced up as a dark shadow passed over the vineyard where she was checking the new crop that was almost ready for harvesting. The vineyards had been in Cassa de Rola's family for centuries. Each generation nurtured the plants that provided a lucrative income for them and the small settlement nearby.

On the other side of the mountains lay the desert and the Badlands. Generally, either her father or older brother, Packu, were the ones who normally traveled there. That was where the mines and the closest large trader Spaceport were located. It was a lawless area and best left alone.

"Cassa!" A young boy called out in excitement as he ran down the long row. "Cassa! Look!"

"I see it, Jesup," Cassa replied, not looking at her younger brother, but up at the massive ship. A sense of unease washed through her. "Is father back yet?"

"Yes," Jesup replied in a breathless tone. "He didn't look happy, either. It's a Legion Battle cruiser; not one of their old ones either."

"How would you know if it was one of their old ships?" Cassa asked in disapproval. "Have you been talking to the traders down at the market again?"

Jesup shook his head. "No, I heard Packu talking about it. He had a hologram of it and a bunch of other Legion ships."

Cassa's lips tightened. Their brother, Packu, had been listening to the other young men in the village. More and more of the young men and women were leaving the small settlement, making it harder for Cassa's father to keep up with all the work. With the harvesting of the crops coming soon, it would be even harder on them if Packu joined the resistance that was growing.

"Why would they be here?" Cassa mused, watching as it disappeared over the mountains.

"Cassa!"

Cassa grimaced and turned when she heard her name again. Packu, or Pack as the family called him, was running toward her. She frowned when she saw the bag he was carrying. Placing her hands on her hips, she knew she was already shaking her head in denial before he drew to a stop.

"I'm leaving," Pack said, his face tight with determination.

"The Legion Battle cruiser," she started to say.

Pack nodded, his face held a grim expression. "That is why I'm leaving," he interrupted. "They are recruiting any male old enough to fight. I won't join them in destroying another world, much less my own."

"Father will tell them that you are needed here, Pack," Cassa argued. "It will be hard enough as it is to harvest the crop this year. Without your help, it will be almost impossible."

"I don't have a choice, Cassa," Pack replied in a quiet voice. "None of us do. The Legion is taking over the entire star system. If we don't stop them now, no one will be able to."

"It's not our fight," Cassa whispered as fear of losing Pack swept through her and she shook her head in denial. "Our planet is small compared to the others. Let the Gallant Order stop them. That is why it was formed."

Pack shook his head and began to back up when he heard his name being called by one of his friends. He turned and waved his hand to let them know that he would be there in a moment. Turning back to Cassa, he gave her a wistful grin and reached out to ruffle Jesup's dark hair.

"They need help," Pack murmured. "Father understands. This is different, Cassa. If it wasn't, I would stay, but it is more dangerous to do nothing this time."

Cassa's eyes burned as she stared up at her brother. While Pack was old enough to go off on his own, she was worried what the growing unrest would do to their family. Turning her head, she blinked away the tears before she turned back to gaze up at him.

"Promise you'll be careful," she replied in a quiet voice, lifting her hand to touch his cheek.

"I will. I'll let you know what is going on if I can," Pack said, turning away.

Cassa watched as he walked away. A part of her feared it would be the last time she saw him. What concerned her was the fact that deep down she knew he was right. The Legion was spreading like a disease through the star system. The Gallant was run by a group of old men who were powerless to stop the new force that had risen up quickly, swallowing up the smaller regions before moving to the larger ones.

"When I get old enough, I'm going to join the Gallant, as well," Jesup said with a voice filled with envy.

"I hope by then, this will all be a distant memory," Cassa whispered, watching as Pack strode off with his friends toward the village. "Come, we have to find out how much help we will have this harvest. You'll have to work, as well."

"Aw, Cassa," Jesup complained, kicking at a clump of dirt.

"No arguments," Cassa retorted in a firm voice, even as her lips twitched in amusement. "You can help protect me from the Legion troops."

Jesup grinned up at her and nodded. "Always," he laughed. "I'll race you to the house."

Cassa watched as Jesup took off at a run. With a shout, she raced after him, knowing she would never catch up. She slowed as she neared the house, glancing up at the sky as another ship took off; this time leaving from the rural port near the village. Pushing away the fear threatening to overwhelm her, she turned and entered the small building that she called home.

* * *

Later that evening, Cassa slipped out of the house for some fresh air and some time to reflect on what was happening. Her father hadn't talked much during dinner. Jesup on the other hand, had. Most of it had been about the Legion Battle Cruiser that had flown over the valley.

The house seemed empty without Pack there. Normally, her two brothers kept the meals interesting with their lively talks of what was happening in the village and at the desert Spaceport. Her father had allowed Jesup to go with him on his visit last month and her little brother had talked non-stop about everything he had seen.

Cassa ran her hands down the off-white, long sleeve tunic that covered her dark brown trousers. Bending down, she picked up the coat that she had placed on the low rock wall. It was chillier than she expected with the breeze. She pulled it on before she sat down on the edge.

Staring out at the vineyard, she turned her head when she heard the quiet sound of footsteps approaching. A soft smile pulled at her lips when she saw it was her father. She sighed when she saw that he was moving slower than normal.

"It is a beautiful evening," she murmured, turning to gaze back up at the stars.

"It is," Jemar responded as he came to a stop next to her.

"Sit," Cassa said affectionately, patting the space next to her. "You've overdone it again. You need to let us do more."

Jemar released a soft sigh as he sat down beside her. "The Spaceport is in an uproar. Everyone was trying to get out before the Legion Battle Cruiser arrived," he replied, pulling his pipe out of his front pocket and filling it. "Those with unaccounted trade did not want it confiscated."

Cass was silent for a moment before she turned to look at her father. Concern tore at her. The Gallant Order had kept the peace for centuries. The Legion was relatively new in comparison, but it had grown fast and strong under the command of the new director. Even in the isolated valley that they lived in, she had heard accounts of some of the horrors inflicted on those that didn't agree with the Legion's policies.

"What do you think will happen?" Cassa asked, studying her father's tired face.

"I heard that six more star systems have fallen," her father replied with a shake of his head. "The Legion has taken over the governments despite the protests of the Gallant Order."

"Isn't there anyone who can stop Lord Andronikos? I don't understand how he could have come to power so quickly," Cassa said with a shake of her head.

"The Legion's forces have gained strength over the last thirty years while the Gallant Order has grown old and tired," Jemar replied. "Lord Andronikos was young and power hungry, then. He came in just as several star systems were in trouble. He said the words they wanted to hear and he made sure that he had the right men in place to take over when the planets failed. He spent years building an unstoppable military force and recruiting followers. I fear nothing can stop him now."

"Not even the rebel forces supporting the Gallant Order?" Cassa asked. "Pack…"

"Your brother has joined a hopeless cause, I fear. The number that has risen up to resist are too few, too unorganized, and I fear too late to stop the Legion from expanding," Jemar stated. "Unless something happens soon, I fear Telsa Terra will be the next to fall. The presence of the Legion Battle Cruiser is proof of that."

Cassa leaned over and hugged her father. She could feel his worry. There would be little they could do to fight against such a force. She released her father when he pulled back and stood up.

"Don't stay out too late. There is a lot that needs to be done tomorrow. I've decided to start harvesting a few weeks early. It is the only way we will get it done before the berries dry out," Jemar instructed before turning back to the house.

Cassa watched as her father disappeared and the lights went out. Turning back to stare up at the sky, she released a soft sigh and pulled her coat tighter around her to keep the chill of the night air at bay. Deep down, she knew her father was right. The presence of the Legion Battle Cruiser was a bad omen for her small world.

She stood and was about to turn back toward the house when a flash of light caught her attention. Her eyes widened when the light lasted longer than was normal for a meteor. She followed the movement of the object, surprised when she vaguely caught the outline of something detaching from the top and a row of colorful lights along the side appeared. Glancing back at the house, she decided not to disturb her father.

Cassa hurried to the dome-shaped repair building. Jumping down the stairs, she grabbed the binoculars off the shelf and raced back to the entrance. With a flick of her finger, she released the covers over the ends and lifted them to her eyes. It took a few precious seconds before she focused on the object as it floated down toward the ground.

"What is that?" She muttered, zooming in.

A large box, outlined in flashing red and green lights floated under a huge parachute. She had never seen anything like it before. She switched on the tracking mode of the binoculars so she could get an accurate location of the box. Only when it disappeared from sight did she lower the glasses.

Biting her lip, she glanced at the house once more. Her father's soft snores could be heard through the open windows. Cassa glanced down at the coordinates on the binoculars' display. Making a decision, she stepped back down into the repair building.

Grabbing a bag off the shelf, she quickly placed a cutting torch into it. She pulled a helmet off the shelf and slipped it on. She would need it to see at night. The last thing she picked up was a stun rod. It shot small bursts of electrical charges. Outside the perimeter of the fence there were large creatures that roamed the forests.

Sliding her leg over the land skid, she turned the power on. She touched the visor to lower the eye shield. The doors to the shed opened as she moved closer to them. Twisting the hand control, she depressed the accelerator and shot out of the building.

Cassa headed down the long road leading into the de Rola vineyard. She turned when the road divided into four different sections, taking the right hand toward the forest and mountains. A half hour later, she slowed to a stop. In front of her was the fencing that separated the vineyard from the forest.

"You've come this far," she whispered.

Reaching into the pocket of her coat, she pulled out the control for the fence. With a flick of her finger, the section in front of her disappeared. Cassa powered the land skid through the opening before pressing the button again to reseal the fence. She dropped the controller back into her pocket and pulled out the binoculars.

Lifting the visor, she lifted the glasses to her eyes and scanned the area. Re-establishing the location of the object, she replaced the glasses in the holder on the side of the land skid, flipped the visor back down, and pressed the accelerator.

Traveling through the forest was trickier than she expected. It had been years since she had traveled up here. When she was younger, she and Pack had spent weeks exploring during the off-season. She stopped four times to get her bearings before she caught a glimpse of faint light shining in the darkness.

Weaving around the thick trees, she stopped and shut the land skid down when she was within a few meters of it. Cassa slid off the transport and removed her helmet. Placing the helmet on the seat, she frowned up at the unusual object. There was a slight pinging noise coming from it.

She walked around the long container. It hung several feet off the ground, just out of her reach. The parachute was caught in the branches of two of the large trees. Cassa paused, staring up at it.

"If I want to see what's inside, I have to get it down," she muttered under her breath.

Turning back toward the land skid, she opened the back storage compartment. Inside were several long blades that they used for cutting the vines, the cutting torch she had grabbed before leaving, and a hover board for reaching the top of the tall plants. She decided to use one of the long, curved blades. She was afraid the cutting torch would catch the thick, fabric roping on fire. Leaning forward, she pulled the blade and the hover board out.

Sliding her feet into the foot locks, she felt the board activate. Cassa moved her foot and the hover board rose off the ground. She shifted her weight to the left and felt it move slowly in that direction. Once she was high enough to reach the thick cords holding the box in the air, she swung the blade out, slicing through the lines attached to the parachute in one clean sweep.

The box landed on the ground with a soft thud. Cassa touched the control again with her foot and the hover board slowly lowered back to the ground. She quickly bent and touched the release on the foot locks and stepped off of the device. Now that it was on the ground, she had a feeling of misgiving. What if it was a new Legion probe?

Cassa stood staring at the strange box in indecision. Maybe it would have been better to have woken her father. He would know what to do with it. She shook her head. Her father had enough to worry about and so did she. The last thing she should have done is taken off the way she had. Her father was right, there was a lot of work to do tomorrow. She knew where the box was. She would leave it and return home. Tomorrow, she would tell her father about it.

A shiver ran through Cassa as she started to turn away. She had just picked up the hover board when the sound coming from the container suddenly stopped. She turned and swallowed when she saw that the red lights were turning to green. Almost as if in slow-motion, the top of the box emitted a hissing sound and the lid popped open. It was only then that Cassa noticed a clear window on the top of it.

She nervously stepped closer, trying to peer through the clear glass. Her lips parted as she fought to draw in a breath. It wasn't until she was just a few feet from the container that she made out the faint outline of someone inside it.

Her first thought was that the man inside was dead. His face was pale and he was lying so still, that she couldn't imagine him being alive. The fact that he was in a sealed box made her wonder if he had died on board a ship and been ejected. She had heard of such things before.

A gasp escaped her when the man suddenly lifted his hand and ripped off the clear mask covering his nose and mouth. He drew in several long, gasping breaths before his eyelids slowly opened. Cassa blinked in surprise when his gaze locked onto hers through the clear glass.

"Where… Where am I?" The man asked in a hoarse voice.

Cassa blinked again and frowned. The words sounded strained and stilted and held an odd dialect, but she could understand them. Stepping around the container, Cassa kept a wary gaze locked on the man inside.

"Telsa Terra," she replied.

The man struggled to sit up. Cassa stepped closer and gripped his arm with one hand when he started to fall back. Her gaze swept over him. The man's dark brown hair was shaggy and sticking out in all different directions. His eyes were clouded and dazed, as if he was having trouble focusing. He shook his head and an intense frown creased his brow as he stared around the dark forest surrounding them. His gaze moved back to her.

"This isn't Earth," he said more than asked.

Cassa frowned and shook her head. "I have not heard of Earth. Which star system is it located in?" She asked.

"Shit! We really aren't alone," the man muttered.

The softly whispered words didn't make a lot of sense to Cassa. Why was he upset that they were not alone? What planet was this Earth? She had not heard of it before. Was it part of a new system the Legion had overtaken? Her biggest concerns were why the stranger was in the box, where did he come from, and was anyone going to come looking for him.

A noise behind them drew her attention back to the dangers of being in the forest at night. She needed to get them both back behind the protection of the fence. After that, she would figure out what to do with her unexpected find.

"Come," she whispered, reaching for his arm again. "It is not safe here. We must go."

Chapter 9

Josh pushed up and weakly crawled out of the emergency pod. His head was spinning and he felt disoriented. He gripped the sides when his knees gave out under him. The fact that he was still wearing the bottom half of his space suit didn't help.

He glanced at the woman when she grabbed his arm to steady him. She looked like a human, at least in the dark. Pushing upward, he was relieved to feel some of the weakness fade.

"We need to leave," the woman said again, looking around the woods with a frown. "There are beasts in the forest that are dangerous. We need to return to the vineyard."

"I have to get out of this suit," Josh muttered, reaching for the bottom section.

"Just hurry," the woman said with an anxious tone, turning to place the long board and knife that she was holding in the compartment under the seat of a strange looking vehicle.

Josh released the bottom half of the suit and let it drop to the ground. Right now, his legs felt like spaghetti and it was taking everything inside him to remain in an upright position. He grunted when he stumbled. The material was bunched around his ankles. In space, it would have been easy to free his legs, he would have just floated out of it.

It took a moment for him to realize that the tight cuffs at the bottom were part of the problem. Bending, he pulled the straps on them free, loosening the material so that he could step onto the soft, moist leaf-covered ground. A grimace of distaste flashed across his face as the moisture seeped through his socks.

"We need to go now," the woman said, pulling on his arm as she stared behind them in growing alarm.

Josh glanced over his shoulder and nodded. He stumbled after her to the unusual looking device that looked like a motorcycle without wheels. She grabbed a helmet off of the seat, placed it over her head, and quickly slid onto the bike. He climbed onto the back and gripped the edge of the seat.

"Hold on," she instructed.

"I am," he mumbled.

Josh glanced over his shoulder again just as a dark shape with yellow glowing eyes broke through the thick woods on the other side of the emergency pod. His eyes widened when the large, hairy beast snorted at them. The creature was at least ten feet tall at the shoulders and coated in a thick, gray fur.

He returned his gaze to the front. His hands and thighs instinctively gripped the vehicle as it shot forward. Everything blurred in the darkness. He didn't know how the woman knew where she was going, much less avoided the tall trees as they sped through the forest at a neck-breaking speed. He was just thankful she could when he heard the loud crash behind him.

Josh's fuzzy mind spun as he tried to piece together what happened. The last thing he remembered was being ejected into space after the Gliese had passed through the gateway. The ship was breaking apart and he needed to get into an emergency pod. He had loaded the pods containing the rest of the crew.

He turned his gaze immediately back toward the way they had come. Where were the others? Had they survived? If so, had they landed on the same planet?

"Where is Tesla Terra located?" Josh asked.

The woman didn't respond. Josh wasn't sure she could hear him and didn't bother repeating his question. All he could do was hang on and try to figure out where in the hell he was and what he was going to do.

..*

A short time later, he felt the woman slow the vehicle. He could see a strange fence in front of them. Dark red beams stretched between the poles. He sat back when the woman moved. His gaze followed her hand as she pulled a small device out of her pocket and pointed it at the fence. A section of the light disappeared.

His fingers tightened on the side grips embedded in the seat when she moved slowly forward. Once they were on the other side, she did the same thing before pocketing the device. Unable to keep his curiosity at bay any longer, he leaned forward until his mouth was near her ear.

"Where are we?" He asked in a quiet voice.

She briefly glanced over her shoulder, but he couldn't see her face because of the helmet. "My home," she replied in a terse tone before turning around to face the front again.

Josh's gaze swept over the dark rows as they moved silently down the wide road that separated the fields. He quickly looked behind him again when he heard a loud roar and the sound of something hissing. The yellow eyes of the beast from the forest gazed back at him for a moment. The creature snorted before turning and disappearing back into the thick trees.

"It cannot get through the fence," the woman said.

"What is it?" Josh asked, turning back to sit straight in his seat again.

"It is a Tusku," she replied with a shrug. "They are nocturnal and very territorial."

Josh didn't respond. He was too busy trying to absorb the fact that he was not only alive, but on an alien planet somewhere out in the universe. Swallowing, it suddenly dawned on him that if he had survived, the others may have as well.

"Were there any other emergency pods?" He asked, leaning forward.

The woman shook her head. "No, your pod was the only one I saw," she stated.

Josh sat back and pressed his lips together. In the distance, he saw several dome-shaped buildings illuminated by the moonlight. Several minutes later, the woman pulled the strange vehicle into one that was set a short distance from the others.

He slid off after she had powered it down. Turning in a slow circle, his gaze took in everything. He finished his rotation, staring at the woman under the dim light inside the building. His breath caught in his throat when she removed the helmet to reveal dark brown luminous eyes that stared at him with a wary expression.

"Who are you?" He asked in a gruff voice.

She stared at him for several long seconds, her gaze moving slowly down him as if she was trying to understand who and what he was. Her gaze finally returned to his face. A slight frown creased her brow. Her lips pursed together before she released a frustrated sigh. Turning, she walked over to a small shelf and carefully placed the helmet before pivoting to look at him again.

"I am Cassa de Rola. You are in my family's vineyard. Who are you? Are you a Legion soldier?" She demanded, crossing her arms and lifting her chin in defiance.

Josh frowned and shook his head. "No," he started to say before pressing his lips together and turning his head to stare at the strange vehicle that sat several inches off the ground, as if suspended in the air. Releasing a tired breath, he ran his hand through his hair. "I don't know anything about the Legion. My name is Joshua Mason. My… ship was destroyed. I wasn't alone. There were others with me. I need to find them."

Cassa stared at him with a suspicious expression before she finally dropped her arms to her sides. She seemed to be arguing with herself before she released an exasperated huff. Josh's lips twitched at her look of irritation.

"I did not see any other containers such as yours falling from the sky. It is possible I missed them. I will bring you out some clothes and food. You can sleep in the back room. There is a cot and a bathroom back there. In the morning, I will see if my father can send some of the men out to search for your companions. They may have landed on the other side of the mountains," Cassa stated. "Wait here. I will return in a few minutes."

Josh nodded and watched as Cassa gingerly stepped around him and disappeared up a short set of steps. He turned when she was out of sight and began searching the interior area of the shed looking for clues as to where in the hell he might have landed. Moving from shelf to shelf, he picked up objects that were alien, yet familiar. Frustrated when he didn't find anything that looked like a weapon, he turned and stood in silence. He frowned down at the vehicle from earlier.

Stepping closer to it, he ran his hand along the seat. He jumped when his fingers slid across a button and a section of the side opened. Inside was a long metal shape that looked suspiciously like a rifle. Lifting it out, he turned it over in his hands. He was about to raise it to his shoulder when he heard the sound of footsteps on the gravel outside. Replacing the weapon, he silently closed the compartment and stepped away as Cassa appeared at the top of the stairs.

"I brought you some of my brother's clothing," Cassa said as she stepped down the last step. "You and Pack are about the same size. I've also brought you some meat, bread, cheese, and wine. I did not want to wake my father or my little brother, so it will have to do for tonight."

Josh stepped forward and carefully took the items from her with a slight nod of his head. Now that there was light, he could see the faint markings along her brow and down along her left cheek. The small spots highlighted her long dark hair and eyes.

"Thank you," Josh said, glancing down at the clothing and food before looking up at her again. "Thank you for your help."

Cassa gave him a strained smile before turning to look out the doorway. "I must return to the house. We can talk more in the morning," she replied. "My father will know what to do to help you find your friends. I just hope…."

Josh gripped the food and clothing in his left hand and reached out with his right when she stopped talking and turned partially away from him. He had caught the faint look of worry in her eyes.

"You just hope… what?" He quietly asked.

Cassa turned her head so that she could stare him in the eye. "I just hope you are telling the truth about not being with the Legion. I should have asked if they are looking for you. We are a small vineyard. It is just my father, little brother, myself, and a handful of workers from the village. The last thing we need is trouble with the Legion forces."

Josh shook his head and dropped his hand. "I've never heard of the Legion, so I seriously doubt they are looking for me. My friends and I are not a threat to anyone," he promised, taking a step back.

Cassa studied him for several long seconds again before she nodded. He watched as she turned to leave again. She paused to look back at him with a bewildered expression before she shook her head and disappeared into the night. He waited until he couldn't hear her footsteps any longer before he set the items she gave him down on the counter.

Unwrapping the food, he picked up a piece of the meat. It was dark brown with swirls of white through it. He sniffed it before taking a bite. He was surprised by the rich flavor and quickly ate more. He finished the meat and several pieces of cheese, washing it down with some of the smooth, dry wine that was in the flask.

Walking back to the vehicle, he opened the compartment and pulled out the rifle, weighing it in his hands and exploring it. He spent the next thirty minutes learning what each of the buttons on the land skid did. He received a surprise bonus when the thick, leather seat opened and he found an abundance of sharp knives inside.

"This might come in handy," he murmured, pulling a smaller blade out and studying it.

Rising to his feet, he stretched. His gaze moved to the pile of clothing and the pair of boots sitting on the counter. Deciding he would not only feel better, but smell better as well, he picked up the items and walked down the small hallway to the back of the building. At the end, there was an open door. Inside, he could see a long, narrow cot and another room that looked like a bathroom. Stepping inside, he turned and glanced to see if there was a door. A lighted panel next to the doorway drew his attention. He reached out the hand holding the boots. The sound of the door sliding shut behind him made him jump and mutter a small curse. With a shake of his head, he stepped away from the door and walked around the room.

"Where the hell am I?" He muttered, dropping the clothing on the bed and placing the boots next to it. Looking out the small, narrow window, he couldn't help but take a step closer so he could look up at the trio of moons. "Better yet, where in the hell are the others?" He whispered before releasing a sigh and turning toward the bathroom.

Perhaps in the morning he'd find some answers. Right now, he would get cleaned up and explore a little more before then. Until he knew exactly where he was and what the hell to expect, he needed to be on his guard.

Chapter 10

Cassa moved quietly around the kitchen, preparing breakfast for her father, brother, and their unexpected guest. She had already been out to see the strange man this morning and invited him to come to the house for breakfast. She decided that would be a better time for her father to meet Joshua Mason.

"You are up earlier than normal," Jemar said as he stepped into the kitchen.

"Yes," Cassa replied, turning to place a plate of fresh fruit on the table.

"You were up late, as well," he said, pulling the chair out and sitting down.

Cassa looked at him with a startled expression before her lips curved into a soft smile. "I thought you were sleeping," she commented.

"Not as soundly as you thought," her father replied with a shrug. He reached for the plate of fruit and selected several pieces before returning the plate to the center of the table. "It sounded like you took the land skid out."

"I did," Cassa admitted in a clipped tone, glancing up as Jesup hurried into the room with a soft apology. "Jesup…."

"Who is that?" Jesup asked, staring with wide eyes behind Cassa.

Cassa turned and nervously smoothed her hands down over the front of her dark brown tunic.

Swallowing, she stared at the stranger she had found late last night with renewed apprehension. He looked different, more dangerous, dressed in Pack's old clothing. It was ridiculous, but true.

Cassa glanced at her father when she heard his chair slide across the floor. Licking her lips, she stepped around the table so that she would be on the same side as Josh. She glanced nervously at her father. A dark frown creased Jemar's brow as he stared back and forth between her and Josh.

"This is Joshua Mason. He is why I was late coming in last night," Cassa replied in a soft, calm voice that belied her nervousness. "Joshua, this is my father, Jemar de Rola, and my younger brother, Jesup."

"Sir," Joshua said, bowing his head in greeting. "Cassa suggested it would be best if I came to the house this morning. I hope you don't mind."

Cassa waited for her father to make up his mind. She knew he could see that Joshua wasn't like the other strangers that sometimes came to the spaceport on the other side of the mountains. Nor was he like the traders that often came to bargain for their wine.

"Sit," Jemar ordered, slowly sinking back down into his seat. "Cassa, the tea."

"Yes, father," Cassa murmured, stepping back around the table to the stove where she had the tea for the morning meal ready. "I found Joshua last night in the forest on the edge of the mountains. He needs help. I told him you would know what to do."

"The forest is no place to be at night," Jemar said, looking at Josh with a raised eyebrow. "What were you doing there?"

..*

Josh stared at the man sitting across from him. "My ship broke apart and the emergency pod I was in landed in the forest," he explained, deciding it was best to stick as close to the truth as he could. "It is possible the rest of my crew also survived. I need to find them."

Jemar leaned forward, placing his elbows on the table and looking intently at Josh. For a moment, it reminded him of Cassa's scrutiny last night. He could see a slight similarity between Cassa and her father. They had the same dark hair and eyes.

And the same intense stare, he thought to himself.

"How did your ship break apart?" Jemar asked with a puzzled frown. "Where were you coming from?"

Josh's lips tightened for a moment before he shrugged. There was no way he could tell Jemar de Rola that he was from Earth. He didn't know what happened to the gateway. The last thing he wanted to do was put the planet in danger by revealing where he had come from.

"The hull was breached and my crew and I were forced to use the emergency pods. I'm not really sure where I am to tell you the truth. I know that the pods were designed to locate a habitable planet and send out an emergency signal. The life support will technically function for approximately thirty days. I don't know how long I was in space before it landed in the forest," Josh admitted, skipping the last question.

Jemar nodded and frowned. "There are several planets in the solar system that are habitable. Some are more remote than others. I can ask at the spaceport if anyone has seen anything." He paused and picked up his tea, taking a sip and sitting back in his chair. "In the meantime, we are shorthanded. If you need work, we could use the help."

Josh felt Cassa start in surprise. She was staring at her father with a combination of confusion and shock. It was obvious that was not what she was expecting.

"Thank you. I appreciate your offer and I accept," Josh said.

"Please eat, we have a long day ahead of us," Jemar replied, nodding to the food that Cassa had placed on the table. "I will show you around the vineyard after breakfast."

Josh nodded, reaching for the plate of food in front of him. He handed the plate to the young boy sitting to the left of him after he had taken several pieces of fruit and some bread. A smile tugged at his lips at the boy's curious, wide-eyed stare.

"So, how big was your ship?" Jesup asked.

..*

Josh walked beside Jemar as he quietly explained the harvesting process. In the distance, he could see what appeared to be small robots moving down the rows. His eyes widened when he saw a larger robot step over the long line of vines and lift the full bins of fruit. It poured the picked fruit into itself before setting the container back down and moving to the next one.

"We only have seven helpers left. The others have either left the planet or joined the Gallant Order," Jemar stated.

Josh could feel Jemar's intense stare at his comment. He still didn't know who or what the Legion or Gallant Order was. From the few pieces of information he had been able to gather, he was pretty sure they were two opposing governing forces. Cassa's harsh question asking him if he was a member of the Legion told him that she wasn't a huge supporter of that particular group.

"Why would they leave the planet? Where would they go?" Josh asked, pausing to study the large, thick orange fruit that was almost as big as his hand.

Jemar stopped beside him and turned to look at him. "What do you know about the Legion and the Gallant Order?" Jemar asked in a quiet tone.

Josh shrugged. "Not much," he admitted. "I know that Cassa isn't too happy with the Legion."

"My daughter can be very difficult when she isn't happy, Joshua Mason," Jemar chuckled and reached out to cut the fruit from the vine with a sharp, curved blade that looked very similar to the one that Josh had taken last night. "I do not know where you are from, but I can tell that it is not from any of the known galaxies."

Josh stiffened and he cleared his face of any expression. "Why do you say that?" He asked in a cautious tone.

Jemar looked at him with amusement. "You do not deny it," he murmured in approval. "I would have had doubts about you if you had lied. Anyone who lives here, even in the remotest sections of the galaxy, is aware of the power of the Legion, and the struggles of the Gallant Order to stop Lord Andronikos from taking over any more worlds."

"Lord Andronikos?" Josh replied with a raised eyebrow.

Jemar nodded. "He is the director of the Legion and not a man you want as an enemy. Those that have disagreed with him do not live long," he warned.

"What is the Gallant Order?" Josh asked after several long seconds.

"The Gallant Order was once very powerful," Jemar explained. "The Gallant was made up of representatives from each world, knights that swore on their lives to help guide and protect the worlds. As the members grew older, the younger generation thought them old fashion and weak. Andri Andronikos took advantage when one of the planets under the Gallant Order suffered a devastating loss."

"What kind of loss?" Josh asked with a frown.

Jemar's lips tightened in anger. "It was said to be a natural disaster, but I seriously doubt it. The central core of the planet froze. Millions of people died before support could be sent to them," he explained with a sad look in his eyes. "Lord Andronikos accused the Gallant Order of ignoring the pleas of the planet. He drew in large followings and continued to build up his army."

"Why didn't the Gallant try to stop him?" Josh asked in surprise.

Jemar looked out over the fields. "There are few of the original knights left in the Order. We saw what was happening and tried to stop Andronikos. The cost of trying to stop the director came with huge consequences. Unfortunately, we were too few and too old for the wave of support following him," he replied with a hint of resignation in his voice.

"We… You were part of the Gallant; one of the original knights?" Josh asked in surprise.

Jemar released a deep sigh and nodded. "Yes, until the death of my wife," he murmured. "I returned to the valley and the vineyards that belonged to my family. I am too old and the Gallant needs younger men to fight against the Legion's forces."

..*

Later that evening, Josh stood outside of the house in a small garden. He stared up at the moons. It felt strange, yet natural to see three of them. One was nearly full, while the other two were in different stages based on their distance from the planet. In the back of his mind, he was curious about the geological makeup of Tesla Terra. Something told him it was larger than the Earth.

He turned when he heard soft footsteps behind him. His eyes widened when he saw not only Jemar, but Cassa and Jesup walking toward him. Jemar carried a long box in his left hand.

"If you are going to be in our world, Joshua Mason, then it is important that you know how to defend yourself," Jemar stated, placing the long box on the stone planter and opening it. "I have trained all of my children. Now, I will train you."

Josh frowned when he saw four long staffs in the box. Each had an intricate design etched into it. His hand automatically reached out when Jemar held one out to him. He was surprised by how light the staff was considering it looked like it was solid metal.

"The staffs have been in our family for centuries. They were carried by the Knights of the Gallant Order. Each staff was made for a specific family and entrusted to them to be used to serve and protect those less fortunate. There were originally five brothers in the de Rola family that carried them. I have kept the others safe, teaching my own children how to use them," Jemar explained, gently lifting one of the staffs up out of the case and turning toward him.

Josh took a step back when the staff in Jemar's hand suddenly expanded. On each end were two bright, round red orbs that looked as if they contained a fire storm of electricity inside them. He watched intently as Jemar moved with a grace that belied his advanced years. The old man reminded him of the Masters in the old Chinese films he used to watch as a kid.

He didn't take his eyes off of Jemar as he swung the staff. Instead of expressing a loud shout like they did in the movies, Jemar breathed out in long breaths as he thrust. Josh had watched so many martial arts movies as a kid that his father had actually enrolled him in a class down at the local youth center. He had managed to make it to a first degree black belt before girls and cars replaced his interest. He had continued to practice, more out of the enjoyment of the movements than for any other reason. Still, it was years since he had been in any of the competitions and none of them had ever held the moves that Jemar was doing.

A few minutes later, Jemar turned to Josh and retracted the staff. Josh stared into the old man's eyes, seeing a quiet question in them, as if he was asking Josh if he would accept not only the staff, but the responsibility that came with it. Josh glanced down at the beautifully crafted weapon in his hand.

He carefully ran his fingers over the staff, memorizing the feel of it. He felt the small indention where the release was and pressed it. Each end of the staff slid out. He began to slowly twirl the staff, relying on instinct and years of practice to guide him. Instead of mimicking Jemar, Josh moved in graceful sync with the katas from his youth. He discovered as he moved that the position of his hand on the staff controlled the orbs at the ends of it.

After several minutes, he straightened and bowed to Jemar, holding out the now retracted staff. His gaze remained locked with Jemar's inquisitive one. He was surprised when instead of taking the weapon from him, Jemar closed his fingers around Josh's and pressed them to the staff.

"On your world, you were a warrior," Jemar murmured with curiously satisfied insight. Josh hesitated for a moment before he gave a brief nod. The satisfied smile on Jemar's lips confused Josh for a moment. His gaze slipped back to where Cassa and Jesup stood in silence. He stepped back when Jemar turned and reached for the other staffs. "Now, my daughter will show you how to use it correctly."

Josh's gaze flashed to Cassa. A sense of unease swept through him when she moved and lengthened the staff. He noticed that the ends of her staff were glowing green. Stepping to the side, he gave her a brief bow just before their staffs clashed together with a surprising force that told him that Cassa knew what she was doing.

Chapter 11

"Sir, the last of the debris has been retrieved," one of the lower officers aboard the Legion Battle Cruiser stated.

General Roan Landais glanced up from the report he was studying. An intense frown creased his brow at the interruption. He rose from his desk and stepped around it, walking over to the large window so he could stare out at the service ships.

"You are sure it is from the same spaceship?" He asked in a harsh tone.

"Yes, sir. We've received information that five signals were intercepted moving away from the debris," the man stated.

"Have any of the signals been traced yet?" Roan asked, continuing to stare out the window.

"One was reported in the region of Tesla Terra," the man replied.

Roan was silent for several seconds before he raised his hand in dismissal. Once the door shut behind him, he continued staring out the window. He folded his hands behind him, deep in thought.

Turning, he walked back to his desk and sat down. With a flick of his hand, he accessed the secure communication channel to the Director. His gaze flickered to the report next to him.

"What have you found?" Lord Andronikos demanded.

“The last of the pieces have been found,” Roan responded calmly. “I have our engineers recreating the ship, but it looks foreign. There is additional debris mixed with it that appears to match the information you gave me. Unfortunately, there is very little of it that survived whatever happened.”

“And the signals that were intercepted?” Andronikos asked, sitting back in his seat and making a temple of his fingers as he stared back at Roan.

Roan kept his expression blank. It was one of the many skills he had learned early in his career; keep all thoughts and feelings under control at all times. He should have known that the Director would have been informed of the unusual signals that had been detected moving away from the area.

“One was intercepted in the region of Tesla Terra,” Roan responded, repeating the information he had just learned from the other officer. It was obvious that there was a spy on board his Battle Cruiser, something that he would not tolerate. While there was little he could do about it, he would discover who it was and make sure he limited what the person had access to. “Do you wish an investigation?”

Andronikos was silent for a moment before he shook his head. “No, continue to search for the rest of the signals. I want to know where that ship came from and who was on it. Keep me informed.”

“Yes, Lord Andronikos,” Roan said with a bow of his head.

Roan ended the call and turned back to the report he was studying. He glanced at the symbols on one of the pieces of debris. The strange design – Gliese 581 – looked as if it was some type of writing. It was a language he wasn't familiar with and there were no known symbols in the database that matched it. He glanced at the console when it pinged.

"Report," Roan ordered.

"Sir, we have traced another signal," the communications officer reported.

"Plot a course," Roan ordered as he ended the link and rose out of his chair.

When the report was initially sent to Lord Ankronikos, the director had been adamant that Roan oversaw the investigation. Since the recovery of the first pieces, the leader of the Legion had become more demanding and insisted that any findings be immediately reported to him. Roan felt that there was more to the strange ship than he had been briefed on. Striding toward the door of his office, he decided it was time that he personally inspected the new pieces of the unusual spaceship.

***

Josh wiped the sweat from his brow and pulled loose the flask of water attached to his side. He grimaced when he felt the muscles in his arms protest. Between the work in the vineyard and the training sessions in the evenings, he was discovering muscles he hadn't used since leaving Earth.

He took a deep swig of the refreshing liquid before lowering it and wiping a hand across his mouth.

His gaze moved over the large field. He could see Cassa arguing with one of the robots. She was pointing down the row and shaking her finger at it. Amusement swept through him.

During the past couple of weeks, he was slowly discovering more about the unusual, but beautiful alien woman. Cassa was an enigma. She held an air of quiet reserve about her, but there was also an edginess that he found captivating. He couldn't quite figure her out. That was something that had never happened before.

A low chuckle escaped him when she threw her hands up in the air after the small robot turned and headed down the row. The smile froze on his lips when she turned toward him, as if aware that he was watching what was going on. Her lips twisted in response to his observation of her argument.

His gaze followed her as she moved between the rows towards him. Surprise swept through him when he felt a heat building inside him that had nothing to do with the work he was doing. A silent curse escaped him when he realized his body was definitely not immune to Cassa either. He could never remember being this distracted before. She had been in his thoughts, and his dreams, constantly since the first time he saw her through the glass of the emergency pod.

"The robot is malfunctioning," she said with a frustrated sigh. "That is the third time this week. We are already shorthanded."

"Would you like me to take a look at it?" Josh asked, not sure that he could do much, but feeling like he needed to at least offer.

Cassa shook her head. "No, I sent it back to the house. Jesup can take a look at it. He has a knack for repairing them," she murmured, staring up at him with a sudden look of confusion.

Josh took a step closer to her, as if pulled by an invisible string. They were alone in the far fields, working with the V2 Harvest robots while Jesup, Jemar, and a handful of the other workers from the nearby village worked near the processing center closer to the house.

"Cassa," Josh murmured, lifting his hand to brush a strand of her loose hair back from her cheek. His hand continued to slide along her jaw to draw her closer. "I'm going to kiss you."

Her eyes widened and her lips parted on a slight breath of surprise. Josh didn't wait. Bending forward, he captured her lips in a kiss that both surprised and shocked him. A soft groan escaped him and he deepened the kiss when she stepped closer to him and raised her hands to rest them on his shoulders.

The jolt he felt at their first touch shook him. That had definitely never happened before between him and a woman. While it fascinated him, it also raised a warning flag that this could be dangerous. He ignored it and pushed down his reservations even as he pulled her closer.

Several long seconds later, he pulled back. He drew in a deep breath and stared down into her eyes. He saw confusion mixed with desire.

"You are a very strange man, Joshua Mason," Cassa whispered, blinking several times.

"You have no idea," Josh muttered, turning his head when a dark shadow caught his attention out of the corner of his eye. "Fire!"

Cassa's gaze turned to follow where he was staring. Alarm flashed across her face. He released her when she pulled back.

"Legion troops," she whispered in a shaken voice. "Father! Jesup!"

Josh cursed when he saw several low flying ships coming toward them. The ground rocked as they fired on the vineyard, sending up waves of flames. Several of the V2 Harvest robots were caught in the blasts. He turned in time to see Cassa climbing on one of the land skids.

"Cassa!" Josh yelled before cursing when several more blasts almost knocked him off his feet.

He turned and ran toward his land skid. Jumping onto it, he thumbed the control and turned it around. He shot down the row, trying to catch Cassa.

"Son-of-a-…," Josh's curse faded as he weaved through the openings in the vines.

The fields were ablaze. Thick, black smoke obscured the house. Leaning forward, he pressed the accelerator on the land skid down as far as it would go. He could see Cassa's slender figure to the left of him. Turning the handles, he cut out onto the straight road leading back to the house just ahead of her.

Sliding sideways, he blocked the road. Cassa pulled to a stop just inches from him. Josh swung off the land skid and rushed to Cassa. His arm wrapped around her waist just seconds before one of the airships broke through the thick smoke. He twisted and fell as it fired on the two vehicles.

"No!" Cassa cried out as he covered her with his body when they exploded. "Father! Jesup!"

"We can't help them if we are dead," Josh said in a grim voice. "Come on!"

Josh rolled to his feet, pulling Cassa up beside him. They ran down the long row. Fire licked at the vines barely ten feet from them, forcing them to run flat out. He kept his hand wrapped tightly around hers as they practically flew over the uneven ground.

At the far end was the first of a series of repair-charging and storage buildings. He pulled her behind him and flattened her against the side of it. Glancing over his shoulder, he saw that the two airships were moving over the far fields where they had been a short while ago.

Turning his head back to Cassa, he saw the angry tears glittering in her eyes. He could feel her trembling, but she stared back at him with determination. His jaw clenched and he pulled his gaze away from her.

"We have to get to the house. Do you know if there are any weapons in any of the buildings?" He asked in a husky voice that held a thread of steel in it.

"Yes. All of the repair-charging stations hold at least one blaster. It is necessary in case one of the fences goes down. Each land skid is also equipped with one. The next building is a repair-charging station," she whispered. "Follow me."

Josh wanted to argue. Everything in him wanted to protect Cassa, but he knew she knew the location of things far better than he did and time was critical if they were going to reach Jemar, Jesup and the others. He gave her a sharp nod and stepped back.

Josh ran slightly behind Cassa, scanning the area as he ran for the airships and any Legion soldiers. Cassa palmed the door to the next repair-charging station and hurried down the steps. Inside were a land skid and several V2 Harvest robots that were charging. He watched as she pulled open a cabinet. Turning, she tossed him one of the rifles similar to what he had discovered the first night of his arrival. Gripping it, he walked over to the land skid and opened the seat. Inside the compartment, there were a variety of curved blades used by the workers. He quickly removed several of them.

"Take this," Josh said, handing her a long, deadly looking blade.

Cassa gripped it in her free hand. "There are six more buildings before we get to the house. At the rate the Legion airships are destroying things, we may not have much time," she said, moving to a panel on the wall. "I'm going to send the V2 Harvest robots out just in case. I don't want them destroyed if I can help them."

Josh heard the thickness in Cassa's voice. He reached out with his free hand and brushed her cheek in support before turning away. She was right. The last thing they wanted to do was get caught inside one of the buildings. He watched as she opened the door to the repair-charging station and the little robots rolled out.

"I hear one of the airships coming back this way," Josh cautioned through gritted teeth. "Let's move."

He stepped through the door, glancing around before looking up. Shouldering the rifle, he calmly aimed at the airship coming in low back over the fields. He waited, focusing on the right engine. He fired just as it did. He jerked back in surprise when both engines exploded at the same time. The airship rocked before it plummeted to the ground, exploding in a massive fireball. Glancing to his right, he saw Cassa standing with her blaster pressed firmly against her shoulder.

"Remind me never to make you mad," he muttered, turning back around.

"The same for you," she replied, following him.

Together, they ran between the buildings, only pausing when the other airship turned to investigate the one that had crashed. Josh waved his hand for Cassa to move to the next building. They were too close to the house to fire on the airship. Closing the distance to the repair-charging station he was living in, they peered around the edge of the building.

"Sir, one of the airships has crashed," a soldier was saying.

"Find out what happened. Where is the person who was in the pod?" The Legion commander demanded, turning to Jemar and standing with his legs apart and his hands behind his back.

"I do not know what you are talking about," Jemar said in a tired voice. "We are simple people. You have destroyed the vineyard that has been in my family for centuries. The lives of the people in the valley depend on the income from the harvest for their survival."

"I want to know where the person that wore this is," the commander demanded, lifting his hand and snapping his finger to one of the soldiers standing nearby.

A silent curse went through Josh's mind when he saw the clothing he wore under his space suit. He should have destroyed it. Watching, he inched closer.

"I don't know where that came from," Jemar replied with a wave of his hand. "I have workers come and go from the spaceport. I do not keep up with them all, nor what they wear. I never saw any of the men wearing such clothing."

"He is telling the truth, sir," one of the soldiers replied. "The scans are coming back clear."

The commander's face darkened in anger. Josh breathed out a sigh of relief. Jemar must have known that he was being scanned. The old man was smart.

He hadn't lied. He didn't know where the clothing came from because he didn't know about Earth. With a few carefully crafted words, he had been completely honest in everything he said.

"Perhaps you need a little encouragement," the commander said in a clipped tone, nodding to another soldier..

"Father," Jesup cried out, trying to twist free of a soldier that was pulling him to the front of the group.

"Release him!" Jemar ordered, turning toward his youngest son. "He knows nothing."

"He's lying," the soldier holding the scanner replied.

Jemar took several steps toward Jesup before he jerked in surprise, looking down at his stomach. A harsh cry escaped Jesup, drowning out Cassa's horrified denial. The Legion commander stepped back, retracting the blade in his hand.

"Search every building," the commander ordered, turning away.

"What should we do with the prisoners, sir?" The soldier standing next to the commander asked.

"Kill them all except for the boy. He will be reconditioned to serve the Legion," the commander instructed.

"No!" Cassa furiously cried, stepping out from behind the building as the soldiers opened fire on the small group of workers.

The blast from Cassa's rifle struck the Legion commander in the center of his chest. Josh immediately stepped out, firing as well. Fury poured through him and he carefully aimed, making sure that each shot counted.

"Jesup, run!" Cassa yelled, wincing when a blast grazed her arm. "Run!"

The young boy turned and ran for the house. He was almost to the door when a soldier turned and fired on him. Josh watched Jesup jerk and fall before lying still on the walkway. Cassa's grief-stricken cry filled the air. He saw her flash past him, running toward her brother. Turning, he systematically fired on the soldiers.

Out of the corner of his eye, he saw Cassa struggle briefly with one of the soldiers before she pushed far enough away to use the blade he had given her. He fired on another soldier that was aiming for her before turning and focusing on the airship that was coming in at a high rate of speed. He waited until he knew he wouldn't miss. Pulling the trigger, he fired on the incoming ship, striking the left engine. It spiraled out of control, slamming into the ground and sliding before coming to a halt. Josh walked up to it, firing repeatedly through the cracked windshield, striking the two men inside.

Turning slowly, he rotated and scanned the area for any remaining Legion troops. Josh stepped over the bodies littering the area. He quickly checked each of the soldiers lying on the ground; three out of the seven surviving workers helped him.

He paused over the Legion commander. He knelt down and gripped the man's shoulder, rolling him over onto his back. The man was gasping for breath, but Josh knew he wouldn't live much longer. Already, he could hear the death rattle in the man's chest.

"Who… are… you?" The commander demanded in a hoarse, barely audible voice.

Josh stared dispassionately down at the man. He had seen men like him before; men that only lived for the power to control others. His eyes swept down over the man, noting the insignia on the commander's collar.

"Lieutenant Commander Joshua Mason, United States Navy, asshole," Josh replied in a grim voice. "Why are you searching for me?"

"The Director…," the commander choked before his head rolled to the side and his sightless eyes glazed over, frozen in death.

Josh cursed, rising to his feet. He turned when he heard Cassa's soft weeping. She was holding Jesup tightly against her and rocking back and forth. Blood stained the left sleeve of her shirt and the rifle and blade lay by her side. Her head remained bowed over Jesup.

"Cassa," Josh murmured, walking toward her. "Cassa."

She didn't turn her head toward him. He could see her shoulders shaking and her breathing was ragged and harsh. Her fingers were coated with blood. In that moment, he knew the little boy was gone. He dropped down, sitting beside her and wrapping his arm around her.

Several minutes later, she raised her head. She still didn't look at him. Instead, she gazed through tear clouded eyes out over the burning vineyard. Dark streaks marked her face where fresh tears fell. Her hands trembled as she tenderly stroked Jesup's dirty face, as if memorizing it.

"We need to leave," Josh murmured in a gentle voice. "We'll take care of the dead, but it isn't safe to remain here. I'm… sorry, Cassa. I'm so sorry I brought this to your home."

Cassa drew in a deep, shaky breath and wiped her cheek on the sleeve of her shirt. She pulled Jesup closer to her, as if willing him to wake up and tell her that it was all a mistake. Holding him close to her chest, she released the breath she had sucked in and finally spoke.

"It is not your fault, Joshua. It was the Legion. Father…." Her voiced thickened in grief. "Father warned that they would come. He said he feared that nothing could stop them, not even the Gallant Order. He was right."

"Is there somewhere you can go?" Josh asked quietly.

Cassa's lips parted. "I will find my brother, Pack," she whispered, turning to look at him. "I will join the Gallant Order and fight with the rebellion. There is nothing left for me here."

Josh's lips tightened as the heavy weight of responsibility settled on his shoulders. He turned his gaze to look out over the vineyard. The flames were beginning to die down. In the distance, he could see the skeletal remains of a large harvest robot.

"I have to find out if the other members of my crew survived. The Legion commander said something about a Director. If they are alive, they are in danger. I have to find them," Josh stated, turning back to stare at Cassa.

"We will bury my brother, father, and the others; then, we will go find my brother, Pack. He can help us find your missing friends.

Chapter 12

Cassa gently lifted the box containing the Staffs belonging to the Knights of the Gallant Order. Her fingers trembled as she opened it. Inside were the four Staffs. Only one was missing; the one belonging to Pack.

"Cassa," Josh quietly called from the doorway.

Cassa nodded, drawing in a deep breath before she reached into the box and withdrew two of the Staffs. She turned and held one of them out. She saw the puzzled look in Josh's eyes.

"Father was training you to be a Knight of the Gallant Order," she said in a soft voice. "Only a Knight can train an apprentice. The first night he handed the Staff to you, I knew what he was doing."

She watched as Josh took the Staff out of her outstretched hand and gently held it. Reaching out, she curled her fingers around his hand so that his fingers closed around it. He turned his gaze to her.

"I'm…," he started to say, stopping when she raised her other hand and placed the tips of her fingers against his lips.

"He saw something in you, Joshua Mason," Cassa said with a shake of her head. "The Staff is yours, wherever your journey takes you. I will help you find your friends, if they are alive. The journey to Pack will be dangerous. Word of what has happened here will spread quickly and the Legion will not stop until we are dead."

"Cassa," Josh muttered, grabbing her arm as she started to turn.

Cassa turned to look up at him, her head lifting in stiff resistance. They had buried her father and brother just a few short hours ago. The workers that had survived had helped with burying the others before leaving to tell the rest of the villagers what had happened. She knew that they would be fleeing as well. It was only a matter of time before the Legion sent more troops to investigate their missing commander and troops.

After the burial, she had retreated to the house. She had taken a quick bath and doctored her wounds before gathering the supplies they would need for their journey to the Spaceport on the other side of the mountains. It would be a dangerous journey. There would be Legion troops there from the Battle Cruiser. Still, if they were to leave the planet, it was their only choice. There were no ships at the local airstrip.

"Josh…," she started to say.

"No, I need to say this," he interjected, sliding his hand down her arm. "I never meant any harm to come to your family, Cassa. Your father and Jesup…." He paused when he felt the shudder of grief that ran through her body. Pulling her closer, he wrapped his arms around her and held her tightly against him. "I can't tell you how sorry I am for what happened."

"You had no way of knowing what would happen, none of us did. We were already in danger from the Legion before you came," she replied, looking down at the front of his shirt. "I do not regret finding you and bringing you here. I regret my own stupidity for not realizing just how dangerous the Legion had become and my blindness in believing that we were immune to it. No one is, they have proven that. I will not make this mistake again."

"I've seen men like this before, Cassa. They feed on the fear of others. This is war and war does not care who it hurts," Josh warned, lifting her chin so she was forced to look at him. "But, I do. I care and that scares the hell out of me."

A slight, sad smile curved the corner of Cassa's lips. Tears burned brightly in her eyes, but didn't fall. She rose up on her toes and pressed a kiss to his lips.

"We must go. We need to get over the mountain before it grows dark," she said, pulling away.

Josh reached out and ran his fingers down her cheek before giving her a brief nod. Cassa turned and closed the box. She quickly finished packing the last of the items that she wouldn't or couldn't leave behind. With a last glance, she turned away. In her heart, she feared she would never return to the only home she had ever known.

She handed a bag to Josh before picking up the last one. Turning on her heel, she stepped out of the room and made her way through the house. She stiffened her shoulders when she felt the flood of grief threatening to drown her. A shuddering breath escaped her and she pulled the door open and stepped outside.

***

Darkness had fallen by the time they reached the Spaceport. They had barely made it through the forest before the sun set. The darkness worked in their favor. There was a flurry of activity. Cassa had only been to the Spaceport a handful of times, but she knew enough from listening to her father and brother to know where she needed to go.

"Keep your face covered," she warned as she slowed the large land transport. "Word of what happened must have reached the Legion."

Josh nodded. Both of them kept their eyes diverted when six Legion soldiers walked past them. The feeling of relief Cassa felt faded when two more soldiers waved her down. She slowed the transport, gliding to a stop next to the soldier.

"Where are you coming from?" The soldier demanded.

"Los Grapos," Cassa replied, holding up a receipt for the items. "I have cloth for the General Merchant. He is to use it to make some items that we need."

The soldier took the receipt and glanced at the back of the transport. Cassa had piled several bolts of canvas material used for making covers on top of the weapons they had brought. She had also retrieved an order list they might need from the compartment from her father's last trip to the Spaceport a few weeks ago.

"Have you seen anything unusual?" The soldier asked.

"No," Cassa replied with a shrug. "I was not aware that Tesla Terra was under the Legion's control now. What are you looking for?"

The soldier did not respond to her question. Instead, he looked toward Josh and nodded.

"Who is that?" The man asked.

Cassa looked at Josh and smiled. "My husband," she replied. "He suffered an injury in a mining accident two years ago. A severe fire has burned his face and people stare at him. He prefers to keep it covered."

She turned to stare up at the soldier, keeping her face and body calm. She was thankful the man didn't carry a scanner on him. It would have picked up her lie.

"Go ahead," the soldier replied, waving his hand when he saw several other transports arriving.

"Thank you," Cassa replied, holding out her hand for the paper she had given the man. "Pleasant evening to you."

Cassa inched forward before picking up speed. She released an unsteady breath. Her gaze flickered down to where Josh held his hand slightly inside his jacket. The hint of a laser pistol showed.

"Your husband?" Josh asked, glancing at her.

Cassa gave him an uneasy smile. "As my husband, you are less likely to be questioned. Luckily for us, my… father had picked up this for a friend from Los Grapos which is on the far side of the desert, in the opposite direction of the vineyard," she explained.

"What do we do now?" Josh asked, shifting so he could see her face.

Cassa glanced at him before focusing on maneuvering through the marketplace. She glanced at the different figures she passed. Patches of bright light lit the area.

"We find someone to buy the transport," she replied. "My father had several friends here. They will help us."

"Can we trust them?" Josh asked, moving his hand and touching her arm.

Cassa nodded. "Yes," she murmured.

"Can they get us off the planet?" He added.

"Yes. Hutu was a member of the old Gallant Order and a true friend of my father," she replied again, this time in a softer voice.

"This is like something out of a movie," he murmured, glancing at all the unusual figures with a shake of his head. "If you had asked me a month ago if I thought I'd be waking up in an alien world and stuck in the middle of a fight between ruling powers, I would have asked what you were smoking."

A soft chuckle escaped Cassa and she glanced at him. "You do not have different visitors to the Spaceports in your world?" She asked.

"We don't have Spaceports, period," Josh admitted. "The Gliese 581 was the first intergalactic voyage ever done."

Cassa shot Josh a surprised look. "But, how does your planet trade with the neighboring worlds?" She asked with a puzzled frown as she pulled to a stop outside a building with a dim light flickering over the entrance and shut down the land skid.

"Cassa," Josh said in a hesitant voice. He waited until she turned to look at him. His expression serious. "We've never met anyone else. The Earth is the only planet in our Solar System that has life on it… that we know of."

"But… How did you get here?" She asked in confusion.

"There was a strange object discovered a little over ten years ago," Josh admitted. "An international collaboration created the Project Gliese 581g to investigate it. It was the only mission of its kind. It was some type of gateway. My crew and I were sent to inspect it, try to figure out what the hell it was, and return with it if we could." He turned to look down the road at the alien terrain and its residents. "We accidentally activated the gateway and were sucked through it. The Gliese 581, my spaceship, was destroyed. In an effort to save the crew and myself, we used the emergency pods to escape."

"The capsule that I found," Cassa stated more than asked.

"Yes," Josh turned to look back at her. "I have to believe the others survived. All of this…." He waved his hand outward. "We've never seen anything like this except made up in a movie."

"A movie? You said that word before, but I'm not sure what it means," she repeated with a small frown.

"You know, moving images captured and replayed for entertainment," Josh explained.

"Ah, yes. We have those. How many were on your ship?" She asked in a husky voice.

"There were five of us. Julia, Mei, Sergi, and… Ash," Josh murmured, running his hand down over his face. "I should never have allowed Sergi to see if he could repair the damn thing."

Cassa could hear the exhaustion and regret in his voice. She couldn't imagine how she would react if she suddenly awoke in an alien world where everything was foreign to her; a place where species from dozens of different worlds lived together. For the first time, she saw her world through new eyes.

Turning to look at him, she raised her hand to his cheek. Her thumb moved over his skin, enjoying the slight roughness. A shiver went through her when he raised his hand and cupped her hand in his.

"I would like to know more about your world," she whispered. "In return, I will tell you all I can about mine."

Her gaze held his as he leaned closer. She knew he was going to kiss her again. After everything that had happened that day, she needed it. She needed to feel his warmth. She needed it to drive away the cold that had seeped into her soul when she saw her father and brother lying lifeless. Tears burned in her eyes and she closed them, pressing forward and closing the distance between them.

The touch of his firm lips against hers soothed her battered heart. A low sob caught in her throat, captured by his lips. Her eyelashes fluttered open a few minutes later when he pulled back.

"You are an incredible woman," Josh muttered, wiping the tear that escaped from her cheek.

"Hey, what do you want? There is no parking here. You need to move your transport before I blow it out of the way," a voice growled out of the darkness.

"Hutu, it is Cassa de Rola," Cassa called in a soft voice.

"Cassa? Where is your father?" Hutu exclaimed in a startled voice.

"Killed by Legion forces earlier today, as was Jesup," Cassa replied in a strained voice. "We need your help."

"Oh, child," Hutu muttered in anguish. "Come in, come in."

Chapter 13

"The Legion forces are checking every spaceship before they depart and scouring the planet for something they think has landed here," Hutu said twenty minutes later. He placed a cup of hot tea in front of both of them before turning back to pick up a tray with food on it. "They haven't stated what they are looking for, but word spread that the commander of a Battle Cruiser and his troop of men have gone missing."

Cassa nodded. "They came to the vineyard," she said, picking up the hot drink and holding it in her hands. "Josh and I were in the outer vineyard with the V2 Harvest Bots when we saw smoke. They had lit the vineyard on fire."

"Bastards," Hutu muttered under his breath as he sank down into his chair with a heavy sigh. "Do you know why they were there?"

"I believe it was because of me," Josh stated, sitting forward and placing his elbows on the table. "We overheard them asking Jemar about it."

Hutu sat back in his seat and studied Josh for several long moments, a puzzled expression on his face. Josh knew what the man was wondering. Hutu was trying to figure out who the hell he was and what he was doing there. His gaze shot to where Cassa was sitting. She was staring down into her tea with a slightly dazed expression. He could see that she was still in shock about what had happened and hadn't missed the wince when he mentioned her father's name.

"Which leads me to my next question… Who are you and where did you come from? I would know if I had seen or met someone like you before," Hutu stated, resting one arm on the table.

Josh stared at the large male across from him. The man had dark red skin with thick markings, that looked similar to tattoos, visible through the opening of his shirt. Dark brown eyes pierced him, searching and analyzing every aspect of him until Josh felt exposed.

Josh decided he had two ways of dealing with the man, trust him like Cassa did, or just give him enough information to get his help and hope for the best. He hadn't missed the concerned look the male had kept shooting at Cassa, the fact that Hutu had slipped a blaster into his pocket while preparing their meal, or that he had taken a strategic position by sitting straight across from Josh with only one hand visible at any one time. Josh had a feeling that if he glanced under the table, he'd find himself staring down the end of a barrel.

Glancing once more at Cassa, he saw her return his look with one of her own. She nodded her head in encouragement, before dropping her gaze once more to her tea. With a weary sigh, Josh focused on Hutu.

"My name is Joshua Mason. I'm a Lieutenant Commander with the United States Navy. I was chosen to command an experimental intergalactic mission," Josh began, slowly explaining everything in detail.

An hour later, Hutu sat forward with both of his hands folded on the table in front of him, a worried frown creasing his brow. Josh had answered a hundred different questions from the man over the course of the conversation. Cassa had quietly excused herself when he started telling Hutu about what had happened earlier today.

"She has devoted her life to her family since her mother's tragic death," Hutu commented in a soft voice. "Jesup was more like her child than her brother."

"What happened to her mother?" Josh asked.

Hutu released a deep sigh and shook his head. "There is what I know, and there is what I suspect," he admitted, glancing at the closed door where Cassa had disappeared. "What I know is that Jemar and I were sent on a mission to Abelquin in the Durluxing Galaxy. We met with a group of dignitaries a little over ten years ago. They were concerned about the sudden influx of soldiers to their planet. Andri Andronikos had sent a battalion there unbeknownst to the Gallant Order. A skirmish broke out and Jemar and I sided with the Abelquin forces. It was the first major defeat our dear Director suffered. When we returned to Jeslean, the headquarters for the Gallant Order, we presented our findings to the council."

"What happened?" Josh asked with a frown.

Hutu shrugged. "Andronikos received a slap on the hand and was cautioned that such behavior was a direct violation of the Gallant Order. He, of course, denied any knowledge of the situation, stating that he had simply sent troops there to help support the civil unrest, but the commander had defied him and taken matters into his own hands."

"What happened to the commander?" Josh asked, already suspecting the answer.

"He is Andronikos second in command," Hutu admitted. "I was surprised at first, until I realized that there was a connection between the two. General Landais is Andri Andronikos' half-brother."

"What does this all have to do with Cassa's mother?" Josh muttered, shaking his head as he tried to work out the connection.

"Jemar was one of the most vocal opponents against Andronikos. He knew many of the council members and they trusted him. Fear was rising from some of the things Andronikos was saying. Jemar argued that power had corrupted Andronikos who had just been elected as the new director. Shortly after a public confrontation, word reached Jemar that Lesla was found dead," Hutu murmured. "The news almost destroyed Jemar. He had Packu, Cassa, and a new baby, but Lesla had been his world. He resigned his position with the Gallant Order to return to the vineyard."

Josh's mouth tightened and his gaze narrowed on Hutu's face. "How did she die?" He asked in a husky voice.

Hutu sent a sad glance at the closed door where Cassa had retired for the night. "They found her body outside the house. A section of the fence was damaged. The official report stated that a Tusku must have somehow damaged it and made its way in. The investigator suggested that Lesla heard a noise and went to see what it was and was killed."

"But, you don't believe that," Josh stated more than asked.

Hutu looked down at his cold tea and shook his head. "No, I know that is not what happened, and so did Jemar," he responded in a grim voice. "The injuries… a Tusku wouldn't have inflicted those types of wounds. There were also no tracks and the damaged fence was done from the inside, not the outside. It was a message to Jemar warning him that none of his family would be safe from retribution if he continued to stand in the Director's way. It was something we had seen before, but it was the first time Andronikos had attacked an actual Knight of the Gallant Order."

"Something tells me it wasn't the last," Josh reflected.

Hutu glanced at Josh and shook his head again. "No, it was not the last. After that, the Knights began dying in mysterious ways. There were shuttle accidents, unusual medical conditions that had been missed during routine physical exams, unexplained disappearances, and more," Hutu whispered, staring back at Josh.

"What about you? You were a Knight of the Gallant Order. How did you survive?" Josh asked.

Hutu's mouth tightened into a flat line before a small curve lifted the corner and his eyes danced with amusement. Josh's eyes narrowed when he saw the man glance back at him with another assessing gaze. Hutu suddenly rose to his feet and waved for Josh to follow him.

"I am just an old man who now buys and sells junk for a living as far as the Legion is concerned," Hutu stated.

"But, in real life you are still a Knight," Josh muttered, grabbing the hooded coat off the back of his chair and rising to his feet so that he could follow Hutu out the back door.

Hutu chuckled and glanced over his shoulder at Josh. "In real life, I am a General of the Gallant Order and the rebellion," he admitted. "And you, Joshua Mason and your crew, are a prize that the Director wants to get his hands on very, very badly."

..*

Josh didn't know what to say to Hutu's last statement. He didn't understand why this Director would be interested in him or the rest of the Gliese 581 crew. Hell, it wasn't like they could give the guy information about advanced technology, weaponry, or anything else that would be of use.

"Do you know why Andrionikos is looking for us?" Josh asked as they stepped outside.

"Yes and no," Hutu murmured. "Pull the hood over your head. There are those that would betray you in a heartbeat for a few credits."

Josh nodded, pulling the coat on and lifting the hood to cover his head. He kept his head down as they began walking through the streets of the Spaceport. He turned to glance back at Hutu's home, worried about leaving Cassa alone.

"She is safe," Hutu promised. "I have men watching the house."

They walked in silence, turning down several streets before reaching a large, dome-shaped building. Large groups of individuals mingled outside. Josh forced himself to keep his eyes down as much as possible. In reality, all he wanted to do was stare at the different alien forms.

Pushing past a small group, they climbed up the steps and entered the dark interior. A smile tugged at Josh's lips when he realized it was a bar.

It appears that bars are a universal establishment no matter which galaxy you live in, he thought, looking around.

The interior was dim with colorful lights dancing over the long bar. Dozens of patrons filled the seats, with more mingling in the open area, making it difficult for the service bots to deliver the drinks. Individual booths tucked along the sides were also filled.

One booth in particular caught Josh's attention when he saw two unusual men arguing over a woman. One of the men must have said something that upset the woman because she reached out with a long blade and sliced the man's cheek. He jerked and blood splattered the floor near his boots.

"Nice place," Josh muttered under his breath.

"This is a slow night," Hutu chuckled. "This way."

Hutu paused near one of the bartenders. Josh watched as Hutu leaned forward and murmured something in the man's ear. The man glanced at Josh before nodding and lifting the divider so they could step behind the bar. Josh frowned, glancing behind him. The feeling of being watched was suddenly very strong.

"We're being observed," Josh muttered when Hutu paused, waiting for the door to open.

"Do you know who?" Hutu asked, not turning around.

"Third booth from the door, the guy in the red outfit," Josh stated. "Seventh booth from your right, the one in brown as well."

Hutu passed through the door when it opened and turned, waiting for Josh to follow. He murmured something to the bartender who let them through before closing the door behind them. Josh started when the floor under them suddenly began to lower.

"Mercenary spies hired by the Legion. They will be taken care of," Hutu replied.

"How?" Josh asked, frowning as they continued to descend down into the ground.

Hutu chuckled. "The Legion is not the only one who knows how to arrange accidents," he replied.

"Where are we going?" Josh asked with a raised eyebrow.

Hutu grinned. "This is a mining planet. There are hundreds of miles of tunnels scattered throughout the area. It was not difficult to build a business establishment above one. A lot of business is done in a bar."

"And a lot of information exchanged," Josh murmured.

"Yes," Hutu agreed with a loud sigh. "It is a dangerous business. The Legion is known for setting an example of those that resist them."

"We have the same type of men back on my planet," Josh replied. "A wise man, Edmund Burke, once said something to the effect that all evil needs to triumph is for a few good men to do nothing. That's not an exact quote, but it is true, no matter where you live."

"He was a wise man," Hutu said with a nod. "We are here."

'Here' turned out to be an underground compound. A transport was waiting for them when they stepped off the lift. Josh turned and watched as the lift immediately disappeared again. Following Hutu, he climbed into the transport.

"This is just one of many bases located throughout the galaxy," Hutu explained. "Tomorrow, you and Cassa will be escorted to one of the off-world transports. I know that Cassa wishes to meet up with her brother, Pack, but the priority needs to be on locating your other crew members. We have received word that the Legion believes they have located another of your escape pods. A Battle Cruiser has been dispatched to search for it."

"I still don't understand why the Director is so interested in finding us," Josh said, staring down the dimly lit mine shaft. Lights embedded in the walls flickered as they passed by them at a rapid speed. He caught glimpses of other corridors that cut off of the main tunnel. "Our planet is nowhere near as advanced as yours," he reluctantly admitted.

Hutu looked at him with a startled glance before he shook his head. "It is not your technological advancement that the Director is afraid of, Josh."

Josh frowned. "Then, what is it?" He demanded in frustration.

"He is afraid of those that came through the ancient gate. The true rulers of our galaxy. The ancient rulers," Hutu responded, stunning Josh into silence.

Chapter 14

Two hours later, Josh was still silent, only this time it had turned from stunned to grim. He sat in the underground control room, listening to the different reports on troop movements by the Legion. He sat back at the end of the table, his fingers were templed as he stared up at the lighted board while Hutu explained what was going on.

"General Landais' Battle Cruiser has been retrieving parts of an unknown spaceship that was discovered in the Torrian area," Hutu explained.

"Why is Andronikos wasting the time and resources of one of his most successful Generals to retrieve debris?" One of the men sitting around the table asked with a frown. "It doesn't make sense. Landais is one of our most difficult opponents."

A low murmur of agreement swept around the room. Hutu turned to look at the pilot who spoke. His lips were pressed tightly together.

"It isn't the ship that Andronikos wants, it was what was on board the spaceship," Hutu stressed. "There were five emergency pods. Two have been tracked so far, only one has been found. There are three others unaccounted for. It is imperative that we locate those pods before the Legion does."

"Why? We have more important things to do than waste our time looking for trash from a spaceship," another man grumbled. "Our resources are low as it is. Now you want us to waste precious time chasing shadows? Those emergency pods could be anywhere."

"Unless those pods contain a miracle, I have to concur with the others, General Hutu," a woman said. "Since the death of the Premier of the Gallant Order, hope, and resources, continue to fade. I'm afraid I would have to vote against sending out our scouts for your missing pods."

Josh saw Hutu glance at him and shook his head. The feelings of defeat and unease resonated through the room. Hutu would not receive any support from the other leaders.

"Very well," Hutu said. "I will conduct the search myself."

"General!" The voices of dissent rang out as the men and women in the room started to argue.

Josh decided that he'd had enough. Rising out of his seat, he quietly left the room. He walked down the narrow corridor that opened into the main tunnel. He had only taken a few steps down it when someone bumped into him.

"My apologies," a young man stated, taking several steps before he turned and frowned at Josh. "That coat… That is… was my father's coat. I would recognize it anywhere."

Josh took a step back when grief flashed across the man's face before it was replaced with rage. The man reached for the weapon at his waist. Josh recognized the staff a split second before the man moved into a fighting stance. His hand slipped into the pocket of the coat and he withdrew the staff that Cassa had given to him shortly before they left the vineyard.

He barely had time to extend it before the man attacked. The two staffs clashed loudly, each man stepping forward as they strained against each other. Josh pushed forward before taking a quick step to the side. The move knocked the man backwards several steps.

"That staff belongs to my family," the man growled. "Only a Knight of the Gallant Order has the right to use it."

"Your father gave it to me," Josh stated, keeping his eye on the man as he circled around him. He blocked another blow. "Are you Packu?"

The man paused, looking at him with a wary expression. "Who are you?" Pack demanded in a slightly hoarse voice. "My father would never give a staff to an outsider."

Josh blocked another blow, holding the other staff down to the ground before he released it and stepped back several feet. He retracted the staff in his hand, knowing that he was leaving himself open. Grief, rage, and uncertainty flashed across Pack's face as he stared back at Josh.

"My name is Josh Mason," Josh said. "Your sister, Cassa, found me. Your father did give me the staff. He was training me."

Uncertainty warred with hatred. Josh knew that Pack's anger came from grief at losing his father and younger brother. How he had found out so quickly, Josh didn't know.

"He's telling the truth, Pack," Hutu stated, walking slowly toward the two men.

Pack slowly lowered the staff in his hands and retracted it. Josh watched as Pack drew in several deep breaths and lowered his head. When he looked back up, his eyes were hard and cold.

"Where is Cassa?" Pack demanded.

"Safe," Hutu replied, coming to a stop next to Pack. "For now. Come, we must prepare for our mission."

..*

An hour later, they were back at Hutu's residence. Josh quietly watched Cassa nod and sniff at something Pack said. Both of their faces were twisted in grief. He returned his attention back to packing the items Hutu was handing to him.

"As soon as I found out what happened, I made sure that Pack was informed. He was still on the planet, awaiting departure," Hutu murmured. "Knowing Jemar, the boy has been better trained than most of the new recruits. I hope so, anyway. He will need all of those skills if things turn bad."

"Where are we heading?" Josh asked, closing the bag he was packing.

"To find your friends," Hutu said, glancing over his shoulder at where Cassa and Pack were gathering additional supplies. "It is going to be extremely dangerous," he added with a grim smile.

Josh's eyes narrowed. "Why?" He asked suspiciously.

The grin turned to amusement. "We are going to find your friend, hopefully before General Landais does, or steal him from under the General's watchful eye. Neither task is going to be easy and I can guarantee that the General will not be happy," Hutu chuckled dryly

Josh's lips twitched. "You'd have fit right in back home," he retorted.

"Josh," Cassa interrupted. "We have everything."

Pack's face was tight with frustration, but also resignation. It was clear that whatever conversation Cassa and Pack had, it hadn't gone the way Pack wanted. Josh's lips twitched in amusement. From the steely determination in Cassa's eyes, he had a pretty good idea what Pack had been wanting – Cassa to remain behind.

"We're ready as well," he responded.

A sudden knock on the door drew their attention. Hutu motioned for all of them to move to the back room and remain quiet. He peered down at the digital readout in his hand. Walking over to the door, he cracked it.

"Legion troops are heading this way," a man murmured before disappearing.

Hutu turned, his face grim. "Let's go," he muttered, grabbing one of the heavy bags.

Josh took up the rear, making sure that he kept Cassa shielded as they hurried out of the back door. They kept to the shadows. On several occasions they paused and waited when Legion soldiers hurried past them.

"This way," Hutu muttered, nodding to a section of repair bays.

The small group slipped inside when the double doors slid open. Josh's eyes widened when he saw a spaceship inside. Hutu hurried over to the ship and pressed a device to its side. A section underneath began to descend. He turned and glanced at Josh and Cassa.

"You two get the supplies on board," Hutu instructed, dropping the large bags he was carrying. "Pack, you get the locks on that side."

Pack nodded and handed his bag to Josh. Josh bent and grabbed a fourth bag while Cassa carried two up the back platform. He quickly followed her and set them down before retrieving the other two that Hutu had dropped.

The sound of shouting outside of the repair bay drew his attention. He handed one of the bags to Cassa when she returned and drew one of the hand blasters that Hutu had given him.

"Pack, I need you to help me get the engines going," Hutu yelled, running to the platform. "It is time to go."

"This lock is stuck," Pack replied, working the lever back and forth.

"Go help Hutu. I've got this," Josh said, thrusting the bag he was holding at Pack and kneeling down next to the lock. There was a piece of metal jammed in the gears.

Josh swore, glancing over his shoulder. The pounding on the doors spurred him into action. Glancing around, he saw a long metal rod. It looked like what had been jammed into the locking mechanism.

Someone doesn't want anyone leaving, Josh thought grimly as he rose and hurried over to it.

Grabbing the end of the pipe, he returned to the locking mechanism and hooked it in between the two sections and pressed down on the piece trying to work it free. His jaw clenched as he worked it back and forth.

"Let me help," Cassa said, grabbing the end piece.

Josh glanced up at her. "Work the controls back and forth," he suggested. "It is wedged in too tight to work it free."

Josh strained on the bar while Cassa worked the controls back and forth. His gaze kept flickering to the double doors. They were re-enforced to help protect the outer structure in case of a mishap while the ships were being repaired. He had seen the same thing while at the training compound in Dallas. Still, the doors wouldn't last much longer. His fear was proven right when a dark red line formed along the edge.

"Now," Cassa cried, slamming her hand down on the control again.

The gears jerked for a moment before the piece of metal flew out and the lock released. Josh threw the bar to the side and pulled the blaster at his side. Reaching for Cassa's hand, he wrapped his fingers around her wrist and began pulling her toward the spaceship. The loud boom of the door exploding inward made them flinch. Josh's hand rose and he fired several shots at the soldiers trying to squeeze through the narrow entrance.

Cassa ran to the ship and up the platform, firing as well. He heard Cassa yell to Hutu and Pack to get them out of here even as she slammed her hand against the control panel. Josh backed away, continuing to fire until he could no longer see the soldiers.

"We have to get buckled in," Cassa said in an urgent voice, grabbing his arm.

Josh followed Cassa as she ran down a long corridor. He could feel his stomach shift as the spaceship rose at a high rate of speed. Realizing that they weren't going to make it to the cockpit, he caught Cassa's arm and pulled her into a small alcove where a ladder lead to the upper level. He pinned her between his body and the ladder and wrapped his arms around both of them.

"Hold on to me," he ordered quietly in her ear.

Cassa wound her arms around his waist, hugging him tightly against her as the ship shot upward. For a moment, Josh felt weightless. A soft chuckle echoed in his ear.

"The ship's gravity will kick in momentarily," Cassa murmured.

Josh's eyes glittered and he grinned. "This is a little different from back home," he commented.

"What's different about it?" Cassa whispered.

The smile on Josh's lips faded and his gaze grew serious. The sadness still haunted Cassa's eyes, but it had dimmed a little. He knew seeing her brother, Pack, had helped a great deal.

"Think of being in a can with enough explosives to shoot you into space and that about sums it up," he replied, his gaze moving down to her lips. "I'm going to kiss you again."

Cassa's lips parted and her eyes darkened. Her hands splayed across his back and she rose onto her toes. Josh knew that she was just as affected by him as he was with her.

Their lips met in a harsh, desperate kiss. He silently cursed his need to keep them steady. All he wanted to do was run his hands over her, caress her, and wipe the fear and pain away.

It took several long minutes for him to realize that a voice was calling his name. He reluctantly pulled back, pressing several smaller kisses to her lips before he released a sigh. Her gaze reflected her own disappointment.

"I guess we'd better answer them," he murmured.

Cassa nodded, her cheeks flushed from their kiss and the excitement of their escape from the planet. He tested his footing before he stepped back. She had been right – the ship's artificial gravity was working.

"Hey, we need to jump to light speed," Pack yelled. "You two need to be strapped in. We've got Legion fighters coming at us."

"Damn it," Josh growled, grabbing her hand. "Let's go."

Chapter 15

Andri Andronikos stood gazing out of the headquarters on Jeslean. His eyes were narrowed in thought. All but one of the Knights of the Gallant Order were now dead. Andri clenched his fist. The last one had slipped through the fingers of the Legion commander sent to Tesla Terra.

"Enter," Andri ordered when he heard the quiet knock on the outer door.

"Lord Andronikos, the Commander on Tesla Terra is reporting in," his assistant stated with a bow.

Andri turned and nodded. "Send it through," he ordered, returning to his desk.

"Yes, sir," the man replied and stepped back out of the room.

A moment later, the image of the new Commander of the Battle Cruiser he had sent to Tesla Terra faced him. His lips tightened at the man's grim expression. In the background, he could see a haze of smoke in the air and hear the sound of alarms.

"Shut off the alarms," the Commander ordered before returning his attention to Andri. "My apologies, Lord Andronikos."

"What happened?" Andri demanded.

"An empty pod was found, my Lord," the man replied grimly. "Commander Cota decided to investigate it personally. He suspected that whoever was in it might have received help from some peasants in a nearby valley. Shortly afterwards, all contact with Commander Cota and the troops with him were severed. I immediately sent a team to investigate – they were all dead."

Andri's eyes flash with cold rage. His fists clenched again before he relaxed them. This was one of the most blatant attacks to date against the Legion and could not go unpunished.

"What of the peasants?" He asked harshly. "Where they questioned?"

"The vineyards were burned to the ground, though fresh graves were discovered," the man continued. "The vineyards belonged to Jemar de Rola. His name was on one of the fresh graves."

A muscle ticked in Andri's cheek. He knew all too well who Jemar de Rola was. He was silent for several seconds before he spoke again.

"Did you find any evidence of who may have been in the pod that was discovered?" Andri finally hissed.

The man shook his head. "No, but we suspect whoever was in it is with Hutu Gomerant, a trade merchant from the Spaceport. We tracked him and several others to a repair hanger. They lifted off before we could stop them. I ordered the Battle Cruiser to pursue them."

"And…," Andri asked with a cold glare.

The man nervously swallowed. "We engaged them, but they escaped. The transport they were on contained a modified weapons system that we were not expecting. They escaped into hyperspace before we could prevent it."

"Find out where they went and send me all the items that were recovered," Andri ordered, ending the message. He stared down at his desk for several long seconds before he pressed the communications console once again.

"Yes, my Lord," Roan Landais answered.

Andri stared at the cool mask on the face of one of his deadliest Generals. Roan's father had been in his service from the beginning. His father had trained Roan from a small boy to serve the causes of the Legion.

"Have you intercepted the other pod?" Andri asked in a sharp tone.

"Pod? If you are referring to the signal, then no, not yet," Roan responded stiffly. "The one on Tesla Terra has been retrieved?"

"The pod, yes, the contents, no," Andri replied. "Find the pod you are searching for – and the contents. Do not underestimate the danger. General Cota did and he and a troop of Legion soldiers are dead. I want the contents, General."

"Yes, my Lord," Roan replied with a bow of his head.

Andri cut the communications once again. He raised his head and stared out the window. A thoughtful expression crossed his face and he once again touched the communications console. This time a very different face appeared.

"I have a job for you," he said, staring at the shadowy image.

***

Josh's gaze followed Cassa as she moved around the narrow galley on board the *Tracer,* Hutu's modified transport. The battle earlier had caused only minor damage thanks to Hutu's defense systems. Hutu came in wiping the dirt off of his dark red hands.

"Your brother has become a good pilot," he said, nodding to Cassa when she handed him a hot drink. "If I had known earlier, I would have talked to your father about recruiting him sooner."

Pain flashed across Cassa's face and she slid onto the seat next to Josh. Josh immediately wrapped his arm protectively around her. Shooting Hutu a warning glance, he held Cassa close to him.

"What is the real reason the Legion Director wants me and my crew?" Josh demanded. "They were determined to capture us."

Hutu sighed and slipped into the seat across from Josh and Cassa. He glanced at Cassa for a moment before he turned his attention to Josh. Josh could tell the man was having an internal battle with himself.

"A long, long time ago, this region was ruled by an advanced species, more so than what is here now. It is said they studied the stars, wondering what was out there. In time, they built great spaceships and they left Jeslean, the birthplace of the Gallant Order.

Cassa shook her head and laid her hand over Josh's hand. "Surely no one really believes this, it is a child's tale told to children. Before the Legion, it was another monster," she argued.

"It matters not whether it is true, it is what gives people hope. That is something that Lord Andronikos does not want. If the people have hope, they have a reason to fight. Word is already spreading about the strange spaceship that was discovered. No matter how hard the Legion tries to keep it a secret, people will find out. What happened yesterday will only make it more mythical." Hutu paused and looked at Josh. "It is imperative that we discover what happened to your friends before Lord Andronikos' forces do."

"If they are even alive," Josh murmured, glancing down at where Cassa held his hand.

"There were five signals reported, each moving in different directions. Yours and another have been tracked. I have men looking for the other three. If they are alive, we will find them," Hutu promised.

"How do you know so much about what is going on?" Josh asked, tilting his head and staring at Hutu.

"The Legion isn't the only one with spies," Hutu replied. "I will relieve Pack for a while. I suggest you both get some rest. The next few days are going to be dangerous at the most, exciting at the least."

"Why do you say that?" Cassa asked, sliding out from behind the table when Hutu stood up.

Hutu grinned. "We are going to be right under General Landais' nose," he said with a chuckle. "It does not get more dangerous, or exciting, than that."

"I hope you know what you are doing, Hutu," Josh retorted with a grim look.

Hutu's eyes softened for a moment. "I do," he promised. "I want to see how much training Jemar did with you, Pack, and Cassa. I will start tomorrow. I suggest you worry more about that at the moment. If you are to fight and win, you need to be ready."

..*

Josh walked in silence slightly behind Cassa down the narrow corridor. There wasn't much room on the transport, so sleeping accommodations would be tight. He paused, glancing into the narrow room. It was barely big enough for the bunk.

"How are you doing?" He asked quietly, reaching up to touch her cheek when she paused and turned towards him. A trembling smile curved her lips and tears filled her eyes, but she blinked them away. "I never did thank you for your help back there at the Spaceport."

"You never have to thank me for helping you," she murmured. "It will take time. It is still hard to believe that my father and Jes… Jesup are gone. The Legion has a lot to answer for." She glanced down at her hands which were splayed across his chest. "I had heard stories of their brutality. I'm ashamed that I was reluctant to stand up against them."

Josh's hand slid up under her chin and he lifted it. His expression was serious as he stared down at her. He wished there had been some way to shield her from the pain of losing her father and little brother. Deep down, he still fought with his own guilt that he had been partially responsible for bringing this grief to Cassa's family, even if it had been unintentional.

"Never be ashamed of being who you are," he said in a quiet, firm voice. "You are an incredibly beautiful and strong woman."

"Josh," Cassa whispered, gazing up at him. "Just so you know, I'm going to kiss you."

A soft chuckle escaped him before her lips captured the sound. The feelings that had been burning inside him flared into white-hot embers, refusing to be extinguished this time. Life held no guarantees, he and Ash had always known that. The last few weeks, and his growing feelings for Cassa, had just made it more obvious.

"I want…," Josh started to say.

"… You to stay," Cassa's hushed words mixed with his. "Stay with me tonight."

Josh pulled back and stared down at her with a fierce expression. If he stayed, it would be for more than one night – it would be for a lifetime. Cassa was not a woman to be toyed with and discarded. She was the type of woman to make a man realize he was being given a chance at something special the moment he saw her.

"This isn't about one night, Cassa," Josh warned her. "This is about forever."

A sad expression swept across Cassa's face before it cleared. "Then, I accept your forever, Josh," she responded in a soft voice.

Josh stepped forward, pressing Cassa backwards into the long, narrow room. His lips captured hers in a hot passionate kiss that sealed his vow that this was not just a short term relationship, but one that he planned to make permanent.

"You have no idea how hard it has been to keep my hands off of you," he muttered, working the fastenings of her tunic.

"You are not the only one," she whispered, brushing her lips along his jaw.

..*

Josh was surprised by the trembling in his fingers as he carefully pushed Cassa's outer tunic off her shoulders. The faint markings along her forehead and left cheek ran down over her shoulders. He wanted to kiss every one of the marks.

A soft, startled hiss escaped him when Cassa pressed her lips against him and twisted so she could push him back against the closed door. Her hand fumbled for the panel and she locked it. His own hands began moving frantically over her. He pulled far enough back to grab the bottom of her shirt and tugged it over her head. He tossed it to the floor, his eyes narrowing in desire.

"You have no idea how beautiful you are," he murmured.

Cassa raised an eyebrow before she leaned in and pressed a kiss to his lips. "Why don't you show me?" She murmured in invitation before kissing him again.

Josh's mind sizzled as he turned her and pressed her back against the bed. There were times when it was best to take your time and there were times when you just couldn't wait. A soft groan escaped him when she ran her hands up under his shirt.

This was definitely a time when waiting was highly overrated, he thought as he let go of his control.

"You have too many clothes on," she whispered frantically, tugging at his shirt.

Josh released a soft chuckle and sat back, straddling Cassa's slender hips. He quickly pulled his shirt off and tossed it to the floor next to hers. His jaw clenched when she ran her hands over the heated skin of his stomach. The muscles tightened at her touch and his hips jerked forward. The movement caused his already aching body to tighten even more.

His hands moved to the fastening of his trousers. He undid them and scooted off the bed so he could kick them and his boots off. He felt like a schoolboy for a moment, clumsy and uncoordinated. Of course, it didn't help that Cassa was lying back against the pillows watching him with a heated look of desire that was guaranteed to bring his blood to a boil.

Kicking his pants to the side, he glared down at her when her lips lifted in amusement. She knew perfectly well the effect she was having on him. His own lips twitched when she flushed and he saw her nipples harden. Two could play this game.

"Do you like what you see?" He asked in a husky voice, not bothering to hide his arousal. "I certainly do."

Cassa's hands started to move up to cover her breasts, but Josh leaned down and grabbed them. He shook his head and allowed his gaze to run down over her. His hands slid away from hers. Running his palms over her skin, he followed the path of the markings until he could cup her breasts.

"I've never seen anything like this before," he murmured, bending over her so he could press a kiss to one of them.

"The markings you have are very small and scattered," she whispered, arching upward when he pressed another kiss to her side. "I want to kiss them."

It took a moment for Josh to realize she was talking about the few dark freckles he had. The marks on her skin were slightly darker and ran along both sides of her body, up over her shoulders and up her neck before the left side continued up her cheek to her forehead. Each one was about the size of a dime, but instead of being perfectly round, they were uneven. He noticed that each one fit together. It was going to take a while to work his way down each and every delicious one.

He bent to capture one taut nipple between his lips even as his hands moved down to push her trousers off her hips. Her hands grasped his shoulders, her fingers gently kneading them while her hips lifted to help him. A soft moan escaped her and she pulled him over her.

He sucked on the rosy tip, feeling it swell at his rough attention. Her legs moved restlessly and she kicked her trousers away so she could lift her legs to wrap them around his hips. He didn't need any more encouragement. His body was hard and ready for her.

Bracing his arms on either side of her, sweat beaded on his brow when she reached between them and guided him to her slick channel. A shudder swept through both of them as they fought for the slender thread of control they had on their emotions. All hope of that disintegrated when she ran her strong fingers along his cock. His hips jerked forward, pushing deeper into her when she released him. Her hand slid along his side and she gripped his hip, urging him on.

"Oh, Cassa," Josh groaned, closing his eyes when he felt her moist heat slowly surrounding him. "Oh, sweetheart."

He opened his eyes and stared down at her as he buried his cock to the hilt. A long, soft hiss escaped him and he trembled. His jaw clenched when she began to move her hips. The slow, deliberate movements shattered his control and he lowered himself over her so that he could wrap his arms around her and bury his face in her neck.

His own hips began moving, faster and harder. Each stroke becoming rougher and more urgent than the one before. Cassa's uneven breaths echoed through him. Her soft moans growing louder with each thrust until she released a sharp, harsh cry and stiffened.

Josh felt her body shudder and tremble with her release. His arms tighten around her and he continued to drive into her with a frantic urgency that was driven by the primitive need to possess, conquer, and worship the woman in his arms. His head tilted backwards and the muscles in his neck strained as his own body exploded with his release. He could feel his seed emptying into her as his cock pulsed, throbbing in time with her shuddering gasps.

Josh closed his eyes and pressed a kiss to Cassa's shoulder. Her arms tightened around him and her legs slowly slid down along his. He ran his lips along her hot skin, enjoying the silky feel of it.

"I love you, Josh," Cassa replied in a quiet voice, squeezing him tighter to her and pressing her cheek against his hair.

Another shudder ran through Josh at her tender words. He'd had other women tell him that they loved him over the years, but their words never affected him the way her softly spoken confession did. Like finely woven threads of molten silver, they sank into his soul, warming him and sending another wave of primitive feeling through him, this time one of protectiveness.

Lifting his head, he gazed down at her. His throat swelled with emotion, an emotion that choked him, making it impossible for him to speak. He could only hope that she could see the impact her words had on him. Capturing her lips again in a kiss that he hoped conveyed his feelings, he knew that he'd never let her go.

One night will never be enough, he thought as the flame inside him ignited once again.

Chapter 16

"I wondered where you had disappeared to," Pack muttered, walking up behind Josh as he stepped out of the cabin much later.

Josh turned and looked at the younger male. He could see the wary expression in his eyes and the hint of anger. While Cassa didn't blame him for their father and brother's death, something told him that Pack wasn't as forgiving. Drawing in a deep breath, Josh knew that if he didn't resolve the issue that was brewing between the two of them, it could get dangerous.

"Pack," Josh greeted with a grim nod. Pack's face tightened when he moved so he could block the man's way. "I need to talk to you."

"Move," Pack ordered with a dark scowl.

Josh shook his head. "I'm sorry about what happened to your father and Jesup. If I had known that my presence would have jeopardized them in any way, I wouldn't have stayed. The fact is, I didn't. I also can't change the past."

"Your presence has already devastated my family," Pack snarled under his breath. "Instead of turning yourself in to the Legion or parting ways, you drag Cassa into it as well. I don't know where you came from, but you need to return to it."

"I can't," Josh muttered, a flash of regret darkening his gaze. "It isn't that simple. Even if I could, I wouldn't leave without my crew… or Cassa."

"My sister isn't going anywhere with you," Pack growled, reaching out and grabbing the front of Josh's shirt.

Josh immediately gripped Pack's wrists and twisted, throwing the young man off balance as he reversed their position. He stepped closer, pushing Pack back against the wall across from the cabin. He wouldn't let the man wake Cassa.

"Listen to me," Josh snapped in a harsh, soft tone. "I may be stuck in your world, but that doesn't mean I can't take care of myself and your sister. I knew nothing about the Legion until the other day. They brought the fight to me, not the other way around. I don't back down – ever. If they want a war, I'll give them a fucking war. I'm sorry about what happened to Jemar and Jesup. If I could change what happened, I would. You need to understand that fighting with me isn't going to bring them back, though, it will only accomplish two things; hurt Cassa and get us all killed. I won't let either one of those things happen. If you can't get your head out of your ass and understand that, then get out of the way."

Josh stared intently into Pack's eyes. He needed Pack to understand that he wasn't playing a game. He was serious. The Legion had declared war on everything that Josh held dear and he wasn't the type of man to back down from a fight, especially after his night with Cassa.

Pack finally gave him a stiff nod and slumped back against the wall. Josh released him and stepped back. Glancing at the door to his and Cassa's cabin, he was thankful that she was still resting.

"Come on," Josh muttered. "Let's go find Hutu. You can still try to kick my butt during the training. That might help some."

Pack hesitated a moment before he gave Josh a look of uncertainty. "Is it true that my father was training you?" He asked in a quiet voice.

Josh's lips tugged up at the corner. "Yeah, I did well against him, but your sister… Well, let's just say she kicked my butt pretty good," he replied.

A reluctant smile curved Pack's lips in response. "She was always better than me, too," he muttered.

Josh chuckled and shook his head. "Let's go," he said, feeling the release of tension in the other man.

***

Several days later, Josh leaned back against the bulkhead breathing heavily. His gaze roamed over Cassa as she and Pack fought. He absently rubbed his wrist where she had hit him.

"She is good," Hutu murmured in approval, his gaze following the two siblings. "Jemar did well in his training."

"Yes, he did," Josh replied with a grimace as he felt another bruise beginning to form.

An alarm briefly echoed through the ship. With a sigh, Hutu pushed against the side with a wince of his own. He chuckled when Hutu rubbed his left hip, Cassa had flipped the old Knight more than once.

"We have reached the outer rim of Torrian. We'll have to proceed with caution. The area is thick with Legion forces. General Landais' Battle Cruiser has taken up a position near the third moon. We'll come in on the far side. Have you programmed in the signal we are looking for?" Hutu asked.

Josh nodded. "Yes, though it is getting close to the end of the period for the life support, the signal will continue to transmit anywhere from forty-five to sixty days. It is like a black box on an airplane," he explained.

"I will trust you to know," Hutu replied with a shake of his head at the unfamiliar terms.

Josh climbed the narrow steps into the cockpit of the transport and slid into the co-pilot's seat. He reached for the scanner that Hutu had shown him how to use. Punching in the code, a small blip showed up.

"There it is," he said, pointing to the location.

"Mm, that is located in the desert region. There are numerous nomad tribes that live in that area. This will make it slightly more difficult for General Landais' troops," Hutu said in approval.

"Won't that make it more difficult for us as well?" Josh asked with a raised eyebrow.

Hutu shook his head and shot Josh a wry grin. "Not if a native of the planet is the one guiding you," he informed Josh. "Welcome to my home world."

Josh stared for a moment at Hutu before he looked down at the scanner. He wondered vaguely which member of the crew they would find – and if whoever was in the emergency pod survived. Each pod was marked with a number. He had been in Pod Four; while Ash had been in Pod Two, Julia in Pod Three, Mei in Pod One, and Sergi in Pod Five.

Releasing the breath he didn't realize he was holding, he forced himself to remember that he had survived. It was quite possible the others had as well. He listened to Hutu explaining the different regions and species that inhabited the planet. The first view of the planet appeared in the distance. It was slightly larger than the Earth and two-thirds of it was covered in water. For all the water, more than one third of the planet was a desert with most of the inhabitants living in the arid regions.

"While the top is covered in sand and rock, under the desert fresh water rivers are abundant," Hutu was saying.

"Where do most of the inhabitants live?" Josh asked, staring at the large blue and tan planet as they drew closer.

"Some have built homes on the surface, some live along the cliffs of the sandstone mountains, while a few have taken refuge under the sands to build their cities," Hutu explained. "My people are from the underground city. It is much cooler there."

"I can imagine," Josh murmured, staring at the brightly lit surface. "What are the temperature ranges?"

Hutu shrugged. "Anywhere from below freezing at night to hot enough to boil your blood during the day. Special clothing helps to keep that from happening. Having the right kind of skin is also useful," he commented, holding up a dark red arm.

..*

Several hours later, Josh lifted a scanner to his eyes. He lay on the hot sand and searched the horizon. In the distance, he could see several large space ships. They were twice the size of Hutu's ship.

"There is at least four of them," Hutu snorted. "It looks like search teams have already departed the ship. There are only a few soldiers guarding them."

"The signal I've got is coming from the east," Josh noted, glancing down at the tracking device Hutu had programmed in his hand.

"That area is filled with deep canyons," Hutu replied, sliding back down the sand dune. "I need to meet with some of the resistance stationed here. It will be too dangerous for the three of you to come with me. We won't have much time. Pack has been here before. Jemar allowed him to travel with me one summer. It is imperative that I meet with my contacts while we are here, especially with General Landais' presence on the planet."

"We'll find the pod and return to the ship," Josh replied with a nod.

"I will meet you back there in three days. That should give all of us enough time to finish our business," Hutu said.

"Be safe, Hutu," Cassa murmured, stepping up to hug the old Knight. "You are in just as much danger as the rest of us."

Hutu chuckled and squeezed Cassa before releasing her. "Yes, but I blend in here better than you do. Three days," he said again with a nod before he turned and began moving away at a swift jog.

Josh watched in appreciation at how easily the man moved across the sand. Even though it was still early morning, the temperature was already beginning to rise. The long sleeves and hat that Hutu had given each of them would help keep them cool, but it would still be dangerous if they were caught out in the middle of the day. They would need to reach the canyons by then to find the cooler shadows cast by the high walls.

"Let's go," Josh said with a nod to Pack. "You lead. Cassa and I will follow behind you."

Pack nodded and headed across the sand to two land skids. Josh adjusted the cover over his head to shield his face before pulling down the protective goggles. He waited for Cassa and Pack to do the same.

Sliding on to the land skid, he fired it up and waited until Cassa had wrapped her arms securely around his waist before depressing the accelerator. The land skid zipped across the sand. The terrain was relatively flat, making the journey easier. Further up they would encounter a rockier terrain that would slow them down.

"The reading is still strong," Cassa said through the communication device attached to their ears. "Turn more to the Northwest."

Pack adjusted his track to follow the directions that Cassa called out. It took close to two hours before they reached the outer rim of the deep canyons that extended out from the desert. It turned out to be just in time when Cassa hissed a warning in their ear.

"Legion scouts," she muttered, glancing over her shoulder. "We need to find cover."

"There is a section of rock just ahead," Pack responded in a grim voice. "I think it is wide enough to hide the land skids underneath."

Both men leaned forward, pushing the land skids to their maximum speed. They barely slowed in time before they slipped under the large rock overhang. Sliding off the land skids, they quickly grabbed the sand colored covers. The three of them worked quickly to cover the land skids so that they were camouflaged.

Kneeling under the cover, they peered through the thin fabric as two large scout ships flew closer. Josh felt Cassa press up against him, her hand gripping the long range blaster in her left hand.

"The cover should shield us from any scans," she whispered.

Josh's lips curved up and he raised an eyebrow at the blaster. Her lips twitched in response. She pulled her gaze from him and back to the two ships.

"Even if it didn't, I know how lethal you can be with one of those," he replied in a soft voice, focusing on the twin ships. "I'm glad."

Warmth twisted his gut when he felt her briefly press her lips against his shoulder. This woman continued to amaze him. His gaze followed the ships as they passed overhead. They waited until they couldn't hear the rumble of the scouts before they carefully crawled out from under the overhang.

"We'll have to go on foot from here," Pack said, slinging his rifle over his shoulder. "Hutu never brought me beyond this point. He did give me a map showing a way down, though. He said we needed to keep an eye out for the Canyon Dwellers. They are a tribe that live in different sections of the canyons. They aren't very welcoming to strangers."

Josh grimaced. It looked like they were in for hostile encounters both above and below. Striding after Pack and Cassa, he glanced in the distance at the Scout ships. He grimly hoped that they didn't return before they found the emergency pod.

Chapter 17

Josh wiped the sweat from his brow and took a drink from his canteen. His gaze swept the high walls of the canyon. It had taken them almost an hour to get to the bottom of the first layer of canyons.

"Hutu said there should be shallow springs or a water source located inside the various caves that dot the area," Cassa said as she sat down next to him on a low rock.

"How much further to the signal?" Josh asked, glancing at the scanner in Cassa's hand.

Cassa handed it to him. "Just over a kilometer, but that doesn't mean much in this area. It is good that the frequency of the signal changed after it landed. Hopefully, General Landais won't be aware of that. All he has is the initial signal that he was tracking," she replied with a tired sigh.

Josh shifted the scanner to his other hand and reached over to gently grasp Cassa's fingers in his. He could feel the roughness from years of work, but instead of finding it unattractive, he found it gave him a deeper respect for her. He lifted her hand to his lips and pressed a kiss to the back of her fingers.

"You are an incredible woman," he said in a quiet voice.

Cassa's gaze softened. "I never thought to find a man I would want to spend my life with until I met you," she murmured, turning her gaze to focus on the long, winding canyon. "After our mother was killed, I didn't really have time. Jes… Jesup was so young and needed me." Her voice faltered and thickened when she spoke of her younger brother. She pulled her hand free and angrily wiped at her eyes. "It didn't help that so many of the young men and women were leaving to join either the resistance or the Legion. The only thing that saved Pack from being taken by the Legion forces was that he was with Hutu that summer. They left me alone as there was no one to take care of Jesup. Father was still away at the time."

Josh reached over and cupped her cheek. He leaned forward, brushing his lips against her slightly parted ones when she turned her head toward him. A soft sound escaped Cassa and she opened for him, allowing him to deepen the kiss. The firm pressure of her lips against his pulled an instant reaction from him. This again was a foreign feeling to anything he had experienced before. A silent curse escaped him and he pulled back.

"We need to find Pack," he murmured, rising from his seat on the rock.

***

Cassa nodded and stood. She quickly adjusted her headscarf to cover her face and lowered the goggles to protect her eyes. She turned to reach for her rifle, stiffening when she felt a sudden sharp sting to her left hip. A startled cry escaped her, drawing Josh's attention. His low curse was silenced when his eyes suddenly glazed and he collapsed to the ground beside her. Cassa tried to pull the long, thin dart from her hip even as the world spun dizzily around her.

She quickly looked up and stared in frustration at the dark shadows emerging from several sections of the rocks. She stumbled, placing her hand on the rock to steady herself. A low feral growl escaped her when her legs gave out from under her.

"Non-det! Non-det!" Don't! Don't. She struggled to shout. "We need your help. Please, Hutu Gomerant… Please," Cassa whispered to one of the shadows that came to stand over her as the world grew dark.

..*

Josh blinked several times in an effort to clear his vision. He instinctively moved one hand to run down his face. A dark frown creased his brow and his head snapped up when he realized that he couldn't move his arms.

His gaze swept the area where he was tied to a stake in the ground. Turning his head, he saw Pack sitting on the ground next to him. He was also tied to a long pole. A dark bruise shadowed Pack's left cheek.

"You look like shit," Josh remarked.

Pack turned to look at him and grinned. "That's what happens when you take five of them by surprise," he remarked casually.

"Where's Cassa?" Josh forced past his dry throat.

Pack nodded toward one of the caves further up on the cliff. "I saw them take her up there," he said in a tight voice. "She was unconscious."

Josh twisted his wrists in an effort to see how tight the ropes were. He winced when the rough cord cut into his flesh. His gaze moved to the section of rock where Pack said Cassa had been taken.

"I have a knife in my boot," Josh said in a soft, determined voice. "I'm going to twist around on the pole. Try to pull it out and cut the ropes holding you."

Pack nodded. "I'll let you know if anyone comes," he muttered. "I don't know what we're going to do when we get free. There has to be a hundred of them."

"We'll worry about that after we get loose," Josh responded, twisting around on the pole. "Right now all I care about is Cassa."

Pack glanced at him. "You really do care about her, don't you?" He asked in a quiet voice.

Josh gave him a sharp nod. He was focusing his energy on getting free. His gaze swept around the area, trying to determine the best way to escape. They were in the middle of a long canyon. Most of it was in the shadows of a group of large rock overhangs. Cut into the walls were buildings that reminded him of the Cliff Dwellers of Mesa Verde.

"Hold up," Pack muttered in a low, sharp voice. "A group is heading our way."

Josh leaned his head back against the pole and waited. He stared down the long winding canyon. A small group of women worked along one of the shelfs cut into the wall. They were talking and watching him. Pack was right when he said it wasn't going to be easy escaping.

"He is my brother," Cassa's warm voice was explaining. "The other is our friend."

Josh's head jerked around and he struggled to see Cassa. She was talking to several men who were walking beside her. One of them said something and she nodded.

"Yes, my father was Jemar de Rola," she replied in a husky voice.

"Release them," one of the men ordered with a wave of his hand.

Josh waited impatiently as his hands were free. The moment they were, he rose to his feet and turned toward Cassa. She broke through the group and ran toward him. His arms wrapped around her and he held her close to him for a moment before he turned and placed her protectively behind him. Pack came up to stand behind the both of them. This position placed Cassa between them, not that it would do much good with the number of weapons pointed in their direction.

"What's going on?" Josh asked, glancing warily at the three men standing in front of them.

"It will be alright," Cassa murmured, resting her hand on his shoulder. "They know Hutu and they knew my father. This is Jubotu. He is the leader of the tribe."

Josh's gaze locked on the tall, stately looking man. He was dressed from head to foot in a long, sand-colored outfit that blended in perfectly with the canyon walls. It wasn't difficult to see how easy it would be to miss these shadow warriors.

"Come with me," Jubotu said with a wave of his hand. "We have what you are seeking."

Josh started when the man spoke. It took a moment for what he was saying to sink in. When it did, his stomach tightened.

"Where is it?" He asked in a slightly harsh voice.

Jubotu waved again. Josh started forward, followed by Cassa and Pack. He ignored the dry burning in his throat as they wound deeper into the canyon. He slowed when he saw the man disappear into one of the low caves. There was no way that the emergency pod could have landed in there. It would've had to have been moved.

Josh bowed his head and stepped inside the cool interior. He waited a fraction of a second for his eyes to adjust to the dimmer interior. Soft lighting shone upward, illuminating the cave. The sound of water dripping captured his attention. Just as Hutu had said, there was a pool of water that ran from an underground spring before disappearing down a narrow channel cut in the rock.

"We found it several moons ago," Jubotu said. "We brought it here until we could determine what was in it. First, you must drink. You have been in the heat for too long."

Josh nodded and tried to swallow. Almost immediately, a young woman stepped forward with a cup of water for each of them. He nodded his thanks and took the cup from her. Draining it, he handed the cup back to the woman who bowed and moved away.

"Several of the warriors saw it float down from the sky. It took them several days to reach it," Jubotu explained, turning and continuing back through the cave.

"How could the signal reach through the rocks if they have it back here?" Pack asked in a soft voice.

"I'm not sure," Josh said, glancing around. "The devices are designed to send a signal in some of the harshest environments on my world."

Josh followed the man through several more passages before they came to one that had an opening in the roof. In the center, he could see the familiar shape of one of the Gliese's emergency pods. Hurrying toward it, his gaze swept over the large number two printed on it.

"Ash," Josh muttered, hurrying around the other side and pressing the release button. "Ash…."

His voice died when the top opened to reveal an empty interior. He glanced up at the man who had led them here. His jaw worked in frustration.

"Where is he? There would have been a man like me, only with darker skin, inside," he demanded.

Jubotu stepped forward. "There was nothing. This is how we found it," he stated. "The desert covers the tracks of any that travel across it within hours. Your man must have escaped."

Josh bowed his head and closed his eyes. Ash was alive. He had made it and escaped from the pod. It wouldn't take long for his friend to realize that he was on an alien planet. The question was… Where had Ash gone?

"What is located in the area where the pod was found?" Josh asked.

"There are three cities that he could have possibly traveled to," Jubotu said with a frown. "The largest is Nobo Sands. The other two, Nobo Cliff and Nobo Cavern are small."

Pack frowned. "I've been to all three," he said. "I can search Nobo Cliff and Nobo Cavern in a day. If you and Cassa could take Nobo Sands, I could meet you there by tomorrow afternoon."

"That is the only way if we are going to locate him. Hutu is at Nobo Sands," Cassa said with a frown. "We can meet up with him there, as well."

"How long will it take us to get there?" Josh asked.

"We'll be traveling during the hottest part of the day. It will make it difficult. The land skids might overheat, not to mention it will be hard on us, even with the proper clothing," Pack responded.

"There is another way," Jubotu stated with a wave of his hand. "The rivers that run under the sands also provide a passage for my people. I will send two of my warriors to guide you through them. If you get lost, you may never be found."

"Thank you, Jubotu," Cassa said, stepping forward and grasping the older man's rough hands.

"Your father was a great warrior, child. He would be proud of you and your brother. The Legion wish to control us as they control other worlds, but we will not give in," Jubotu stated proudly before he held out a small metal box to Josh.

Josh took the box with a frown, turning it over in his hand. "Neither will we," he assured Jubotu with a puzzled frown.

"They are the same type of darts that we used to capture you," Jubotu stated. "Sometimes it is not necessary, or wise, to kill. I have had your land transports brought down to hide them. You will use transports better suited for the tunnels. My men will show you the way," Jubotu said with a wave of his hand at two men dressed in the lightweight covering of the Canyon Dwellers. "Good luck on your journey, warrior."

Josh nodded his head and turned on his heel. He and Cassa followed one of the men while Pack disappeared in a different direction with the other. In minutes, they had wound through a series of tunnels before emerging in a wider one. Josh was surprised to see the advanced technology in the huge cavern. Men and women worked side by side.

"General Hutu has been overseeing our resistance here," the man explained. "We have been learning to fight in the air. The Legion does not want to fight us on the surface."

Josh's lips twitched in amusement at the man's sneer. He could appreciate the Legion's decision. It was difficult enough to fight on another's home turf.

The fact that most of the planet had an underground maze of tunnels that they utilized would make it even more of a strategic nightmare. It would be like trying to fight a colony of prairie dogs. You'd never know where they were going to pop up next.

"This is all very deceptive," Cassa noted, glancing around at the large underground structure. "How did you get all the equipment in here?"

The warrior pointed to the large rock area above them. Josh could appreciate the camouflage covering. From above, it would blend in with the rest of the desert terrain.

"We have had to monitor our movements since the Legion Battle Cruiser arrived," the warrior said with a glum look. "I am learning how to fly. It is more fun than running over the desert."

Josh chuckled. "Yes, it is," he replied.

The young warrior stopped and looked at Josh. "You are a flyer," He said more than asked.

Josh glanced at some of the sleek fighters. They were different from the aircraft he flew, yet there were a lot of similarities as well. For a moment, his fingers itched to get behind the controls.

"Back on my world, I was a very good flyer," he said in a light tone. "How long will it take us to get to Nobo Sands?"

"Several hours," the warrior said, turning and striding past the land skid. "You cannot take your transport. Some of the tunnels are not very wide. We use a different type."

Josh's gaze moved over the smaller, sleeker transport that the warrior slid onto. It only had room for one person and looked like an exercise bike back home, only more compact. He carefully climbed on to another one. It didn't take him long to realize it used the same concept as the land skid. He controlled the acceleration with his foot and the braking system with his hands. Once started, it rose several inches off the ground. He used his body to balance it.

"Are you ready?" The warrior asked.

Josh's eyes glinted with excitement and determination. At least one other member of the Gliese 581 team was alive. That meant there was an excellent chance the others survived, as well. He gave the warrior a sharp nod and pressed down on the accelerator. Cassa moved in front of him and he took up the rear as they began the winding journey underground. The further into the tunnels they went, the better he understood the extent to which the Gallant Order was taking to prepare for war.

Chapter 18

The journey took a little over two hours. There was a minor obstruction in one of the tunnels. The debris forced them to take a slightly longer route. In the end, they came up just outside the city to the east, instead of the south.

"Look!" Cassa exclaimed, staring at the massive row of gun ships dropping troops off. "The area is flooded with Legion troops."

"I must return and tell Jubotu what is happening," the warrior said. "There has never been this type of Legion presence on our planet before."

"Thank you for your help," Josh replied in a grim voice. "We'll take it from here."

"General Hutu would be in the center of the city. Look for Sandsabar," the warrior said.

"I know where it is," Cassa replied. "Mother and I came here once before Jesup was born. It is not a place you forget."

Josh didn't say anything. His gaze paused on the rows of gun ships. They were ten deep and twenty wide. He estimated that they carried at least one hundred and fifty men per ship. Several took off as they made their way around the perimeter.

"I've never seen so many Legion troops before," Cassa whispered. "General Landais' Battle Cruiser must be larger than the ones I've seen before."

"Stay to the edge and walk like nothing is happening," Josh muttered as they melted into the crowds of pedestrians. "There are four coming up on your right, turn left."

Together, they turned before they reached the four soldiers that were randomly stopping people. Fortunately, they blended in with their headscarfs, eye protection, and clothing. Josh loosely held Cassa's elbow as they hurried down the narrow alley to the next street. He paused, glancing around before he nodded to her.

"Which way?" He asked.

"Right, then left," she replied softly. "How are we going to find your friend? There are thousands of people here. I forgot just how large a city it was and it has grown more since I was last here. He will not understand the dangers."

Josh pressed his lips firmly together and bowed his head as they passed several more soldiers. He waited until they were far enough away so that they couldn't overhear him before he responded to her question. One thing he did know was that Ash would recognize the dangers and know how to handle himself.

"Ash is smart," Josh murmured. "He'll know how to blend in, even here. The key is figuring out where he would go. He'd need clothing, weapons, and information."

"But, he would need to get them without being seen," Cassa summarized. "There is a small settlement on the outer edge of the city. It is in the same direction as he would have been traveling."

"We'll start there," Josh said with a nod.

"I'll let Pack know where to meet us," Cassa murmured, turning toward Josh to conceal the soft glow of the tablet and quickly sending a coded message to her brother. Almost immediately, she received a reply. "He said no one had seen any strangers at Nobo Caverns. He will go to the Cliffs, but he believes it will be the same. It is slightly further than both of these cities."

Josh frowned when he saw someone hurrying up to a soldier. He jerked his head to Cassa to move closer so they could hear what was being said. The man speaking to the soldier didn't look like a local inhabitant.

"Tell your commander that someone stole some clothing and a weapon from a home in the Baska District two days ago. A strange man was spotted moving away from the home," the man was saying. "Where are my credits for the information?"

"You will get the credits if what you say proves correct," the soldier stated. "What did the man look like?"

"I don't know," the informant snapped. "Dark skin – brown – not red, with short black hair. He was wearing an unusual suit with an emblem on it. The woman said it was made of different colors and had stars on it. She did not know what the symbols meant and would not give it to me without payment in return."

"Give us the exact location and we will pass on the information," the soldier replied.

The informant shook his head. "I'll take you there. I want payment like I was promised for information," he growled.

"Lead the way," the soldier said, waving his hand to two additional members of the Legion forces.

Josh waited until they had passed by him and Cassa before he motioned for her to follow them. They kept the men in their sight while staying far enough behind to be unnoticed. Josh immediately recognized that they were just north of the landing area of the gunships.

"There," the informant said, pointing to a small structure.

"Stay here," the soldier ordered.

Josh and Cassa watched as two of the three soldiers walked toward the building. One of the men banged on the outer door. A moment later, it cracked open.

They were too far away to hear what was being said, but the hand gestures gave him a fairly good idea of where Ash might have gone. Pulling back, he nodded to Cassa. Together, they quickly melted back into the shadows of the alley.

"He would need food, water, and information," Josh said, glancing around at the different buildings. "A market or series of stores would be ideal. He could cover up, yet find the items he would need to survive."

"There is the center market about five streets from here," Cassa replied, glancing down at the map that Hutu had given her. "My mother and I loved going there. It is very large and usually crowded late into the evening."

"I'll follow you," Josh murmured.

* * *

They had to stop and change direction several times. Legion forces patrolled the area at most of the main crossings. Cassa grabbed several large baskets as they walked by the back entrance to a restaurant and handed him one, showing him how to carry it like a local. She then guided him to a small group that was walking together.

Josh glanced around the market. Large crowds of residents milled around, bartering with the shopkeepers. Ash could easily find the items he required, all he needed was a deft hand to pocket some of it. The market wasn't much different from some of the places they had visited back home.

Frustration built inside him. Ash could be anywhere! He started to turn when he felt someone bump into him.

"Remove your goggles and present identification," a Legion soldier demanded.

Josh turned toward the man. Out of the corner of his eye, he saw Cassa slip away into the crowd. He knew she wouldn't go far, but it was important that they both not be detained. His gaze swept the crowd. The soldier appeared to be alone.

"I said remove your goggles and present identification," the soldier repeated.

Josh dropped the basket he was carrying and started to reach up to remove his goggles. Instead of removing his eye covering, he struck the man in the throat with his elbow. The man choked and tried to bring up his weapon, but Josh stepped into him and grabbed his wrist. He applied pressure and twisted, at the same time, he struck the man again, this time in the jaw.

The moment the man started to sink down to the ground, Josh bent and grabbed his weapon. The small crowd that had started to gather pushed past him when they heard a shout from further down the crowded corridor. Josh glanced behind him to see several soldiers fighting to get through the mass of bodies.

Turning on his heel, he quickly caught up to Cassa who silently stood waiting for him near an alley between two carts. He pushed through the crowd toward her. The moment he stepped between the carts, the merchants pushed them together and started shouting out their products for sale. He and Cassa pressed back into the shadows and watched as the soldiers gathered around their fallen comrade.

"We need to find Hutu," Cassa whispered. "Word of what the soldiers found out will quickly spread, not to mention what just happened. It is too dangerous for us to be on the streets. He might have heard something."

Josh pressed his lips together and turned to follow Cassa down the alley. He tossed the stolen weapon into a large basket as they passed by, not wanting to be seen with a Legion weapon. Without breaking stride, they melted into the crowd again.

..*

Roan Landais stood aboard his Legion Battle Cruiser, staring down at the planet. He lifted his hand to the communicator attached to his ear when it chimed. Turning, he ignored the men and women who stood at attention as he walked past them and into his office located off the bridge.

"What have you found?" He demanded, walking across to his desk and bringing up the image of his field commander on the planet.

"One of our informants was able to locate information on some stolen clothing and a missing knife. The resident said she saw a strange male running away from her home. She found this lying on the ground."

Roan frowned at the unusual symbol on the cloth. He touched his finger to the lighted keys on his desk, capturing the image. He would have it delivered to him later for analysis. Until then, he would search the data basis for any information that might match the pattern, symbols, and language on the circle.

"What else?" He asked, leaning back in his chair.

The commander's jaw tightened before he spoke again. "One of the soldiers was attacked in the marketplace. He said he stopped a man and ordered him to remove his goggles and present identification. The male attacked him. Whoever it was took his weapon, but it was later found in an alley not far from the attack. The merchants claimed not to have seen the male, but one witness said he met up with a woman in the alley."

"Was the soldier able to get a visual on the male?" Roan asked impatiently.

The commander shook his head. "No, sir," the man replied. "I have increased checkpoints and doubled the guards so none travel alone."

"Very good. Keep me posted and send what was found immediately," Roan ordered, cutting communications the moment the commander replied.

Leaning forward, he pulled up the image he had captured and enlarged it. He studied the position of the stars on it, not recognizing them, before he looked at the other symbols. There were three of them, each different than the next, yet linked together with the image of a spaceship unlike anything he had ever seen before.

Sitting back in his seat, he stared at it for a long time. Touching the keys in front of him, he loaded the image into the database and began the scan. There were literally billions, if not trillions, of pieces of information stored in the Legion's database about every species in the known star systems. He knew it would take several hours for the scan to be completed.

With an unusual reluctance, he slid the screen to the side and tapped the communications icon. He impatiently waited for his call to be answered. Soon, an all too familiar face appeared before him.

"What have you learned?" Andri demanded in irritation.

Roan's chin lifted. His security measures were beginning to work. He concealed the satisfaction he felt at discovering the spy among his crew.

"An item was found. I am running a scan on it now for more information. One of the soldiers was attacked in the marketplace. The attacker escaped, but I believe the two are related," Roan replied.

"And General Gomerant?" Andri asked.

Roan raised an eyebrow. "The old Gallant General?" He asked in surprise. "He hasn't been seen."

"He is a Knight of the Gallant Order. He is there," Andri replied in a clipped tone. "I want him found and brought to me."

Roan bowed his head in acknowledgement. He stared at the blank screen in front of him. Pushing his chair back, he rose and walked over to the large windows. He stood, staring down at the planet with a frown. What did the debris, signal, unusual emblem, an attack on one of his men, and an Old Knight of the Gallant have in common?

Turning, he returned to his seat. Slipping an encryptor disk out of his pocket, he placed it on the side of his computer. Once he was satisfied that his search would be concealed, he tapped in his command.

An hour later, he removed the device and returned it to his pocket. The scan he had initiated was also complete, much to his surprise. The muscle in his jaw twitched as he rose from his chair and stretched. Adjusting his uniform, he decided it was time he took a more active role in the search down on the planet.

Touching the screen, he turned it off before rounding the desk and heading for the door. He had found more questions than answers over the past hour. He wanted answers and something told him that the old Knight might be able to provide him with a few. One thing was for certain – he would have a conversation with the old Knight before he turned the man over to the Director.

Chapter 19

Josh cursed when he saw the group of Legion soldiers standing outside of the Sandsabar. It was similar to the bar where Hutu had guided them back on Tesla Terra. He watched as several patrons the size of small children came out of the bar. They were arguing with a large female. It was obvious that the woman was in charge of the establishment.

"I'll be back," Cassa murmured, removing her protective eye gear now that the sun had gone down.

"Where are you going?" Josh hissed, reaching to hold her back.

"We need a distraction to get inside," Cassa replied with a smile. "I'm about to create one."

Josh gritted his teeth in frustration before he forced his jaw to relax. Cassa strode across the busy road as if she owned it. He had to give her credit, when she wanted to do something, she did it in style.

His eyebrows rose when he heard her angry voice. She was talking fast and pointing down the street. It was hard to hear what she was saying above the noise of the other patrons and pedestrians, but he picked up enough to figure it out.

"Stole… Tall… I don't know! I've never seen anyone like him… Wearing unusual clothing… Took my…."

He shook his head and walked toward her when the group of six soldiers took off down the road, scattering startled pedestrians in their wake. The woman who had shooed the small, noisy group away a few minutes ago stood staring at Cassa in amusement. Josh walked up just as Cassa was quietly asking the woman if she had seen Hutu.

"We are friends of his...," Cassa was saying.

"I do not think if you were his enemy that you would introduce yourself as such," the woman pointed out with her hands on her hips.

Josh reached up and removed his goggles. He gripped the cloth covering the lower half of his face and pulled it down as well. It was obvious from his features that he was not a local inhabitant.

"Ah," the woman said with an inquisitive look when she saw Josh wrap a protective arm around Cassa. "Cover your face, human. Hutu might be expecting you, but there are others who would just as soon capture you for the bounty the Legion has on your head. Follow me."

Josh grimaced and nodded. He replaced the cloth over half of his face and adjusted his head covering to hide the rest. The goggles would not only look out of place inside the bar and draw attention to him, but also hinder his vision in the dim interior.

He followed the woman and Cassa up the steps and into the bar. He paused at the entrance, quickly assessing the interior. It was crowded with a wide range of species. In the far back corner, he saw Hutu's large form seated facing the entrance. Their gazes connected across the distance and he could see the surprise and concern in the other man's eyes.

Hutu leaned forward and spoke to whoever was sitting across from him. At this angle, Josh couldn't see the person's face. A moment later, Hutu slid out of the booth and walked toward the back.

The woman cut a path through the bar. Patrons quickly stepped to the side to get out of her way. Cassa followed the woman while Josh took up the rear, scanning the crowd in curiosity.

He was almost to the end of the bar when one of the men sitting there rose and bumped into him. Josh's gaze flashed to the man's face and a sense of unease filled him when the man refused to look at him. Josh turned and watched as the man quickly pushed his way through the crowd toward the entrance.

Turning back, he casually slid his hand into the pocket of his covering. He ran his fingers along the inside several times before he released a frustrated breath. His fingers closed around a small, round object. He pulled his hand free of his pocket and dropped the small device into a semi-empty glass as a waiter walked by him. He walked down a narrow corridor and turned into a large back room.

"Cassa," Hutu exclaimed, pulling her into his arms. "Where is Pack? I was not expecting you both to come here, though I am not surprised now that I have heard the news. It is not safe for either of you to be here."

"I will watch the bar and alert you if any of the Legion troops come," the woman informed Hutu with a slight bow.

"Thank you, Devona," Hutu replied.

"We might want to take our meeting somewhere else," Josh said in a grim voice. "Someone tried to plant some kind of device on me as we were coming through the bar."

Hutu's gaze grew dark with concern. "Do you still have it?" He asked, taking a step closer to where Josh was standing near the door.

"No, I dropped it in a glass as a waiter passed by," Josh replied. "The man took off out of the bar."

Devona turned to look at Hutu. "He is right. It is not safe for you here," she said, holding out a small, flat card to Hutu. "Take this. It will open the doors through to the next building. You can cut through them. If you take the stairs at the far end to the roof, you can cross over the buildings before returning to the street level."

"What about Pack?" Cassa asked in concern. "He is on his way here."

"We will contact him," Hutu assured her. "Devona…."

"I will take care of it, General," Devona replied, turning toward the door. She paused and peered down at her wrist. A light was flashing on the wristband she was wearing. "You must go now. Legion forces are approaching."

Josh stood to the side so that Hutu could pass him. Cassa quickly followed. He stepped out into the corridor and glanced toward the entrance. Devona was waving her hands and yelling. The movement prevented the soldiers from seeing them. Josh turned and hurried out the back door.

The night had grown much colder in just the few minutes they had been inside the bar. Josh adjusted the cloth over his nose and mouth to keep the vapor from his breath from revealing his location. The three of them hurried across the narrow alley. Hutu pressed the disk Devona had given him to the panel. The door immediately opened. Once inside, Hutu swiped the card once again over the panel, sealing it behind them.

"This way," Hutu murmured.

The building looked like a large warehouse for clothing. Spools of cloth hung from large racks. The way they were positioned left a narrow path between each row.

They silently threaded their way through the dark building, pausing occasionally when they heard the sound of voices. The loud boom of an explosion signaled that they were no longer alone. The red beams of lights behind them and to the front of them had them changing course. Josh and Cassa slid behind one large array of cloth and knelt down while Hutu slipped behind another. The flash of a red light swept back and forth, searching the area.

Hutu jerked his head and nodded toward the far side of the building where a set of stairs led upward. Josh touched Cassa's arm and motioned for her to follow Hutu. She frowned at him and shook her head. Pulling his knife out of his boot, he pressed a tense, firm kiss to her lips before motioning again.

Josh moved off in the opposite direction. There was no way they could make it up to the roof without some type of diversion. He paused at the end of the long row. His gaze swept over the area. There were eight beams of light. Picking the one closest to him, he silently moved behind a hanging section of cloth. He used the knife in his hand to cut through a thick cord. He replaced his knife, not wanting to kill if he didn't have to, and waited for the soldier walking toward him.

The flash of light skidded past his left shoulder. Josh skillfully palmed one of the small darts out of the kit that Jubotu had given him before they left earlier this morning. The man paused in front of the bolt of material and turned away to check on the location of his comrades.

Josh took advantage of the man's distraction. He reached up and covered the man's mouth with his right hand. He pressed the dart into the man's side between the two body plates he was wearing for protection. He barely had time to grab the rifle in the man's left hand. Holding the beam steady when the man grew limp, he slipped the rifle out of the soldier's grasp and pulled the unconscious body behind the covering before lowering it to the floor.

He knelt beside the man and quickly tied him with the cord he had cut. Knowing he didn't have much time before the soldier's comrades would miss him, he pulled the helmet off the unconscious man. The young face behind the cover of the helmet made it easier to accept his decision to not kill first if he could avoid it.

He quickly removed his headscarf and pulled on the helmet. Pulling the breast and back vest off the man, he slid his arms through it and attached them at the side. Next, he loaded the blowgun with almost a dozen of the tiny, but potent, darts. Grabbing the rifle lying next to the unconscious man, he rose to his feet and turned on the weapon.

He was just stepping out from behind the cloth when one of the men motioned to him. He tapped his ear, acting like the communicator wasn't working properly, and swept the red beam of light in the man's eyes as if by accident. It was enough that the man turned his head away to keep from being blinded. Josh took advantage of the exposed neck and blew one of the darts.

The man's hand slapped to his neck and he turned in annoyance before his knees gave out and he lay sprawled on the floor. Josh casually walked over and kicked the rifle under a rack of cloth. Turning, he moved closer to his next target. He had eliminated six men before the other two realized what was going on. He was moving closer to the seventh man when the man yelled. Josh raised his hand to tap his helmet, but this time the man didn't react like the first.

"Remove your helmet," the man ordered.

Josh lifted the rifle and fired, sending the man back into a long table. The fire immediately drew the last man's attention. He spun around and ducked under one of the racks. Running down the aisle, he rose up just far enough to fire in the direction the man had been before darting to the left.

He cursed when the material in front of him suddenly exploded into fire. He turned to the right with a soft curse. There was another soldier he had missed.

Josh ran between two rows of cloth, staying low. He could see the flash of red light, but couldn't risk firing until he knew the location of the second man. He turned to the left and pressed his back against the low table. He checked the weapon he had taken from the first soldier and pocketed the blow dart. This time it was kill or be killed.

Controlling his breathing, Josh listened carefully. The slight squeak of leather pulled his attention to the right. In the dim light filtering in through the open doors, Josh saw the shadow before the light reflected off the rifle casing. Rising up, he started to fire a quick burst, but the man fell before he could. He turned in the direction that he anticipated the attack had come from and fired two rapid shots before sinking down to the floor again.

A series of dull thuds resonated through the area a second before the cloth around him exploded. Rolling to the far side of the aisle to escape the intense heat, he stayed close to the ground and crawled along the edge of the table. The sound of a low, menacing hiss sounded above him, drawing his attention to the table that was still burning. Josh rolled again, this time onto his back, and fired upward.

The figure jumped across to the other table with blurring speed. Josh twisted to follow before he froze when a bright red beam suddenly centered on his chest. He lifted his chin and waited as the figure dressed all in black rose to its feet above him.

"Drop the weapon and remove the helmet," the dark form ordered.

Josh held his hands out and dropped the rifle he was holding. This wasn't a Legion soldier. Lifting his hands in a slow, careful movement, he pulled the helmet off his head.

"What now?" Josh replied with an arrogant grin.

"You are not like they described," the man stated.

Josh stared intently at the beam still pointed at him. He gripped the helmet and calculated his chances of striking the man before he ended up with a hole in his chest. The odds weren't good. A lot depended on how much the man wanted him alive.

"No, I guess not," Josh responded with a stiff shrug.

"Where are you from and where is the other male?" The man demanded, stepping down off of the table.

Josh warily sat up before rising to his feet when the male motioned for him to stand. He held the helmet firmly in his left hand. His gaze flickered past the man when he saw another shadow. The man must have sensed the movement as well because he started to turn. The moment he did, Josh threw the helmet at him, catching him in the jaw.

The move caught the man off-balance. Josh rushed the creature, catching him around the middle. They toppled against one of the tables, each struggling to get a better grip on the other. A blow to his side sent a wave of pain through Josh, but he pushed it away and swung upward, catching the male under the chin.

Josh jerked away when the male fell back far enough to reveal a deadly blade in his hand. Reaching down, Josh gripped the Knight of the Gallant Order staff and extended it. The two of them moved around each other where the row opened up in the long, main aisle. Josh's gaze warily followed the man's movement. This guy knew what he was doing.

"Why didn't you kill me?" Josh asked, circling to the right.

"You are worth more alive, than dead, but now that I know there are more than one of you, I don't think that will be an issue," the male snarled. "Where did you get a Gallant weapon?"

Josh stepped into the man, striking at him. The staff flashed at the end, sending out a powerful burst that threw the man back across the floor several feet. Twirling the staff over his head, he watched the man struggle to rise to his feet.

He immediately adjusted the staff to a shield when he saw the pistol in the man's hand. Brilliant flashes of light bursted in front of him. He was about to respond when the pistol aimed at him suddenly dropped from the man's limp hand. Josh watched as the dark form collapsed face forward.

The frown disappeared when he saw Hutu step out of the darkness. The dark scowl reappeared and he raised an eyebrow, glancing around for Cassa. Hutu stopped next to the dark figure and glared down at it with distaste.

"Turbinta trash," Hutu muttered. "An assassin from the lowest pits of the galaxy."

"Did you kill him?" Josh asked.

Hutu reached down and ripped the half shield helmet off the assassin's head. "Her," he muttered. "I will. They don't stop. There are only two things they care about; credits and making the kill. They'll even do the kill without the credits if it comes down to honor. Their reputation is based on the fact that they never miss their target."

Josh reached out and grabbed Hutu's hand when he raised his pistol and pointed it down at the unconscious female. There were a lot of things he would do, but killing an unconscious woman was not one of them. His logic fought with the knowledge that Hutu was right, it could be a fatal mistake in the long run, but it was one he was willing to chance.

"Leave her," Josh ordered. "We need to get out of here. The sedative I gave the other soldiers will be wearing off and more will come once they fail to report in.

"We aren't in your world, Josh," Hutu warned.

Josh briefly glanced at the forest green face of the woman and gave Hutu a wry smile. If the female wasn't enough of a reminder, Hutu's dark red skin and broad features were. Shaking his head, he turned back toward the staircase.

"I'm well aware that I'm not back on Earth," Josh replied in a hard tone. "Where's Cassa?"

"Watching for additional troops on the roof," Hutu replied, glancing at his wrist with a grimace. "Speaking of which, they are coming."

Josh closed the staff and returned it to his hip. Picking up speed, he took the stairs leading up to the roof two at a time. They slipped out of the door and crossed to the edge where Cassa was waiting.

"There are about twenty of them coming down the street," Cassa informed them in a soft, urgent voice.

Hutu looked over the side and released a muttered curse. His face was grim when he turned to look at Cassa and Josh. Curious to see what would pull that kind of reaction out of Hutu, he peered over the side. In the center of the group of soldiers another man walked. Josh could tell by the man's stride and his bearing that he was someone of importance.

"Who is that?" Josh asked, pulling back from the edge.

"General Landais," Hutu growled. "We have got to get out of here now!"

Josh glanced one more time down at the figure. The group had stopped, almost as if aware that they were being observed. He drew back when the Legion General suddenly looked up at the roof. He knew the man couldn't see him, but he didn't know if he had any kind of technology that might detect their presence on the roof.

"Josh," Cassa's soft voice whispered. "This way."

Josh nodded, turned and followed her.

Chapter 20

Roan Landais knelt down beside the body of the dead soldier. A puzzled frown creased his brow as he assessed the skillful slice along the man's throat before he rose to his feet. His gaze moved over the interior of the warehouse. Turning, he glanced at his ground field commander.

"What have you found?" He asked in a cold, calm tone.

"Six of the men were knocked unconscious, but otherwise unharmed. One was wounded with a blast to the shoulder, but will live. He said that he fired on the rebel when he realized that the male was not one of the other soldiers," the commander replied. "This is the only one that the rebels killed."

Roan didn't reply. Brushing past the commander, he walked to a large section of burned cloth. Touching it, he frowned. Something wasn't right. Why knock the other soldiers out, but kill the one? The other soldier he understood. The soldier admitted firing on the rebel first.

The scant description the informant from the bar had given didn't match the description of the man that had stolen the clothing. Was it possible the male was from the other capsule they had located on Tesla Terra? Reports of his escape with Hutu Gomerant made it a logical guess. Was he the one responsible for killing the other Legion captain and the troops at the vineyard? Once again, he felt like he had more questions than answers.

A glimmer of metal caught his attention and he bent to pick up the item partially hidden under one of the tables. Wrapping his fingers around the cold blade, the frown on his face turned to a dark scowl of anger.

"Assassin," he hissed, recognizing the knife as a Turbinta assassin blade.

Turning, he stared back in the direction of the dead soldier. His lips tightened in aggravation. He would lay his command on the line that the assassin wasn't working with the rebels. He would have the healer aboard the ship do an autopsy and compare the wound on the dead man with the knife.

No, someone had sent the assassin after the same target he was searching for. There was only one person he knew that would hire a Turbinta assassin. It would appear now that he was in a race to find the contents of the capsules.

"Sir, there is a way up to the roof," the commander informed him, coming to a standstill in front of him.

"They escaped over the rooftops," Roan stated. "Close off this section of the city and inspect every building. Do not allow any flights to leave without checking them first."

"Yes, sir," the commander said.

Roan watched the commander give the orders to his men. He turned toward the back door leading into the building. The bar was across the narrow alley. The only way into the building would have been with a special, coded key. He walked back through the warehouse, scanning it. His thoughts turned to Hutu Gomerant. The Old Knight of the Gallant Order had been a mentor to his father. Roan had known the man and respected him as a leader and a fighter. The man had retired to trade used parts in a small spaceport several years ago. It would appear Hutu Gomerant wasn't as retired as he portrayed.

Roan touched the control attached to his ear when he heard it chime. "What is it?" He demanded, pausing in his exploration of the building.

"Sir, we have picked up one of the men on the list," the voice responded.

"Transport him to the Battle Cruiser. I will return shortly," Roan ordered.

"Yes, sir," the voice on the other end responded.

Roan turned and looked across the area. The seven men that had been knocked out or injured would receive medical attention before they were sent for additional training. From what he had learned, one man had been responsible for the act. That, combined with the knowledge that this man also defeated a Turbinta assassin, was enough to set off his internal alarms. Whoever, or whatever, came in the capsule needed to be treated with extreme caution.

Roan stood gazing out the door of the warehouse. He slowly turned and looked toward the staircase in the far corner. His expression thoughtful.

"Who are you and where did you come from?" He murmured before he looked at the commander.

"Make sure this does not happen again. If it does, I will hold you personally responsible."

The commander paled. "Yes, General," the commander said with a curt bow.

Roan continued out of the building. At least one of the rebels had been apprehended. He would get the information he needed from that man.

..*

"No!" Cassa cried in anger where she sat at a low table in the back of a merchant's shop several hours later. She impatiently wiped at the tear that ran down her cheek. "How could he have been caught? He was being careful. He followed Jubotu's instructions."

"A group of Legion soldiers searched the caravan that Pack was traveling with," Hutu explained with a heavy sigh. "One of the members turned him in. The Director has increased the bounty on all of us. That, combined with the increased number of soldiers sent by General Landais, has made it virtually impossible to enter or leave the city. As it is, I am not sure how we will get out."

Josh stepped up to stand behind Cassa. Devona had just contacted them and informed them that Pack had been captured by Legion soldiers. He was to be moved to General Landais' Battle Cruiser. He rested his hands on her shoulders when she bowed her head and drew deep, calming breaths. He could feel her shoulders stiffen before her head rose up again.

"I am going after him," Cassa said with determination. "I will not lose the rest of my family to the Legion."

Hutu nodded. "We will go after him. The question is how to get aboard General Landais' ship without being seen," he muttered.

Josh frowned, staring at Hutu with a thoughtful expression. His mind played back to an old movie he had seen as a boy. What if….

"What if we didn't try not to be seen? What if we just walked on board as if…," his voice faded when Hutu snorted.

"You want us to just walk aboard General Landais' Battle Crusier? It is impossible!" Hutu exclaimed.

"Why? It would be the last thing that he or the Legion would expect," Josh replied with a determined grin. "We just need a way to get on the ship."

Hutu raised an eyebrow. "We'd need a couple of Legion uniforms," he murmured in a thoughtful tone.

"Can you get them?" Cassa asked with wide, hopeful eyes.

"Possibly," Hutu muttered in a thoughtful tone. "Devona can help."

"Does the Legion have any maintenance ships here?" Josh asked.

"Yes, there were several here to work on the gunships," Hutu replied.

"We'll need a way off the ship once we get on," Josh explained. "Those would be less conspicuous and we can use it to escape."

"Yes, but there is no way that it can outrun one of the Legion's fighters," Hutu replied with a frown.

"Hopefully, we'll be off the Battle Cruiser long before they are aware of what is happening," Josh said with a grin. "Personally, I don't plan on getting caught."

Hutu stared at Josh with a thoughtful look for several long seconds before he placed his hands on the small table and leaned forward. Josh could see the other man's mind furiously working through the different scenarios. Finally, Hutu nodded.

"We will need my ship," he stated.

"I have an idea," Cassa said, looking back and forth between the two men. "It is crazy, but this just might work."

..*

The sun was just starting to peek over the horizon when the small trio arrived on the outskirts of where they had started two days before. Devona had appropriated the needed uniforms that they would need. Josh glanced at Hutu as he hurried toward them.

"Are you ready for this?" He asked.

"Yes, there is a maintenance shuttle off to the side," Hutu said.

"Yes, but it has a crew," Cassa replied in a quiet voice. "I have been watching those arriving and departing from the shuttle at the end of the line. It was there only two days ago. It was in for repairs and was just returned to the line."

"How can you tell?" Hutu asked with a frown.

Cassa looked up and gave the old Knight a serene smile. "I hacked into their programming," she replied, holding up her tablet. "Both father and mother believed that it was best to know our enemies. While I was not in favor of fighting against the Legion forces, I was not opposed to learning their programming systems."

"How did you get access to the Legion's programming?" Hutu asked in surprise.

Cassa's gaze flickered to Josh and she gave a bittersweet shrug. "I… One of my former friends was recruited by the Legion. While he has not been happy about it, the recruitment gave him opportunities to expand his skills. We attended the same classes and we kept in touch after mother died. It gave me something to do. While my brothers were better at the mechanical aspects of running the harvest bots back home, I was better at programming them."

"It is a good thing that you had Jesup to care for, otherwise the Legion would have pressed you into service whether you wished to go or not. Their history of recruiting through force is well-known throughout the galaxy," Hutu stated.

A hard look came into Cassa's eyes and she turned her face away to stare at the rows of Legion ships, but not before Josh caught the look of intense grief in her eyes. He saw her lips tighten and she glanced down at the tablet in her hands. He stepped closer and touched her shoulder when she drew in a deep breath and turned back to look at Hutu.

"They still forced me when they killed my father and Jesup. Only… this time I will do everything in my power to stop them," she replied in a quiet voice that held a hint of steely determination. "I've assigned the maintenance shuttle to three fictitious workers and have the new access code. We need to leave now. The code changes in a couple of hours and I'm not sure if I can get it in time to reprogram the computer."

..*

Josh adjusted his helmet and pulled on his gloves. With a curt nod to the others, he stepped out from behind the containers where they had taken refuge. Walking at a steady pace, he knew that Cassa would come out next, followed by Hutu. He bent and grabbed a silver container and carried it toward the maintenance shuttle that Cassa had pointed out. A satisfied smirk curled his lips when the back platform door opened as he approached.

He glanced over his shoulder when he was halfway up the platform and saw Cassa walking toward the shuttle. Her long, self-assured stride didn't break when almost a dozen Legion soldiers marched by. He continued up the ramp and set the container down inside. Turning, he waited for Cassa to walk up the platform. Within minutes, Hutu was at the controls with Josh in the co-pilot seat.

"Why don't you take us up?" Hutu asked, glancing at Josh. "I will show you what you need to know about this ship."

Josh nodded, taking control. Hutu had worked with him while he was on the other ship. It didn't take him long to get familiar with the controls. In many ways, it was easier than the jets he had flown back home.

"I hope this works," Hutu muttered almost an hour later when they navigated through the thin ring surrounding the planet and caught their first up-close view of the new Legion Battle Cruiser. "If not, we are going to need a faster ship."

"It will work," Cassa replied in a soft voice behind them. "It has to."

Chapter 21

"Shuttle 3825, confirm access," the voice requested.

"L39786, this is Shuttle 3825, the confirmation number is Legion 3825...," Josh listened as Hutu responded to the request in a calm, concise tone.

There was a brief delay before they were given permission to proceed. Josh glanced at Cassa. He could see she was worried that she might have the wrong information.

"Confirmed, proceed to lower supply bay. Update your confirmation request list," the voice replied before cutting the communications.

Josh winked at Cassa when she blew out a breath of air and fell back in her seat. She grinned at him for a moment before she returned her focus to the tablet in her hand. Josh released the control of the shuttle to Hutu, deciding it would be better for the Gallant general to guide the shuttle into the landing bay on board the massive Legion Battle Cruiser.

"I forgot to ask you if you heard about any strange aliens in Nobo Sands," Josh commented to Hutu as the shuttle turned to align with the open door of the ship. "Jubotu found the emergency pod. It was the one my friend, Ash, was in. We overheard a woman telling a soldier that he had stolen some clothing. I was hoping you might have heard something."

Hutu shook his head. "No. No one has reported seeing anything unusual. If Devona or any of the other rebel forces had heard of a strange alien male, they would have notified me. I have already talked to Devona. We will find your man, Josh, before the Legion does," he vowed, bringing the shuttle in for a landing. "Cassa, have you located Pack yet?"

Cassa shook her head. "No," she murmured, focusing on the tablet. "Their system is encrypted. I'm trying an old program that my friend developed. As much as I hate to admit it, it helps having a friend in the Legion forces." She paused for a moment before she looked up at them with a triumphant look in her eyes. "It worked. He's being held in Cell Block U41. It is on this level."

Hutu nodded and grinned. "Perhaps this will be easier than we thought," he said, shutting down the engines, rising from his seat, and grabbing the helmet from the side shelf.

Josh rose and waited for Cassa to rise as well. He grabbed the stolen helmet and adjusted it over his head. Rolling his shoulders, he followed the others to the back of the shuttle.

"Do you know where we are going?" He asked, peering over Cassa's shoulder at the screen before his eyes widened. "Nice!" He murmured in her ear when he saw the map of the ship.

"You haven't seen anything yet," she responded with determination. "By the time I get done with this ship, General Landais is going to know that it has been hacked."

"Remind me to never piss you off," Josh chuckled.

She turned her head toward him. He couldn't see her eyes because of the helmet she was wearing, but he knew what would be in them – determination and defiance. He felt his body react and winced. Now was not the time to be thinking about things like how beautiful she was and how much he wanted to show her.

"I am not quite sure what that means, but if it means what I think it does, then you'd better not," she teased before turning back around. "I'll lead the way."

Josh chuckled at her teasing. "I'll just enjoy the view," he murmured.

..*

"You there, come with me," a voice ordered almost as soon as they left the shuttle.

All three of them turned around. A man in a dark gray uniform was staring at Hutu. A look of irritation crossed the man's face.

"I need you to take these supplies to the bridge," the man continued, pointing to a service bot. "You two report to the Cell Block. There is an issue with the disposal unit there."

"Yes, sir," Hutu's muffled voice replied. He waited until the man moved away before he spoke. "There is no way I can pass by this opportunity," he murmured to Cassa and Josh. "This is a perfect chance for the Gallant Order to learn more. I will catch up with you back at the shuttle."

"Hutu," Cassa hissed in dismay.

Josh watched as Hutu ordered the Service bot to take him to the Bridge. He could feel Cassa's frustration, but he also understood that this was the perfect opportunity as a soldier.

"He will be alright. He knows what he is doing," Josh murmured. He wanted to pull her into his arms and hold her close. That would definitely not be the smart thing to do in the middle of a mission. For a moment, he had to silently shake his head at his reaction. This was another first in his life – wanting to comfort a woman in the middle of a mission. "Let's go find Pack and get him out of here," he added in a gruff voice.

Cassa waited a brief second before she nodded and turned to lead the way to the Cell Block. Once again, Josh was reminded that this was a woman with a determination of steel. His love and admiration for her continued to grow.

Love! He thought in shock and disbelief. *I'm in love with her. That is what all these crazy, mixed up feelings are!*

His gaze moved down her straight back. Even in the uniform, he could picture her curves hidden beneath. His mind flashed back in a whirlwind of images since he first met her and he realized that he had been captured by her strength, courage, and beauty from the very beginning. He had known their joining had been different from anything he had experienced before, but he never expected it to be love.

Josh closed the distance between them. This placed the mission on a completely different level as far as he was concerned. They were still going to rescue Pack and find the rest of the crew from the Gliese, but now his top priority had changed. Now, it was to protect Cassa at all cost.

..*

Josh and Cassa moved through the corridors. They focused on where they were going, ignoring the others they passed along the way. Turning to the left, they paused outside the cell block.

"What do we do now?" Cassa whispered.

Josh glanced at the closed door and shrugged. "We tell them that we are here to fix the issue that was reported, I knock them out and put them in one of the cells, we release Pack, get Hutu, and run like hell," he said.

Cassa lifted her visor and stared at him with an expression that said 'Really? That easy?' before pulling it back down again. His lips twitched. He hoped it would be that easy, but he knew from experience that it seldom turned out that way.

"So, do we just knock on the door or what?" He asked.

"No, we do this," she stated, pressing the tablet against the panel and placing her palm against it.

"How did you do that?" Josh asked when the door slid open.

"I told you, I have a friend who isn't happy about being recruited," Cassa murmured, stepping through the open door. "He just happens to be assigned to this ship."

"He's... Just how close a friend, is he?" Josh demanded, following her.

Cassa glanced over her shoulder before refocusing on the two men that were standing in the center of a circular control station. Josh stared after her. He couldn't see her expression because of the helmet and it frustrated him. He was shocked to realize he was feeling jealous. Reaching out, he turned her around.

"How close of a friend is he?" Josh asked in a husky voice.

"What are you doing here?" One of the men demanded.

Josh ignored him. His gaze was focused on Cassa, or what he could see of her. He felt her shoulders tremble.

"I asked you...," the man started to say before he crumbled to the floor.

Josh stepped back, drawing his own weapon from his side to shoot one of the guards, but Cassa had already stunned the second one as well. He turned back to her as she bent forward and pulled her helmet off. She stared at him with an amused expression.

"He was my best friend growing up, but only a friend," she replied with a slight laugh. "You will understand when you meet him."

"Meet him?" Josh asked in confusion. "What do you mean when I meet him?"

"I told you I had a crazy idea. I just didn't tell you everything until I was sure it would work," she said with a shrug. "Let's find Pack."

"I think I'd like to know a little more about this crazy idea," Josh muttered.

Josh quickly pulled the two guards down the narrow corridor while Cassa figured out a way to open the cell doors. He was just starting to straighten when the door in front of him opened. He glanced in and blinked in surprise when he saw Pack sitting on the narrow bench.

"I found him," he called out.

"Josh?" Pack said in surprise, rising off the bench before he blinked again when he saw the bodies of the guards. "Don't tell me… Cassa is here."

"How did you guess?" Josh asked in wry amusement, pulling his helmet off. "Help me pull them into your cell."

Pack quickly hurried over to pull one of the guards into the cell. He stepped aside as Josh deposited the other body. Together they stepped out of the cell. A moment later, the door sealed and locked.

"How did you get here? I can't believe it," Pack muttered, turning to stare at his sister. "Cassa, are you crazy?! Do you know how dangerous this is?" Pack turned back to glare at him. "I thought you said you would protect her? Dragging her onto a Legion

Battle Cruiser is not what I would call protection! It is insanity."

Josh could hear the hint of fear and anger in Pack's voice. He understood the younger man's frustration. He also knew that there would have been no stopping Cassa.

"She has a plan," Josh replied dryly. "Besides, I wasn't about to leave her behind on the planet."

"I wouldn't let him if he tried," Cassa retorted. Her fingers were flying across the keyboard. "I just need a few more minutes."

"What are you doing?" Pack asked, stepping up next to her. His eyes widened in disbelief as he looked down at what she was doing. "Are you serious?! General Landais is going to kill you!"

Cassa glanced at her brother. Her lips were tight with anger and satisfaction. She turned her attention back to the screen. Josh watched in fascination as her fingers flew across the keys.

"She's amazing," Josh murmured under his breath.

"She's tenacious," Pack said in exasperation. "She's also going to get us killed if we don't get moving."

Cassa's head snapped up and she glared at Pack. "I am NOT going to get us killed," she retorted. "I'm making sure that doesn't happen. By the way, Squeals is on board."

"Squeals!" Pack groaned and ran a hand down his face. "You know he has been with the Legion for almost ten years now. How do you know you can still trust him?"

Cassa glared at Pack again and pressed her lips together. Josh raised an eyebrow at her silence. He glanced at Pack.

"Who is Squeals?" He asked Pack.

Pack rubbed at the bruises on his wrists. "He was one of Cassa's old admirers," he said with a grimace. "He wanted to marry her."

"I said no. We were eight years old at the time," Cassa replied in a clipped tone. "We make much better friends than we would lovers, anyway."

Pack flushed. "He was scared of father," he explained. "Every time father was home, Bantu would squeal in terror. We started calling him Squeals."

"He was five years old when that happened," Cassa replied, glaring at her brother. "Finished."

"He has loved her ever since," Pack said, cupping his hands and pressing them to his chest.

Cassa slapped her brother in the arm as she walked by him. "Maybe I should have left you here," she muttered. "How much did you tell them?"

Pack blanched and rubbed his abused arm in exaggeration. "I didn't tell him anything," he retorted.

"Him?" Josh asked with a raised eyebrow.

Pack nodded. "General Landais," he muttered. "He came in earlier and asked me a ton of questions. When I refused to answer, he said he would get his answers one way or another. He ordered a medical bot to be dispatched. I thought you were it when the door opened."

All three of them turned and froze as the door to the Cell Block suddenly opened. Two men and a small bot entered and stopped. The two men had a confused frown on their faces.

"We were ordered to prepare a prisoner for interrogation," one of the men said, staring at Pack in confusion.

"That would be me," Pack replied with a wave before he reached over to pull the small laser pistol from Josh's hip. He raised his hand and fired at the two men. The small medical bot released a sharp squeal, turned on its wheels, and took off.

"Stop it!" Cassa snapped. "If it reports back, all hope of getting out of here without being seen is lost."

Josh took off after the small bot as it weaved crazily down the corridor. He had almost reached it when a group of soldiers, led by none other than General Landais, rounded the far corner. Josh halted and gazed at the stunned look on the General's face. He reached for his laser pistol only to realize that Pack still had it. Grabbing the staff from his hip, he extended it just as one of the soldiers opened fire on him.

"Cease fire!" General Landais ordered, holding out his hand and staring at Josh with an intense frown.

"Later!" Josh muttered, touching two of his fingers to his brow in salute before he pressed the end of the staff to the small bot.

The powerful charge from the end of the staff sent the bot careening out of control toward the group. For a moment, it reminded Josh of a bowling ball heading drunkenly for the pins at the end of a lane. General Landais jumped to the side, but the men behind him weren't as agile.

Josh didn't bother waiting to see what happened next. He turned on his heel and took off. Pack had heard the General's loud exclamation and was waiting for Josh in the Cell Block.

"What now?" Pack asked in aggravation.

Josh swung the end of the staff into the door panel. The acidic scent of burning wires filled the area and sparks shot out of the destroyed panel. He turned to look at Cassa.

"What now?" He repeated.

"Construction access shaft," she muttered, turning on her heel and running down the corridor where the cells were located. "I saw it on the map. Help me find it!" She ran her hands over the panels between the cells. "It has to be here somewhere!"

"Won't General Landias know about it?" Josh asked, searching another panel.

Cassa shook her head. "Most likely not," she answered, moving to the next panel. "It was only used during the construction of the ship."

"I think I've found it!" Pack said excitedly before he groaned. "It's sealed."

Cassa touched the tablet in her hand. "Squeals, are you there?" She asked urgently.

"Cassa, where are you? You said you'd be at the service bay," a husky voice whispered.

"I need you to unseal the construction access door in the Cell Block on Level U41," she ordered, glancing at the door.

"Construction access door?" The voice hissed. "Hold on."

"Hurry, Squeals," Pack said.

"I'm hurrying!" Squeals snapped. "Do you have any idea how difficult it is to circumvent the programming without getting caught on this ship? Don't even get me started on what will happen if General Landais finds out about this. He'll shoot me out into space just so he can watch my head explode."

"Just breathe, Squeals," Cassa interjected, shooting Pack a nasty look. "You know he gets clumsy if he gets nervous."

Josh turned when the door next to him suddenly opened. His eyes widened. He quickly swung the staff around, touching the end against the chest of one of the guards that they had placed into the cell earlier. The man flew back into his companion.

"Wrong door, Squeals," Pack shouted above the banging on the outer door. "We really need you to open the right panel."

"I'm trying," Squeals snapped angrily.

"Yes! That's it!" Cassa cried out when the panel door started to open. "What's wrong? Open it the rest of the way," she demanded.

"It's stuck," Squeals replied. "I'll close it and try to open it again."

"Now, would be good," Pack urged, glancing at where the outer door was beginning to glow a bright red. "Now, Squeals."

Josh was about to put his two cents in when the panel door suddenly opened. Cassa breathed an urgent thank you to her friend on the other end before slipping the tablet into the side pocket of her uniform and grabbing the ladder. Pack followed her. Josh stepped over the gap into the maintenance tube and onto the ladder. He stared up the long tube. Behind him, the door closed again. He began climbing silently. He was almost a floor above when he heard a dull thump as the double doors to the cell block blew open. A smile curved his lips. They weren't out of the Battle Cruiser yet, but it was a huge ship and it wouldn't be that easy to find them, especially with Cassa on their side. He just hoped Hutu was keeping a low profile.

Chapter 22

Hutu paused in the doorway to the bridge. He murmured for the supply bot to deliver its payload. He watched as it whizzed around the room, stopping on occasion to deliver a preprogrammed order before continuing on to the next section.

Hutu casually leaned over and placed another sensor under the closest console to him. Sliding his hand back into his pocket, he removed another one and started to follow the bot. He paused when a side door opened. Bowing his head, he scooted back as far as his large frame would allow him to move and peered out of the low shield as General Landais walked toward him.

He turned slightly when one of the security ensigns next to him stood and stepped forward when the General called to him. There was a tense moment when General Landais turned to stare at him with a puzzled look. Landais started toward him, but stopped when the supply bot rolled up and stopped in front of Hutu and beeped to let him know that it was finished with its assignment.

With a shake of his head, Landais turned away. "Follow me," the General ordered to the five men who came to stand next to him.

Hutu turned and watched Landais exit the bridge. Bending, Hutu gave a quiet order for the small bot to escort him to the service bay. He had placed as many sensors in the area as he could. It would have to be enough. He would deposit more on his return trip to the service bay.

He was almost back to the shuttle when the red alert went off. With a curse, he knew that Josh, Cassa, and Pack had been discovered. Taking off at a run, he abandoned caution. He turned the corner and headed for one of the service lifts. He entered it, followed by the small service bot that suddenly seemed attached to him.

He started to order it to return to duty when four soldiers entered the service lift. He pressed to the back and bowed his head. A silent curse flowed through his mind when they pushed back against him.

"Rebels have been reported in the Cell Block," one of the soldiers stated.

"I thought that was where they were supposed to be," another joked.

"Yes, but not outside the cells," a third soldier muttered. "The General has ordered a lockdown of the ship."

"A lockdown!" The fourth one said just as the lights in the lift flickered and went out. "What the…."

The emergency lights came on illuminating the interior of the lift in a soft red glow. The first soldier turned to look at Hutu in irritation as the lift slowed. Hutu kept his gaze down.

"You," the man said. "You work in maintenance, what is going on?"

Hutu slowly lifted his head and grinned. “Surprise,” he said, striking out and catching the soldier in the jaw.

In the tight confines of the lift, the soldiers didn’t stand a chance against the powerful Knight of the Gallant. Hutu pushed back against one of the soldiers, holding him in place, while he fought with the other two still standing.

He grunted when one of the men landed a punch to his side. Bringing up his elbow, he snapped it back against the man he had pinned against the back wall. Swinging around, he caught another in the stomach while the other fell backwards over the small service bot that was beeping and trying to get out of the way.

Pulling his Staff from his side, he partially extended it and pressed it against both men. He sent a powerful shock through each man. They dropped to the floor with a solid thump.

Hutu’s eyes danced in amusement when the little bot pressed into the corner of the lift and shook. He bent and stared at the small mechanical sensor that made up its eye. While the ‘bots’ didn’t have emotions, they were programmed to have reactions. Obviously whoever programmed this one went a step further.

“It is alright, my little friend. I have no quarrel with you,” Hutu stated. “Now, can you escort me to the service bay from our current location if I get us out of here?”

The little bot bobbed up and down and beeped. Hutu stood up with a satisfied grunt and stared at the doors. Pressing the end of the staff to the panel, he outlined it. The metal glowed brightly as he cut through it. The outer cover of the panel dropped to the floor with a loud ringing sound. Hutu stared at the mass of wires inside with a frown. He glanced down at the little bot and raised an eyebrow at it.

"Do you know which wires will open this?" Hutu asked in amusement when the little bot rose up to scan the panel.

Two thin arms came out. The bot moved several wires before snipping one and touching it to a circuit board. Hutu grunted, impressed, when the doors suddenly opened.

"Well, if I must be stuck on a Legion Battle Cruiser, I prefer to be stuck with a handy service bot such as yourself," he informed the small bot. "Come, I think you might be useful."

The bot took off down the corridor. Hutu followed it, pausing at times when soldiers passed him. He adjusted his helmet outside the service bay and walked quickly across to the shuttle they had arrived on. He stopped halfway up the platform when a Legion soldier suddenly stepped out of the back of the shuttle. The tall, thin male looked at him with an irritated glare.

"What are you doing here?" The man demanded. "This shuttle is out of commission. I have a repair team coming."

Hutu tilted his head and stared at the soldier. There was something vaguely familiar about him. He frowned, about to say something when the service bot charged up the ramp to the man.

"Bolt," the man said with an easy grin before it faded and he stared at Hutu again. "You heard me. I already have a team coming to work on this shuttle."

"Squeals?" Hutu suddenly asked in recognition. "Aren't you the little boy who followed Cassa everywhere?"

The man jerked back and looked warily around before staring back at Hutu with an intense expression. Hutu saw him nervously swallow and wave for him to step further into the shuttle. It was only when they were out of sight of the rest of the crew that the man spoke in a low, rushed voice.

"Who are you? Are you with Cassa and Pack?" The man demanded.

Hutu lifted his hand and removed his helmet. Bantu's jaw sagged in disbelief and he hissed. Running a hand down his face, Hutu watched the younger man pale.

"A Gallant Knight! I'm so dead," Bantu groaned. "You do realize that you, Cassa, and Pack are like the most wanted fugitives in the galaxy, don't you?"

"How did you get involved?" Hutu asked.

"Cassa and I have kept in touch. I'm just doing this for her… and because it is good to show the Legion that they aren't all powerful," Bantu muttered with a heavy sigh.

Hutu chuckled. "Is the little bot yours?" He asked with a nod toward the bot which was rocking back and forth and watching Bantu.

Bantu grinned. "Yes, I'm in charge of programming them. This one was an experiment," he admitted.

Hutu turned when the lights flashed again. "Do you know how to fly this thing?" He asked grimly.

"Yes," Bantu replied, turning toward the front. "I've set the bay shields to release on my command," he added. "You know, if General Landais ever catches me, I'll be dead."

Hutu slapped Bantu on the shoulder, sending the young man forward from the blow. "I guess this is your welcome to the rebellion," he chuckled. "I see them coming. Fire up the shuttle."

"You know the fighters are going to shoot us down before we make it to the planet," Bantu replied in resignation. "This is not how I expected my day to begin."

Hutu ignored Bantu and focused on firing at the two soldiers who rushed toward the fleeing trio. Both men dropped to the floor. The move drew the attention of the other members of the crew.

"Hurry," Hutu shouted.

"Go! Go! Go!" Josh yelled in return, running up the platform behind Cassa and Pack.

Hutu decided it was time to take control of the shuttle. He slapped his hand on the platform control and turned toward the cockpit. Pack was already sliding into the co-pilot's seat.

"Move, Bantu," Hutu shouted, heading for the pilot's seat. "We are going to be moving a little faster than you are used to."

Bantu practically fell out of the seat as he scrambled to get out of Hutu's way. Hutu ignored the man. He slid into the pilot's seat and quickly gripped the controls.

"Cassa, do your magic," Hutu called over his shoulder. "We are about to have company."

"Not if I can help it," Cassa muttered. "We're clear. Go, Hutu. It won't take long for them to figure out what I've done and try to bypass it."

"What did you do?" Bantu asked, curiously glancing down at the tablet.

"Hello, Bantu," Cassa said with a strained smile. "I've locked down the fighter bay doors and have taken the weapons system offline.

"Isn't that the program I was playing with a few years ago?" He asked, practically falling in her lap when the shuttle tilted at a crazy angle.

"Strap in," Josh snapped.

Bantu looked up, startled, and nervously swallowed at the look of warning in Josh's eyes. He nodded and sat back in his seat, grabbing at the straps. The loud roar of the engines drowned out any other conversation.

***

The shuttle swept through the doors of the service bay just as they were about to close. Josh swore he could hear the sound of metal on metal. Darkness engulfed them. In the corner across from him, a slight movement drew his attention to the service bot locked to the floor.

"Where are the fighters? They should be all over us," Bantu whispered.

Cassa shook her head. "Not if they are locked down inside the Battle Cruiser," she stated.

"Hang on," Hutu called over his shoulder. "We have some ground fighters headed this way."

"Can you get to the moon before they get here?" Josh asked, rising out of his seat.

"It will be close," Hutu responded.

Josh watched as Hutu skillfully maneuvered the shuttle toward the thin layer of debris circling the planet. They would lose themselves in it. There were several small 'satellite moons' caught in the gravitational pull between the larger moons and the planet.

"It still amazes me that your spaceships can maneuver through debris like this without getting damaged," Josh murmured.

Pack glanced at him with a puzzled frown. "Your ships cannot?" He asked in surprise.

Josh shook his head. "Not yet," he replied in a light tone.

"How are we going to get to the *Tracer*? It is still on the planet," Pack asked.

Hutu nodded to the moon. "The rings move in a tight, but fast circle around the planet," he explained. "I had Jubotu move my ship to a remote location on the other side of the planet. We will catch a ride past the Legion forces and escape down to the planet once we are clear."

Pack grinned. "Brilliant strategy," he exclaimed.

"Thank you," Josh responded with an answering grin.

"You thought of it?" Pack asked in surprise, turning to stare at Josh.

Josh resisted the urge to make a sarcastic response and failed. "I do have them on occasion," he retorted dryly.

..*

"Where are they?" Roan demanded in a hard voice.

"The scanners are offline, General," one of the ensigns replied.

"Find them," Roan ordered through gritted teeth. "I want a complete scan of the ship. I want to know how the rebels were able to get on my ship and if they had any help."

He turned toward his office, needing time alone. His mind swept back to the man he had seen in the corridor. There was an arrogance to the alien that irked him.

Walking over to his desk, he picked up the patch that had been discarded down on the planet. Instead of sitting down, he walked over to the window. The emergency lights were still on, casting his office in a dim red haze. It wouldn't have bothered him if it wasn't for the fact that it was another thorn in his side

– proof that not only had the rebels snuck in under his security, but they had escaped with a prisoner and brought an advanced Legion Battle Cruiser to its knees.

His lips twitched in sardonic amusement. The two finger salute continued to play over and over in his mind. Whoever the man was, he had thrown down a challenge that Roan was not about to ignore.

"Who are you?" Roan murmured, lifting the patch up to gaze at it. "More importantly, where did you come from?"

Roan grimaced when the console on his desk pinged. Turning, he drew in a deep, calming breath before he walked over to the desk. He braced himself for what was about to come. Obviously he had not found all of the spies aboard his ship.

"Director," Roan greeted in a stiff voice.

Chapter 23

"After we get back to the ship, where are we heading?" Josh murmured, staring out into space as the satellite moon they had landed on moved around the planet, away from the Legion forces searching for them. "We still haven't found any more clues to where Ash could have gone."

"We will find him," Hutu said confidently. "Devona has her team searching the area. She stated a short range freighter pilot took off shortly before we arrived. One of the service bots noted an additional crew member that was not on the ship's register. She is obtaining video and will send it to us as soon as possible. If it is your friend, we will know where to start."

"What are we going to do in the meantime?" Pack asked.

"We will head to a secret rebel base on one of the outer moons of Tesla Terra," Hutu replied. "It is a desolate place and unlikely to be discovered by the Legion forces. Your father and I started it nearly thirty years ago when we realized what Andronikos was doing."

Josh turned when Cassa came to stand behind him. He wrapped his arm around her and pulled her close. She stared out the front window down at the planet.

"KGO, come in," Devona's voice echoed over the communication console a moment before she appeared on the screen in front of them.

"This is KGO, over," Hutu replied.

"I'm sending the video I've retrieved. Hutu…," Devona paused before she continued. "You should know that the Director ordered the destruction of all cities on Jeslean that support the Gallant Order. He wanted to send a message to any that dare oppose his rule."

"No!" Cassa whispered, her eyes wide with horror.

"My parents are there!" Bantu exclaimed, pushing forward. "We've got to warn them."

Devona's grief stricken face reflected Bantu's and Cassa's distress. She turned when someone spoke behind her. Her lips tightened in anger.

"We gave as much warning as we could. The Legion forces are attacking any vessel fleeing the cities. Legion soldiers are coming. I must leave. Long live the Gallant Order," Devona stated before the screen went blank.

Josh turned Cassa into his arms and held her tightly against him. Everyone was silent as the impact of what the Legion had done sunk in. The murder of hundreds of thousands of innocent lives weighed on their conscience.

Bantu turned and quietly walked back to the bench and sank down. Josh saw the haunted look in the other man's eyes. For a moment, Josh was pulled back to the day he saw his father die. The pain and desolation had been suffocating. The difference was his father had died in a tragic accident. This was genocide.

"The Legion has to be stopped," Josh growled with icy resolve.

"Yes… It does," Hutu replied, reaching for the controls. "It is time to get the *Tracer*. I will try to contact the rebel leaders there. The destruction of the Gallant Order headquarters will be a devastating blow to our cause. If we are lucky, the bases outside of the cities will still be intact."

..*

Josh sat in the small galley aboard the *Tracer* several days later. His fingers absently stroked the rim of the cup in front of him. He jerked back to the present when Cassa walked in. Her cheeks were flushed and she was drawing in deep, calming breaths. An amused smile tugged at Josh's lips.

"How is the training going?" He asked, sliding to the side so she could sit down next to him.

"Better," she replied. "Bantu is rusty, but he is picking it up. He is motivated. He is working on a program to work against the Legion forces."

"His inside knowledge will be an advantage," Josh replied, playing with a strand of her hair that had come loose. "You'll have him in shape before he knows it. I know I should regret ordering the gateway fixed, but I don't. I'm glad I'm here. I just regret that I couldn't have done more to prevent the deaths of your father and brother."

Cassa turned and raised her hand. She tenderly placed her fingers against his lips. She had that familiar, fierce expression on her face again. Josh pressed a kiss against her fingers.

"What has happened is not your fault," Cassa replied in a firm voice. "The Legion's actions belong solely on the shoulders of the Director."

Josh reached up and caught her fingers. He tugged her closer, wrapping his other hand around her neck and leaned forward. He paused a second to stare deeply into her eyes before he pressed a kiss to her slightly parted lips.

Josh started to deepen the kiss when the sound of someone clearing their throat broke through the haze of desire. He slowly ended the kiss and pulled back to glare at Bantu, who was standing in the doorway with his arms folded. Josh took his time releasing Cassa. The message in his touch and in his gaze was clear – she belonged to him.

"What do you want?" Josh asked in a blunt tone.

"Food," Bantu responded with a crooked grin.

Josh didn't miss the look of disappointment when the other man glanced at Cassa. Sitting back in his seat, he cupped Cassa's hand in his and waited as Bantu stepped into the narrow area.

Bantu fixed himself a drink and a plate of food and came to sit down across from them. A moment later, Hutu stepped into the room. He quickly fixed himself something to eat and sat down next to Cassa.

"We will be at the base in a few hours," Hutu replied. "The Legion ships have left Jeslean. We are hoping most of the residents in the cities were able to escape to underground shelters. It will be days before we find out how many survived. Rebel troops have not had a chance to search for other survivors. From the initial reports, eight cities were decimated by the attacks."

"What about the rebel bases?" Josh asked with a frown.

Hutu glanced at Josh. "They remained undetected. A decision was made not to engage the Legion forces," he responded.

"What makes the Gallant forces any different from the Legion if they left the people in those cities to die?" Bantu asked bitterly, pushing his plate away from him.

Josh glanced at Bantu. He could see the grief and guilt on the other man's face. He understood Bantu's anger.

"It would have been suicide to engage the fighters," Josh replied in a calm voice.

Hutu nodded. "The loss of the secret bases there would have been devastating to the Gallant's fight against the Legion. As it is, two of the underground bases will be out of commission for a while. These bases are our only hope of defeating the Director. We've spent years building them while trying to undermine the Legion's defenses. You can help, Bantu," he stated.

"How? I was a Service Bot programmer," Bantu muttered, picking at the food on his plate. "I was never a soldier."

Josh watched as Cassa reached out and gently touched Bantu's hand. He could see the compassion on her face. Once again, a warmth spread through him at her understanding.

"Neither was I, Squeals," she said, using the affectionate nickname she had for him. "Remember what we were able to do on General Landais' Battle Cruiser? We can do this. We have to do this – for our parents, for… Jesup, for our people."

"Why wasn't he stopped before? Why didn't the Knights of the Gallant Order stop Lord Andronikos when they had the chance?" Bantu whispered in a strained voice.

"Bad men have come to power using force, deceit, and treachery for thousands of years," Josh replied in a blunt tone. "There will always be men like Andronikos, just as there will always be good men willing to stand up against them. Are you willing to do whatever it takes to stop him?"

Silence descended around the table as everyone thought about what he had said. He bowed his head as he thought about his question. The gauntlet was not just for Bantu, but for himself as well. What was he willing to risk to stand up to a man like Andronikos? This had not started out as his war, but it became personal when the Director attacked Cassa's family searching for him and the rest of the crew of the Gliese. His jaw tightened and he looked up at Bantu with a steely gaze and waited.

"Yes," Bantu replied in a quiet voice filled with resolve. "I resisted it when the Legion came and took me from my family nearly ten years ago. I learned very quickly what happened to those that didn't follow their rules. Over the years, I've done what I can to help the resistance." His gaze flickered to Cassa before he looked down at the table. "I know it wasn't much, but I knew sharing things with Cassa would get back to her father. I've never been much of a soldier," he continued, looking up at Josh. "Until now. If my family… if they are dead, I have nothing to lose anyway."

Josh didn't miss Bantu's second glance at Cassa. Turning his attention to Hutu, Josh thought of what they knew so far. The video that Devona sent had cemented the fact that Ash was alive. The image had been grainy, but Josh would know his friend's easy gait anywhere.

"Once we've reach the base, we can coordinate with the teams we have around the galaxy to find the freighter your friend was on. Devona erased the video stored on the service bot, but that is no guarantee that there weren't others. If we found information about your man, so can the Legion," Hutu said, pushing back and rising to his feet. "I need to relieve Pack."

Josh nodded and rose. "I'd like to go over the video again and see if there is anything else I can discover," he said.

"I'll help you," Cassa murmured, standing.

Josh reached for her hand. "Thank you," he murmured as they stepped out of the narrow galley.

"For what?" She asked in surprise.

Josh turned her so that her back was against the wall. "For being you," he whispered. He covered her lips with his, giving her the long, deep kiss that he had started earlier. A soft sigh escaped him when he released her lips and pulled back. Turning his head, he returned Bantu's sardonic stare with one of his own. "You have terrible timing," he muttered to the other man where he was standing in the doorway.

"Not from my perspective," Bantu retorted, turning on his heel. "You should get a room."

"We have one!" Josh snapped before releasing a surprised chuckle when Bantu raised his hand and extended his middle finger. "I'll be damned! You use that gesture, too?!"

Chapter 24

Several hours later, Josh walked along the wide corridors inside the Tesla Terra One rebel base. The variety of species on the other planets were nothing compared to what he was seeing here. All of them were working toward the same goal – freedom.

He turned when he heard his name called. Cassa was hurrying toward him. She had changed into a heavier tunic and pants. The moon was covered in ice and deadly storms made landing and taking off difficult at best, impossible at worst. He had been shocked when Hutu had asked him to sit in the copilot seat so he could see the base first hand.

***

"It looks like Antarctica on steroids," Josh remembered mumbling as they broke through the thin atmosphere.

Hutu chuckled. "I do not know what your Antarctica or steroids are, but from the sound of it, they must be impressive," he reflected.

"Yeah, you could say that," Josh muttered.

Josh was surprised when he saw a line of lights along the frozen surface. Hutu had followed the line to a thick, snow-covered mountain. At first, the blizzard made it difficult to see that the side of the mountain had opened into a long, wide hanger. They passed through a protective shield that hung like an invisible curtain across the entrance to the cavernous area where hundreds of fighters were lined up.

"What you see has taken years of planning," Hutu murmured. "Time is running out, though. The Legion forces grow more powerful every day and more and more planets are falling under the Director's iron fist. If we do not strike soon, I fear nothing will stop him."

"You don't have to convince me, Hutu," Josh responded in a quiet voice as Hutu landed the *Tracer*. "I've seen first hand what the Legion can do. As I told Pack, the Legion brought the war to me. It's personal now."

Hutu shut down the engines and turned to him. Josh held the old Knight's thoughtful gaze. He saw the look of approval and something else – almost like a sense of relief in the man's eyes.

"You are a good man, Josh. The Gallant Order is very fortunate to have you here," Hutu finally said, rising from his seat. "Come now. I will introduce you to some of the best fighters in the galaxy."

* * *

"You look warm," Josh commented, returning to the present and wrapping his arm around Cassa's waist as she came to stand near him. "And rested."

"You left me alone," she teased. "Of course, I was able to get some sleep. What are you doing?"

"Learning," Josh admitted, staring around the vast area. "In some ways, this is very reminiscent of my world, if you take out the fact that there are aliens, spaceships, and that we are on a frozen moon."

"Oh, not that different at all," she murmured, trying to keep a straight face. "Do you miss it? Your world?"

Josh stopped in the middle of the hanger and looked around. Did he miss the Earth? He thought about it for a moment. In some ways, it seemed more like a dream than a reality. Tilting his head, he brushed his hand along her cheek.

"No, I don't miss it," he said with a slight frown. "I want to find the members of my crew and stop the Legion forces. I've been so focused on that, I haven't thought about Earth."

Cassa bit her lip and bowed her head. "When this is over, if you find your crew, do you think you will want to return?" She asked in a slightly husky tone.

Josh slid his hand down under her chin and lifted it so that she could look into his eyes. He ran his thumb along her bottom lip. His eyes swept over the markings that ran across her forehead and down along her cheek. Bending, he brushed a light kiss along her lips before following the markings along her cheek to her forehead. When he had kissed each section, he drew her into his arms and held her close to his body – to his heart.

"No. I've found where I belong," he said, gazing over her head at the fighters and the men, women, and service bots that worked on them. "I told you this was forever, Cassa. I meant it. I love you."

He felt the shudder that ran through her body before she relaxed against him and wrapped her arms around him. Releasing a deep sigh, he reluctantly released her when he felt a faint vibration and stepped back. He glanced down at the communicator Hutu had given him.

"There is to be a meeting," he said. "I was going to come get you. Hutu wants to meet with the leaders down on the planet. We are going to head down there to coordinate a plan of attack against the Legion forces and see what we can do to help the survivors on Jeslean."

Cassa nodded. "I heard Pack talking about it," she admitted.

"Josh," Hutu said, walking toward him with a grim expression on his face.

"What is it?" Josh asked with a frown.

"We've just received word that Andronikos has ordered Legion Battle Cruisers to destroy additional cities found to be harboring rebel forces. This time, though, he has instructed that every major city on the planet be leveled," Hutu said.

"Which one?" Josh asked.

"Tesla Terra," Hutu responded. "Not only that, the short range freighter that your friend was last seen on has been located."

"Where?"Josh demanded.

"Heading for Telsa Terra," Hutu stated, holding out a helmet and uniform. "We need every pilot that we have. A decision has been made to strike back. Will you fight beside us?"

Josh reached for the uniform and helmet. He glanced down at it for a moment. His jaw tightened and he nodded.

"Of course," Josh stated.

"Good. You are going to need some time in one of the fighters. Gear up. I will meet you back here in ten minutes to take you out. We don't have much time," Hutu stated. He turned and hurriedly walked away.

Cassa stepped back. "I'll make sure your fighter bot is ready," she said. "Good luck."

"Cassa," Josh murmured, catching her arm when she started to turn away.

"Yes," she whispered, looking up at him, her eyes filled with emotion.

"I want you to know that meant it when I said I love you," Josh said in a gruff voice. "I'm coming back."

A slight smile pulled at the corner of her lips. "You'd better," she said, pulling and walking away with a strong, confident stride.

"Damn, I'm a lucky man," Josh muttered before he turned to locate the fighter that matched the symbol on his helmet.

***

"This is Phantom One, coming in to refuel," Josh said.

"Phantom One, clear for entry," the voice on the other end stated.

Josh eased the fighter around and cut through the sheets of icy sleet. Hutu had started out slow, giving Josh time to get familiar with the fighter. It hadn't taken long for Josh to realize that the spacecraft was actually easier to fly and more maneuverable than the jets he had flown back home.

Josh chuckled when he heard Hutu's mutterings over his comlink. Josh had introduced Hutu to a modern day dog fight. It was not something the General had encountered before.

He carefully turned the craft in the air with the help of the Fighter bot and landed the spacecraft. Almost immediately, work crews swarmed the fighter and were preparing it for its next mission. He waited as the cockpit slid back and released his helmet, pulling it off.

"You are crazy!" Hutu growled, stomping toward him with a good-natured grin on his face. "You are also very good."

Josh laughed as he climbed out of the cockpit and waited for the lift to lower him to the ground. He stepped off and slapped Hutu on the shoulder. The old Knight wasn't half-bad himself.

"I liked that one maneuver you did," Josh commented. "That was pretty tricky coming up out of the canyon that way, especially with those ice shelves hanging down."

"It didn't stop you from following me," Hutu retorted dryly. "You had me locked on the entire time."

Josh laughed again. "Ash and I used to take bets on who could shoot a BB through a one inch pipe and hit the target at the other end," he replied. "We didn't have much choice after my dad banned us from shooting the weather vane with the .22 rifle he had."

"You were one of those types of children," Hutu muttered.

Josh slung his arm around Hutu's shoulders. "You have no idea," he admitted with a grin. "Of course, having Ash to hang with made it more fun," he added dropping his arm. "Is there any way to contact the freighter?" He asked.

Hutu shook his head. "Their communication systems must be down. All efforts to reach them have been in vain. I'm afraid they are going to arrive to a less than warm welcome," he responded in a heavy voice.

"Surely they will know?" Josh murmured with a dark scowl. "There has to be some way of contacting them – warning them – about what is headed this way."

Hutu shook his head. "Only if they get here first," he replied, turning when he heard his name.

"General, the other members of the Gallant Order have arrived and are waiting for you," the man said, glancing curiously at Josh.

"We are on our way," Hutu responded.

Josh followed Hutu back through the hanger to the staging area. His gaze swept the room, narrowing in on where Cassa was talking to one of the military personnel he had seen shortly before they left Tesla Terra the first time. Pack was also there, talking with several other pilots. He was dressed in a a dark green uniform similar to the one Josh and Hutu were wearing.

Cassa must have felt his gaze on her because she glanced up. For a brief second, Josh felt like they were the only two people in the room. He bowed his head to her when she started at the touch of the person talking to her.

..*

"General," the group said, coming to attention when Hutu stepped up to the screen.

"General Tailsman," Hutu acknowledged, stepping up to the front.

Josh stood in the back as General Tailsman began explaining what they knew of the Legion's movement. Two Battle Cruisers, almost a thousand fighters, and just as many ground troops were estimated to be among the group converging on the planet. Inside information stated that after the Battle Cruiser and the fighters completed the initial assault, the ground troops were to move in and eliminate any survivors.

"We are expecting them to arrive within the next few hours," Hutu interjected, stepping forward. "Our bases on the planet are ready. Those that agreed to be evacuated have been."

Josh frowned. "What about those that are supporting the Legion? Have measures been taken to prevent them from warning the Legion that the rebels are expecting them?" He asked, remembering the spy from the bar.

"Yes," General Tailsman responded. "Additional security has been increased since the attack on General de Rola's family."

Josh glanced at where Pack and Cassa were standing. He saw Pack wrap his arm around his sister and give her a hug. He could feel the tension in the room at the reminder of what happened to their father and brother.

"Your presence has been a catalyst for the rebel forces," General Tailsman informed him.

Josh stiffened in surprise when he saw heads turning to stare at him. He had noticed the odd looks in the hanger and the quiet greetings as he walked through the corridors earlier. He had not realized what it meant, though.

"Why would my presence be a catalyst?" Josh asked with a puzzled frown.

"You give us hope," General Tailsman replied in a quiet voice.

"Hope?" Josh repeated, stunned.

He glanced around the room. Everyone in it was staring back at him in silence. His gaze took in the expressions of quiet respect and determination. He finally paused on Hutu, staring back at the old Knight with a frown.

"You are believed to be one of the original Knights of the Gallant Order, returned to help defeat the Legion and restore order to the galaxy, Josh," Hutu said, stepping through the crowded room toward him. "You strike fear in the Director, something no one has ever seen before. He is desperate to find you and destroy the hope that has been spreading through the star system since your ship was discovered. Word of it and your defeat of the Legion forces at the vineyard offers the hope of freedom to the people. This is not something that should be ignored."

"Hutu," Josh spoke in a low voice so only the old Knight could hear him. "You know that I'm not who they think I am."

"How do you know that you aren't?" Hutu asked. "You give hope where there was none before, Josh. I would say that is pretty incredible in itself. I am an old man now, my time here is growing short. I am the last of the old Order. You are the first of the new one. Give them hope, Josh. Give them the power to believe that there is a way to defeat the Legion and they will."

Josh tore his gaze from the old Knight and glanced around the room. He saw the truth behind Hutu's quietly spoken words. During his time in the military, he had seen missions, thought to be impossible, succeed because those fighting believed they could win. His forefathers had proven that centuries before.

His gaze locked on Cassa's face. He could see the belief in her gaze. He could also see the fear that she was trying to hide. Acceptance swept through him when he saw her head bow and she smiled back at him. Pulling his gaze away from her, he stared at the images of the Legion Battle Cruisers. A plan began to form in his mind as resolve sunk in.

"I have a plan," he said as his mind ran through the information that had been shared. "Bantu, Cassa, we are going to need your expertise on the Legion's programming."

Chapter 25

Roan Landais stepped into the office of the Director. His lips were pressed together in anger. He had toured the areas of destruction on the planet before making his way to the New Legions, one of the largest and newest cities on Jeslean.

Removing his hat, he tucked it under his arm as he walked into the room. Andri Andronikos stood with his back to it, looking out over the city and citizens that he ruled with the same ruthlessness that he commanded his forces. Roan's gaze moved around the room, pausing on the other man sitting in one of the plush chairs by a hologram fireplace. He hid his grimace of distaste. This meeting was going to be more difficult than he anticipated.

"Roan," Andri murmured, not turning around.

"Director," Roan replied stiffly.

Roan knew his greeting was short and stiff. At the moment, he really didn't give a damn. He resented being beckoned to Jeslean like an errant cadet. The fact that two of the most influential men in his life were both there didn't make the situation any better.

Standing at attention just inside the door, he kept his gaze focused on the black coated figure by the window. His mind was not on the man, though. No, his mind was replaying the destruction he had witnessed upon his arrival.

Silence reigned for several long minutes before Andri released a sigh and turned to look at him. Roan kept his attention focused on the expressionless face, trying to gauge the situation. Andri walked over to a bar and poured a drink. Suspicion and dread began to build inside Roan. He knew for a fact that the Director did not drink. His hand automatically reached for the glass when it was held out to him.

"Sit down," Andri ordered, turning and walking back to the window.

Roan walked over to the second plush chair. He placed the small glass of liquor on the table next to him, along with his hat, before he sat down. His gaze brushed over the older man sitting across from him in silence.

"What happened?" The man asked.

Roan turned to look at him. "There was a traitor on board my ship, a maintenance programmer. He must have helped the rebels gain access and shut down critical systems. I have a team working on correcting the issue and developing security to make sure it does not happen again," he replied in an emotionless voice.

"Who is the traitor?" The man asked in a deceptively calm tone.

"Bantu de Gaul," Roan stated.

"See that his family is punished – publicly," the Director ordered, not turning around.

Roan stiffened before he relaxed. "It has already been done," he replied.

He didn't mention that he had discovered that Bantu's parents had been living in one of the devastated cities. It was unlikely that they had survived. The current number of fatalities was over two hundred thousand and rising.

The Director turned and gazed at Roan with an intense stare for several seconds before he walked over to the table next to Roan and picked up the glass of liquor. He continued back to the bar and poured the liquid down the sink. Roan listened as the water from the sink briefly came on before it shut back off. A moment later, Andri walked by him again.

"What of the rebels? Did you learn anything from the prisoner before he escaped?" Andri asked nonchalantly when he resumed his position by the tinted window.

Roan forced himself to relax and leaned back in his chair. "His name is Packu de Rola. He is Jemar de Rola's oldest son. He refused to say anything other than his name. I was in the process of using alternative methods to secure information when he escaped. As for the other rebels…." Roan's voice faded as he remembered the strange male and his cocky salute.

"You were saying," the man across from him demanded.

Roan's gaze refocused on the Director's face. "There was a strange male. He was… Different," Roan finally said.

“What do you mean by different?” The Director demanded in a harsh tone, turning and stepping closer to Roan. “What made him different?”

“It was more than his features. It was the way he carried himself. He was confident, cocky. He also carried the Staff belonging to a Knight of the Gallant Order,” Roan said in a quiet voice.

“That is impossible! There is only one Knight of the Order left,” the man across from him exclaimed. “A Staff will not work unless it is passed from one Knight to the next, even the two that we managed to retrieve would not work. When we tried to re-engineer one of them, the Staff exploded, killing everyone in the lab.”

Roan’s jaw tightened. “I know what I saw,” he stated in an icy tone.

“It will not matter,” the Director replied with a wave of his hand. “Legion Battle Cruisers will be arriving on Tesla Terra any time now. I’ve ordered the destruction of every city on the planet to set an example of what happens to anyone who dares to stand against the Legion. One old Knight and this stranger will not stand in the way.”

Roan rose from his chair. His hands curled at his side before he forced them to relax. Even so, he could feel the muscle in his jaw twitching with anger.

“Director, the destruction of every man, woman, and child on Tesla Terra could have negative effects to the Legion and to your rule,” Roan cautioned in a stiff voice. “Already, the leveling of the cities here on

Jeslean will have long term effects. Surely that is enough to show the strength of the Legion."

Roan could tell his words were falling on deaf ears. He stiffened when the man across from him rose and stared at him. Glancing down, he bowed his head.

"I only speak to give a different perspective, my Lord," Roan said, looking down at the gleaming tiled floor.

"You are not growing weak, are you, General?" The Director asked in a deceptively calm voice.

Roan straightened and looked back with cold, hard eyes. "No, my Lord. My only thought was for the future of the Legion," he stated.

"Your concern is noted. A new report has come in that another signal has been located. I want you to retrieve the capsule and the contents. It is imperative that you do not fail this time," the Director ordered with a wave of his hand in dismissal.

"Yes, my Lord," Roan murmured, picking up his hat and bowing again before walking toward the door.

"Roan," the Director called in a hard voice.

Roan turned at the door and waited. "Yes, my Lord," he said.

"Do not disappoint me again," the Director warned in a soft tone. "I will not be so forgiving the next time."

"Yes, my Lord," Roan replied, bowing one last time before he opened the door and walked out.

He paused outside the door. For a moment before the door closed, he could hear the conversation between the two men. He pressed his hand against the door so that it didn't quite close all the way.

"I thought you were going to kill him. Do you question his loyalty?" The older man in the room asked.

"I planned to at first. Do you believe he will turn against the Legion?" Andri asked, studying the other man.

"No, he will not betray you. I have trained him to follow in our footsteps since his birth. If he does betray you, I will kill him myself," the man stated.

"Like father, like son," Andri chuckled.

"And like his uncle," Coleridge Landais stated.

"Yes. He is. It is a good thing he was not thirsty," Andri replied with a slightly amused tone.

Roan released the door and silently stepped away. Striding down the corridor, he ignored those that he passed. He knew what they were thinking and didn't care. Lifting the communicator that he had removed when he entered the room, he spoke in a sharp tone.

"Prepare to leave the planet," he ordered.

..*

"Are you ready?" Josh asked Pack.

Pack gave him a crooked grin. "Yes," he said, glancing over his shoulder at Bantu. "What about you?"

Josh saw Bantu swallow and nod. The other man looked pale and his hands shook, but he hadn't bailed out on them… Yet. He still had his doubts. The problem was if Bantu couldn't do this, there was only one other person who could, and Cassa was already assigned to the other dangerous mission.

"Bantu, are you sure you can do this?" Cassa asked in a quiet voice. "If not, perhaps I can…."

"No," Bantu and Josh both snapped out at the same time.

"No," Bantu said stubbornly. "I've got this. I know the ships and the way around better than anyone else. I just need Pack to get me there. I can do it after that."

"Each Battle Cruiser has a protective shield. Pack, you and Bantu will take out the first ship while Cassa and I take out the second," Josh said. "Remember, the plan."

"Yeah, get lost in the confusion and try not to get blown up before we reach our target," Pack replied dryly. "That sounds easy enough."

Josh hated to admit it, but he agreed with Pack. It was a crazy idea. What was even crazier was that he was putting Cassa in the middle of it. Unfortunately, there were only the two of them with the expertise to bring those shields down and, in order to do it, they had to get on the Battle Cruisers to tap into the computer systems.

"We'll come up from under and behind them," Josh said, pointing to the diagram he had drawn of the ships, the moon, and the planet. "Hutu and the other rebel forces will draw attention away from us."

"They are going to be hard pressed to protect this base and the planet," Cassa murmured.

"We've requested re-enforcements," Hutu interjected coming up behind them. "It will be close. They will not arrive before the battle begins, but if all goes well, they will be here before it ends."

"What about the bases on the planet?" Josh asked.

"They are prepared and waiting. The fighters have been positioned in the far desert and will come in on three different sides of the attacking Legion forces. Ground troops will also engage any air or ground units that attack," Hutu said.

They all looked up when the lights dimmed and the red lights warning of the Legion's approach began to flash. They were out of time. This could be either the beginning or the end of the rebellion.

"Are you ready?" Josh asked, turning to Cassa who was dressed in a dark green uniform.

Cassa gave him a reassuring smile and touched his cheek. "Yes," she said, realizing that she was ready. "My father knew that this day would come. He prepared me for it, even when I hoped he was wrong."

Josh reached up and laid his hand over hers, pressing it against his cheek. Once again, he was reminded of what an amazing woman she was. It was hard to remember what his life was like before he met her.

"I love you," he murmured.

Cassa's gaze softened and she reached up to brush a kiss against his lips. "I love you, as well, Joshua Mason," she said.

The sound of clearing throats drew their attention. Pack and Bantu were both looking at them with pained expressions. Josh's lips twitched when Pack turned to look at the other man.

"If you are expecting me to get all soft on you, kiss you, and tell you I love you, you are going to be waiting a long, long time," Pack remarked sardonically to Bantu. "Like forever."

"Thank you for that," Bantu retorted with a roll of his eyes. "Let's go. Suddenly, this isn't as bad as I thought it would be."

"They're just jealous," Cassa chuckled, winking at Josh before she turned and headed to the shuttles they would be using instead of fighters. "Let's show them how this should be done."

***

"Phantom One, locked in position," Josh stated in his comlink.

"Phantom Two, locked in position," Pack added a moment later. "Storm is increasing."

"Affirmative, Phantom Two. Legion fleet is almost in range, hold position until signaled," base ordered on the communication channels set up to prevent the Legion from intercepting their messages.

Josh glanced out the cockpit of the shuttle before looking down at the display. The small Service Bot that Bantu had programmed for them was updating information every few minutes. Wind speeds had increased and blinding sheets of sleet cut a diagonal path along the surface of the moon.

"If the storm increases, will it affect the fighters?" Cassa asked in a worried voice.

"It could," Josh responded. "It will also help to conceal the base from the Legion fighters, though. Cassa released a shaky sigh. "Are you okay?"

"Yes," she finally answered, staring out at the storm. "If you were to ask me before if I ever thought I would find myself in the middle of a battle with the Legion, I would have laughed at you. I never really realized how sheltered I was in the valley."

Josh chuckled. "If you were to ask me if I ever thought I would end up in the middle of an alien battle between two factions, I would have escorted you to the nearest hospital for evaluation," he mused. "I have to admit, I have no regrets. I just hope that after this is over, I can find the rest of my crew. It would be nice to know that they survived."

"Phantom One, prepare for departure," base suddenly instructed.

"Phantom One, copy that," Josh responded.

The familiar adrenaline rush that Josh felt before a mission began to course through him. He checked the readings on the display and sent instructions to the Service Bot to de-ice the thrusters. Wrapping his hands around the controls, he slowly pulled back and increased power to the engines. The shuttle rose like a ghostly figure through the icy spears of sleet.

"Phantom Two, lifting off," Pack stated in a calm voice. "Long live the Gallant Order."

Chapter 26

Josh broke through the thin atmosphere of the moon and angled the shuttle toward the Battle Cruisers. Already he could see the streams of Legion fighters pouring out of the two massive spaceships. Six smaller support ships, a third of the size of the Battle Cruisers, were aligned before the two ships.

He and Pack kept a low profile, hidden by the moon. Cassa's swiftly drawn breath echoed in the cockpit. Josh could appreciate her concern. While he already knew how large the Battle Cruisers were, seeing them for the first time with the fleet and with hundreds of fighters pouring out of them was a sight he would never forget.

"Josh," Cassa whispered when she saw two bursts of light from the bottom turret cannons.

They watched in horrid fascination as twin bolts of energy hit the planet below. Josh could hear Pack's soft curse in his ear. The fight had begun.

"This is going to get nasty, Cassa," Josh warned.

Hundreds of fighters suddenly swept past them. Hidden by the dark side of the moon, the Gallant rebel forces surged toward the Legion fighters. Below them, lights flashed around the planet. Josh and Pack turned away from the mass and focused on their target. They needed to disable the shields on the Battle Cruisers. Until then, the rebellion would be limited in the damage they could do while the Legion continued firing on the planet from above.

"Phantom Two, you have a Legion fighter coming up on your tail," Josh warned, coming into position to cover Pack and Bantu when one of the Legion fighters broke off and headed for them. "He's on your left. Stay in position, I'm coming in to cover you."

"Affirmative, Phantom One," Pack replied.

Josh watched as Pack weaved back and forth to keep from being locked on. Pressing the shuttle forward, Josh came up behind the Legion fighter. The moment he was in range, Cassa opened fire. They watched as the fighter spun out of control, barely missing one of the smaller escort ships.

"Josh, to the right," Cassa warned, swiveling her seat and taking aim.

"Good shot!" Josh exclaimed when Cassa cut the other fighter down in a brilliant explosion.

"Phantom One, take position, watch out for the turret guns underneath," base warned. "Phantom Two, GKL Team is drawing fire away, proceed to contact."

"Phantom Two, affirmative," Pack replied, tilting and moving toward the first Battle Cruiser. "Josh, protect my sister."

"I will, Pack," Josh promised. "We'll see you when this is over."

Josh turned his focus onto the second Battle Cruiser. The plan was for them to connect and enter through a remote access chute that was protected from the mounted guns. Several years before, Bantu had stumbled across one of the original engineers of the Battle Cruisers in a bar. The two had struck up a conversation that had proven to be very informative. Bantu explained that it was a serious design flaw that had been covered up by the original designers. The problem was that the only way to access and connect with it was by using a service shuttle.

"It was just one of those strange bits of information that you never forget. I remember checking out the chute to make sure the old man was telling me the truth. You can imagine my surprise when I found out that he was!" Bantu had shared when they were planning the attack. "The thing is, it was made for a service shuttle. They are the only type of spacecraft designed to fit into the space and connect. That was another reason the engineers didn't say anything. They figured that during a battle, no one would be using a service shuttle."

"Do we have access to any of these shuttles?" Josh remembered asking.

"Yes," Pack had answered. "We use them to transport items from the planet to the moon."

"We'll need to modify them with some weapons," Hutu suggested. "It shouldn't take long."

It hadn't. Within hours, the modifications to two of the shuttles had been completed. Now, the only thing Josh wished they could have done was add more horsepower to them. Trying to do combat between the shuttles and a Legion fighter was like locating a flea on a Mammoth's ass.

"Phantom One, you have a clear path," the Base communications officer announced.

"Roger, Base," Josh replied.

"Josh, there is a channel wide enough for the shuttle. If you stay in it, we should be able to remain undetected and out of sight from the fighters," Cassa said, swiveling around in her seat to get a better view.

"I see it," Josh responded. "Keep an eye out for any stragglers, Cassa. We'll be sitting ducks if they catch us."

"One of the things you will have to do when this is over is to teach me some of your phrases," Cassa replied with a humorous chuckle. "I do not know what a sitting duck is, but I believe I know what you mean. I will keep an eye out for any more Legion fighters."

"There are a few that I'll have to make sure I share," Josh replied.

"I look forward to learning them," Cassa whispered, staring up at the underbelly of the Battle Cruiser. "It is so huge."

"Second new phrase to remember, Cassa. The bigger they are, the harder they fall," Josh said in a reassuring tone. "I see the chute Bantu was talking about."

Josh focused on bringing the shuttle into alignment. The section was very narrow and would leave little room for error. Seeing it up close, he could understand why the original engineers decided it wouldn't be a factor since only the boxy service shuttles could fit in the tight, rectangular section. Josh was thankful for the training he had received back in Houston as he fired the thrusters. A part of him wished that Ash was here. His friend was a pro at doing this. As it was, Josh knew that it would take all of his skills to maneuver them safely to the connecting hatch.

"Cassa, bring the weapons in," Josh ordered, lightly touching the controls as they drew closer to the underbelly of the Battle Cruiser.

"Done," Cassa replied.

Several minutes later, the shuttle gently bumped against the chute connection. Josh could hear Cassa sealing the tube between the two spaceships. He quickly unstrapped and gave the order for the modified Fighter Bot to stand ready for a rapid departure.

Josh rose from the pilot's seat once the shuttle was transferred to the Fighter Bot. He quickly exited the cabin and strode back to where Cassa was waiting for him near the top access hatch. She gave him a calm, reassuring smile.

"Stay close to me," he ordered in a husky voice. "If things take a turn for the worse, get back to the shuttle and get out of here."

She nodded and stepped to the side. "We need to get to the access panel on E214. It is four levels up. This will take us up two levels before we have to work our way to the next levels. Fortunately, this is not a main section of the ship. If we are lucky, there will be very few personnel along the way."

Josh ran his fingers across her cheek. "You are ignoring my instructions," he murmured.

Cassa shook her head. "No, I'm not. I'm just choosing to believe that nothing will go wrong. I won't leave you behind, Josh. We have a mission. I want to focus on completing it without thinking about what could happen. If I thought about it, I wouldn't be able to do what needs to be done," she softly admitted.

For a moment, déjà vu struck him as his father's haunting words swept through him. Drawing in a deep breath, he brushed a kiss across Cassa's lips. She was right, of course. He had never let the dangers of a mission stop him before. Once again, he felt that swift flood of fear run through him at the thought of something happening to her. He quickly locked it away.

"Have I told you lately how much I love you?" He murmured before stepping back. "Stay close."

"I will," she promised.

Josh climbed up the ladder and pressed the release for the hatch. It slid back to reveal the bottom access into the Battle Cruiser. He reached down when he felt Cassa's hand and took the small device that Bantu had given them. Placing it against the outer control panel, he pressed the screen. It lit up with dancing patterns, scrolling in dizzying speed before a series of symbols appeared and the lock on the hatch disengaged.

"We're in," Josh murmured, handing the device back to Cassa.

"Bantu is a genius," Cassa replied, climbing up the ladder behind him. "The Legion has no idea what he is capable of."

"I hope they never find out," Josh retorted, pulling himself up through the narrow access tunnel.

He reached down and helped Cassa up. Releasing her hand, he started down the path he had memorized from the blueprint that Bantu had pulled up from the database he had stored when he deserted. Turning left, he came to the end where the panel opened into the first main corridor.

The low hum of the ship echoed around them. Deciding he had no choice but to chance discovery, he pushed against the release on the panel. It silently slid open. Josh glanced back and forth and motioned for Cassa to follow him. So far, so good. Now, if only the rest of the mission turned out as smoothly.

..*

"I thought you said this would work," Pack hissed to Bantu.

"It will, I just need more time," Bantu muttered, staring at the screen. "This isn't something you can rush, Pack. If I screw up, I could blow the whole damn ship up!"

Pack turned to look at Bantu with an expression of disbelief. He blinked several times as it slowly sunk in. Drawing in a deep breath, he leaned down to stare at his friend.

"Are you saying you can program the ship to self-destruct?" Pack asked in a calm voice.

Bantu scowled. "Of course I can," he snapped. "Each ship has a self-destruct sequence! It is part of the safety protocol."

This time it was Pack's turned to scowl. How the hell was blowing up your own ship a part of the safety protocol? It opened up a whole new idiom in the word vulnerability for the Battle Cruisers!

"Why didn't you tell us that before?" Pack demanded in a low voice.

"What? Why would I want to blow up the ship when I am on it?" Bantu asked in a puzzled tone. "It isn't like it gives you a lot of time to evacuate. Everyone is supposed to do that before the commander starts the countdown."

"Where did you learn about this?" Pack hissed.

"There aren't a lot of challenges involved in just programming Service Bots all day, every day, you know. I was bored! I spent ten years doing nothing else. It was fun seeing what else I could do. I discovered the coding when I hacked into Commander Meagoes files about a year after I was taken," Bantu replied.

"Did you hack into General Landais' files?" Pack pressed, squatting down next to the bank of servers that Bantu was working on.

Pack watched Bantu nervously swallow. "No, he does all of his own encrypting. I saw what he did to those that tried stuff on his ship. It wasn't pretty,"

Bantu muttered. "Getting sucked out into space is not how I wanted to end up."

""Bantu, this is better than shutting down the shields. This would cripple the attack forces. Can you hack in and get the code for the self-destruct for these two ships?" Pack asked.

"Yes… Yes, I think so," Bantu stuttered. "It may take a little while."

"Try. I'll notify Josh and Cassa," Pack said.

Bantu nodded and accessed the encrypted file he had programmed several years before. He wasn't even sure it would still work. He had tried it on each ship up until his last assignment. One of the other programmers had told him how General Landais once discovered that someone was trying to hack into his personal files. He had found the person and ejected them out into space, making sure it was broadcast to the entire crew. The ninety seconds it took for the man to die was ninety seconds longer than Bantu wanted to watch on the recorded transmission. He had spent the first six months on board having nightmares of being cast out into space.

Pack stood up and stepped away from the bank of servers. He glanced around the corner to make sure the door was still sealed before he pressed the code to contact Josh and Cassa. He wasn't sure if it would work this deep inside the ship, he could only hope that it did and that they hadn't been captured.

"Go ahead," Josh said in a barely audible voice.

"Bantu may have a way to access a self-destruct sequence programmed into the ship's computer,"

Pack responded, glancing back at Bantu who nodded and gave him a thumbs up signal. "Correction, he has a program that can open it."

"Can Cassa access it?" Josh asked in a harsh tone.

Pack turned and looked at Bantu. "Can Cassa access the file?" He asked.

"Yes," Bantu replied with a sharp nod. "Let me talk to her."

"He wants to talk to Cassa," Pack said.

"Tell me what to do, Bantu," Cassa's soft voice asked.

Bantu glanced at Pack and turned his back to him. "Go to file CLB1. The password is CassalovesBantu," he muttered, shooting a fierce glare at Pack when he snorted. "Upload the file. It will search for the ship's self-destruct program and match it with the commander's code. You'll have to manually input the sequence three times before it will activate. They really should have used a voice activation as well. It would have helped a little."

"We'll be sure to recommend that to the next Legion ship's commander before we blow his ship up," Josh retorted dryly.

Pack grinned when he saw Bantu grimace after he realized that Josh was listening in. If they survived this, he would have to try to introduce Bantu to a few other women. It was clear that Cassa was no longer available.

"Listen, once you find the sequence, you only have a minute to type the self-destruct numbers in. If you don't, an alarm will trigger unless you type in the words cancel command. I almost got caught the first time I did it."

"I've got it," Cassa replied in a soft voice. "It is searching."

"Bantu, we've got company," Pack whispered when he heard the sound of the door opening.

"Three times, Cassa," Bantu muttered urgently. "Oh, and you'll only have fifteen minutes to get out!"

Pack heard Bantu's muffled curse when he cut the communications between them. He nodded to Bantu to continue with what he was doing. Slipping around the other side, he went in search of their visitor.

Chapter 27

Cassa briefly glanced up to see Josh looking down the narrow corridor in the ship's server room. Returning her attention to the running program, her fingers were flying over her tablet as she went ahead and sent the command to disable the shields just in case she couldn't activate the self-destruct sequence. She drew in a swift breath before she looked up at him again and grinned.

"I've got it," she informed him with a triumphant look.

"I never had a doubt," Josh replied with a wink.

Cassa glanced back down at her tablet and quickly accessed the file, matching it to the commander's file. Once she had it, she typed in the passcode three times before she changed the commander's password so that he couldn't access his files and cancel the command. She quickly disconnected the cable between her computer and the server and rose to her feet.

"It's done," she said. "Contact Hutu and tell him the shield is down."

"Won't the Legion know?" Josh asked with a frown.

Cassa shook her head. "I told you, Bantu is a genius. They won't know until the first blast hits," she said.

Both of them started when an alarm sounded and the ship's on board computer spoke. "Warning – Self-destruct sequence has been activated. All personnel must immediately evacuate. Warning, self-destruct sequence has been activated."

"We have fifteen minutes," Cassa whispered, her eyes wide as she realized the program worked.

"Time to leave," Josh replied grimly, turning on his heel.

They were almost to the door when it opened. He didn't pause. Raising his arm, he fired two shots with his pistol. Grabbing Cassa's hand, he began running.

They barely paused as they shot through the doorway from the server room into the corridor. Fortunately, the corridor was empty. Josh released Cassa's hand and turned right, heading back they way they had come.

They took off down the long, curved corridor at a fast run. Both of them kept their weapons drawn and ready. They quickly slipped into the access tunnel that would take them two levels down. There they would have to use the main corridors again to reach the access tunnel to the shuttle.

"Hold up," Josh whispered, holding his hand out to stop Cassa from going any further.

Several soldiers ran down the corridor. Josh and Cassa pressed back against one of the metal beams. Once the men passed them, they ducked around it and begun running again. They were almost to the end when eight more soldiers came around the corner. For a moment, everyone stood frozen before chaos exploded.

"Halt!" One of the men yelled, lifting his arm.

Josh raised his arm, but Cassa had already fired. Laser fire exploded around them, forcing them back into the recess of one of the doorways. Three of the men collapsed. Josh jerked back when a rain of hot fire exploded around him.

"Nine minutes," Cassa called in frustration. "I refuse to be blown up!"

Cassa reached for the Staff at her waist and pulled it free. Extending it, she drew in a deep breath and stepped out into the corridor. She ignored Josh's sharp curse and waited. It didn't take long before one of the soldiers leaned out and fired at her. Cassa countered, absorbing the shot with the end of the Staff and sending it back at the man. A small, sizzling hole opened up in the center of the man's forehead.

"What the….! When were you going to tell me that the Staff could do that?" Josh growled, sliding his pistol back into the holster at his side and pulling his Staff free.

"It was going to be your next lesson," Cassa responded, catching another charge and sending it ricocheting around the corner. A second later, another body fell forward. "We… don't… have… time… for… this!" She bit out as she stepped forward.

"No shit!" Josh muttered, watching in amazement as she took out another soldier.

By the time they reached the corner, the remaining two soldiers were in fast retreat. Glancing at each other, Cassa and Josh took off behind them. They slid to a stop halfway down the third corridor in front of the access chute panel.

"Come on," Josh muttered as it slowly rose.

Once it was far enough up to squeeze through, he motioned for Cassa to go ahead of him. She jumped through the narrow space, grabbing the ladder. Holding on, she hooked her feet on the outer railing and let gravity take control of her descent.

"Phantom One, engage the engines, prepare for emergency departure," Josh shouted, following Cassa's move.

"CLB4, open the hatch!" Cassa ordered in a breathless voice, landing nimbly on the roof of the shuttle. "Three minutes," she said, waiting for the hatch to open.

"Stop!" A voice echoed from above them.

Cassa glanced up and stared at the face of a soldier looking down at her. Raising her Staff, she fired a bolt from the end. The man rocked back in surprise before he started to fall.

"Oh!" She hissed in surprise when Josh cursed again and grabbed her.

He dropped her through the opening before swinging down behind her. He closed the circular access a split second before the body hit the closed hatch with a nauseating thump. Cassa turned and rushed toward the cockpit. She stumbled, almost falling, when the shuttled disconnected from the Battle Cruiser. She would have flown upward if Josh hadn't wrapped his arm around her waist and held her down using some of the piping along the walls.

Cassa released a soft groan that was drowned by the screeching of metal against metal as the shuttle did a free fall from the narrow confines. Once free, Josh released her and turned.

Cassa slid into the seat next to him as he took control of the shuttle. Pushing the small transport as fast as he could, he knew there was no way they could put enough distance between them and the massive time bomb before it exploded.

"Maximum shields," Josh ordered. "Strap in."

"Base, this is Phantom One requesting all Gallant fighters to clear the area," Cassa said in an urgent voice. "Base…."

"Josh, we're clear!" Pack said. "You've got to put more distance between you."

"I know that!" Josh growled, just as a brilliant light lit up the darkness. "Aw, shit."

Josh tugged at the harness and barely snapped it closed when the first wave from the explosion hit them. In his peripheral vision, he saw the swarms of Legion fighters and shuttles that were pouring out of the Battle Cruiser caught in the same wave. He saw several collide with each other and explode.

His head turned and he reached for Cassa. Her hand grasped his for a brief second before they were thrown forward with enough force to make his vision dance with dark spots. Those spots grew when the second wave hit. The power flickered before going out.

At least it shut the alarms up, Josh thought as his head fell forward and his eyelids closed.

Chapter 28

"Josh! Dude, wake up! Hey, man, are you still alive?" A familiar voice was asking.

The corner of Josh's mouth twitched. He had never really wondered if there was a heaven or hell, at least not in the past twenty plus years, but now he wondered if there just might be. He should have known that Ash would end up next to him.

A frown creased his brow and he forced his eyelids to open. He winced when the bright light struck his pupils, increasing the ache in his head. Lifting a hand to push it away, he was surprised when he encountered warm skin and thick muscles.

"Turn… off… the… damn… spotlight," Josh finally forced out in a husky voice. "Cassa…."

"She's okay. Kella, is with her," the voice said. "Damn, but you are a sight for sore eyes."

Josh groaned and forced his eyes open. Ash's grinning face was just a few inches from his. A painful scowl darkened Josh's face as he stared up at his best friend.

"I swear if you kiss me, I'll knock the shit out of you," Josh threatened.

Ash's loud laughter echoed through the cockpit of the shuttle. Josh winced when Ash bent forward and wrapped his arm around his shoulders to help him sit up. Josh grunted and rested his arms on his knees, breathing deeply through his nose while he waited for the world to stop spinning.

"You know, I could almost do it," Ash muttered, twisting around to sit down next to Josh.

Josh slowly lifted his head and stared at Ash's dark face. There was a new scar above his left eye, probably from when the Gliese 581 went through the gate and Ash's face connected with the control console. He was dressed in a tan colored shirt and dark brown trousers. They were almost the same color as his skin. A pair of matching dark brown boots and vest finished off his outfit.

"The only thing you're missing is the hat and you could be Harrison Ford… with one hell-of a tan, that is," Josh muttered with a slight smile. "What could you almost do?"

Ash leaned back and drew his knees up. "Kiss you," he admitted. "I thought I was the only one alive."

Josh saw the smile fade from Ash's eyes as he looked around the damaged shuttle. His gaze rose to the front window and he frowned. Instead of being in space, he saw that his and Cassa's ruined shuttle was inside of another ship.

"Where are we?" Josh asked, returning his gaze to Ash.

Ash glanced up over his shoulder, the good-natured grin back on his face. He looked back at Josh and shrugged. He was about to answer when he paused and looked over Josh's shoulder. Curious, Josh twisted and looked up at the figure leaning against the frame of the doorway leading to the cockpit. A harsh curse tore from his throat when he saw the smiling face looking down at him.

"Greetings, Joshua Mason," the woman said, folding her arms across her chest.

Josh struggled to his feet, swaying. His hand groped along his hip for the Staff. The figure shifted warily and took a step back.

"Hey, Josh, whoa. Kella's alright," Ash exclaimed in an urgent voice, stepping between him and the woman. "She's cool, man."

"Cool?! She tried to kill us!" Josh said, glaring over Ash's shoulder at the tall, lean woman. "She's a Turbinta assassin."

"Kella? An assassin? Naw, she's a freighter pilot," Ash said in confusion, glancing at the woman standing behind him. "She saved my life."

"No," Josh growled, pushing Ash to the side. "She tried to kill me in the warehouse. We fought and I knocked her out. Hutu was going to kill her, but I stopped him. I shouldn't have."

"Listen, you must be mistaken!" Ash argued, looking back and forth between the two. "Tell him, Kella. Tell him that you didn't try to kill him."

"Yes, I did," Kella responded with a shrug. "That was what I was paid to do."

"See, she… What? Are you nuts? You can't kill my friend!" Ash bit out, turning to glare at the woman.

"It was what I was paid to do," Kella retorted with a shrug. "Or at least, I would have been paid to do if I had been successful. I came to tell you that the woman wants to see him."

Josh watched as Kella turned sharply on her heel and walked away. Her tanned complexion was lighter than Ash and her thick brown hair was cut short. On each hip, she had a weapon strapped snug against her leg.

"Would you mind telling me what is going on?" Josh asked, leaning back against the chair as a wave of fatigue washed through him.

Ash raised an eyebrow and leaned back beside him. Josh saw the disgruntled expression on his friend's face. He mimicked Ash when the other man folded his arms across his chest.

"Dude, if you don't know, how the hell am I supposed to? Remember? You are the one who always knows the answer to things, Sherlock. I'm just your wingman," Ash muttered. "This is one crazy, messed up world."

Josh dropped his arms and pushed up to stand again. He wanted, needed, to make sure that Cassa was alright. Then, he needed to find out what was happening with the rebel forces. He didn't even know how much time had passed. For the first time in a very long time, Josh just didn't know, but he was going to find out – starting with Cassa.

"Let's go find Cassa and I'll tell you what I know," Josh finally said, stepping forward.

"Sounds good to me," Ash replied under his breath.

* * *

Several hours later, Josh leaned back against the seat in the galley of the freighter. His arm was wrapped protectively around Cassa. She tilted her head and tiredly rested it against his shoulder. Ash stared moodily at the drink in front of him. Hutu watched Kella with an intense, edgy stare while Kella, who sat next to Ash, returned the old Knight's gaze with a steely one of her own.

"If you two keep staring at each other like that, I'm going to send both of you to a corner," Ash finally snapped out.

Josh choked back a chuckle at the exasperated look Kella shot his friend. There was something else in her gaze as well that he almost missed. For once, Josh felt like Ash just might have met his match in the assassin turned savior.

"The Legion forces were quickly defeated after the destruction of the two Battle Cruisers," Hutu continued, ignoring Kella for now.

"Pack…?" Cassa asked in a husky voice, sitting up.

Hutu's expression softened and he gave Cassa a soft, warm smile. "He and Bantu faired much better than you and Josh. They were able to put a significant amount of distance between them and the ships before they self-destructed," he assured her.

"Thank you," Cassa replied in a thick voice.

"What now?" Josh asked. "How will the Legion respond, do you think?"

Hutu's expression hardened. "The repercussion of the battle is already being felt across the galaxy. Word that you, and now another lost Guardian of the Gallant Order has appeared, is spreading. The Director is desperate to find the others. General Landais has vanished. He met with the Director yesterday before the battle. He returned to his ship, but left again in a lone fighter shortly after handing temporary control over to his second-in-command. No one has seen or heard from him since. It is believed he is searching for another signal that may have been intercepted," Hutu explained.

"There were two more," Kella suddenly said, glancing around the table.

"Two more?" Josh asked with a raised eyebrow.

Kella glanced at Ash's frozen expression and sighed. "I picked up information about two more signals," she repeated with a shrug.

"Are they the same signals that Landais is hunting for?" Josh asked, leaning forward.

Kella glanced at Ash again and shook her head. "No," she replied in a soft voice. "The last sighting of Landais had him heading in the opposite direction. These… They were headed for Turbinta."

Hutu's fists clenched. "We have to find them," he said, starting to rise out of his seat.

"If you went there, every assassin on the planet would be after you," Kella stated in a blunt tone. "It is the same for you. The Director has placed a very high reward on your heads."

"We can't just leave them," Ash snapped impatiently.

Kella turned her dark brown eyes to Ash. "I never said that you should," she pointed out in a soft voice.

"Then, what do you suggest? That you go and look for them?" Hutu snorted angrily.

Kella turned her eyes to Hutu and tilted her head. Josh saw the appraising look that she gave the old Knight before she broke the contact. She reached for the drink on the table in front of her and finished it before she answered Hutu's questions.

"Yes, but not alone," she said, glancing again at Ash. "Ash will go with me. If they are on the planet, I'll find them. Your people won't know me, but they will know Ash, though, if he were to go with me." She turned her dark gaze toward Josh. "The old Knight is right. The Director will be hunting for the others. He is also correct when he said the Director is scared. That fear will make him more dangerous. We will find your friends while the Gallant Order keeps the Director and the Legion forces busy."

"Do you think I'd just let you take off with Ash…," Josh started to say when Ash broke in.

"She's right, Josh. This is a strange world. It scared the hell out of me. Sergi might be able to handle it, but Mei and Julia? They aren't military," Ash pointed out.

Josh's lips tightened before he relaxed. Deep down, he knew that Ash was more than capable of taking care of himself. His gaze flickered to Kella. She was staring at Ash with a slightly confused expression in her eyes. This wasn't the look of an assassin who wanted to kill his friend.

"Keep us posted," Josh suddenly said. "Stay out of the Legion's sight and for God's sake, stay out of trouble!"

Ash released a chuckle. "Since when have I ever done that, Sherlock?" He asked with a wry grin.

Josh rose stiffly to his feet and gently helped Cassa to hers. He wrapped his arm around her waist when she started to slide back down. Pressing a kiss to her temple, he nodded to Hutu, who had risen at the same time.

"Let's get back to the base," Josh said. "Cassa and I need to get cleaned up and get some rest before we start planning the next phase of our attack."

Hutu nodded in approval. "You are a natural born leader, Josh. The Gallant Order is lucky to have you," he said in a quiet voice filled with respect.

Josh grimaced when he felt his stiff muscles protest. Right now, he didn't feel like a leader. He felt old and tired.

"You can butter me up after I get some sleep," he retorted with a good-natured grin before he turned to look at Ash. " Be safe."

"Always," Ash said, reaching out and laying his hand on Josh's shoulder. "Watch his back while I'm gone," he added, looking at Hutu.

"And who's going to watch yours?" Josh muttered.

"I will," Kella said in a quiet voice. "Now, if you can all get off my ship, we can leave."

Josh shook his head. "Good luck with this one," he whispered under his breath.

"Hey, I'm the one with all the charm, remember? The ladies can't resist me. She'll be eating out of the palm of my hand before you know it!" Ash teased in a slightly strained tone. "If she doesn't bite it off first."

A soft chuckle escaped Josh and Hutu at Ash's reflective grimace. Ash's gaze followed Kella's taut figure as she walked away. He didn't envy the journey ahead of Ash. He just hoped it was a successful one, and was curious as to who they would find next. In the meantime, they needed to locate General Landais and hope he was on a wild goose chase.

"Let's go back to the base," Cassa murmured softly.

Josh nodded. He tightly held Cassa's hand, unable to let her go. Together they followed Hutu back to his ship. Climbing down the ladder to where the shuttle was docked, he waited and helped Cassa down. They moved to one of the seats and sat down while Hutu made his way to the cockpit.

Soon, they were heading through space to the ice-covered moon base. Looking out of one of the port windows, Josh could see the planet far below. He vaguely wondered how much damage was done and how many lives were lost. For a moment, his thoughts returned to the beautiful vineyard and Jemar and Jesup's smiling faces.

His arms tightened around Cassa. She was half-asleep as she leaned against him. He bent his head and pressed a kiss to her temple.

The Legion has a lot to answer for, he thought, leaning his head back and closing his eyes. His hand moved down to his side and he stroked the Staff that Jemar had given him. *I will need to teach Ash how to use one,* he thought as a smile curved his lips.

Josh never expected his command decision to take the Gliese 581 through the gate would have such a profound effect on not only his life, but so many others. The new Knights of the Gallant Order were about to rise up and show the Director and his forces that they were back with a vengeance. The first awakening of the new Gallant Order had begun.

To be continued…. **First Awakenings.**

If you loved this story by me (S. E. Smith) please leave a review. You can also take a look at additional books and sign up for my newsletter at http://sesmithfl.com to hear about my latest releases or keep in touch using the following links:

Website: http://sesmithfl.com
Newsletter: http://sesmithfl.com/?s=newsletter
Facebook: https://www.facebook.com/se.smith.5
Twitter: https://twitter.com/sesmithfl
Pinterest: http://www.pinterest.com/sesmithfl/
Blog: http://sesmithfl.com/blog/
Forum: http://www.sesmithromance.com/forum/

Additional Books by S. E. Smith

Paranormal and Science Fiction short stories and novellas

For the Love of Tia (Dragon Lords of Valdier Book 4.1)

A Dragonlings' Easter (Dragonlings of Valdier Book 1.1)

A Dragonlings' Haunted Halloween (Dragonlings of Valdier Book 1.2)

A Dragonlings' Magical Christmas (Dragonlings of Valdier Book 1.3)

A Warrior's Heart (Marastin Dow Warriors Book 1.1)

Rescuing Mattie (Lords of Kassis: Book 3.1)

Science Fiction/Paranormal Novels

Cosmos' Gateway Series

Tink's Neverland (Cosmo's Gateway: Book 1)
Hannah's Warrior (Cosmos' Gateway: Book 2)
Tansy's Titan (Cosmos' Gateway: Book 3)

Cosmos' Promise (Cosmos' Gateway: Book 4)
Merrick's Maiden (Cosmos' Gateway Book 5)
Curizan Warrior
Ha'ven's Song (Curizan Warrior: Book 1)
Dragon Lords of Valdier
Abducting Abby (Dragon Lords of Valdier: Book 1)
Capturing Cara (Dragon Lords of Valdier: Book 2)
Tracking Trisha (Dragon Lords of Valdier: Book 3)
Ambushing Ariel (Dragon Lords of Valdier: Book 4)
Cornering Carmen (Dragon Lords of Valdier: Book 5)
Paul's Pursuit (Dragon Lords of Valdier: Book 6)
Twin Dragons (Dragon Lords of Valdier: Book 7)
Jaguin's Love (Dragon Lords of Valdier: Book 8) (coming soon)
The Old Dragon of the Mountain's Christmas (Dragon Lords of Valdier: Book 9)
Lords of Kassis Series
River's Run (Lords of Kassis: Book 1)
Star's Storm (Lords of Kassis: Book 2)
Jo's Journey (Lords of Kassis: Book 3)
Ristéard's Unwilling Empress (Lords of Kassis: Book 4)
Magic, New Mexico Series
Touch of Frost (Magic, New Mexico Book 1)
Taking on Tory (Magic, New Mexico Book 2)
Sarafin Warriors
Choosing Riley (Sarafin Warriors: Book 1)
Viper's Defiant Mate (Sarafin Warriors Book 2)
The Alliance Series
Hunter's Claim (The Alliance: Book 1)

Razor's Traitorous Heart (The Alliance: Book 2)
Dagger's Hope (The Alliance: Book 3)
Challenging Saber (The Allianc Book 4)
Zion Warriors Series
Gracie's Touch (Zion Warriors: Book 1)
Krac's Firebrand (Zion Warriors: Book 2)
Paranormal and Time Travel Novels
Spirit Pass Series
Indiana Wild (Spirit Pass: Book 1)
Spirit Warrior (Spirit Pass Book 2)
Second Chance Series
Lily's Cowboys (Second Chance: Book 1)
Touching Rune (Second Chance: Book 2)

Excerpts of S. E. Smith Books

If you would like to read more S. E. Smith stories, she recommends Abducting Abby, the first in her Dragon Lords of Valdier Series. Or if you prefer a Paranormal or Time Travel with a twist, you can check out Lily's Cowboys or Indiana Wild…

Audiobooks are also available. For a list of available audiobooks and to listen to samples please visit: http://sesmithfl.com/category/books/audio-books/

About S. E. Smith

S.E. Smith is a ***New York Times, USA TODAY, International, and Award-Winning*** Bestselling author of science fiction, romance, fantasy, paranormal, and contemporary works for adults, young adults, and children. She enjoys writing a wide variety of genres that pull her readers into worlds that take them away.